More Holmes
for the
Holidays

EDITED BY

Martin H. Greenberg,
Jon L. Lellenberg, and
Carol-Lynn Waugh

BERKLEY PRIME CRIME, NEW YORK

MORE HOLMES FOR THE HOLIDAYS

A Berkley Prime Crime Book / published by arrangement with
Tekno Books, Jon L. Lellenberg, and Carol-Lynn Waugh

PRINTING HISTORY
Berkley Prime Crime hardcover edition / October 1999
Berkley Prime Crime trade paperback edition / October 2001

Berkley Prime Crime trade paperback ISBN: 0-425-18211-8

Visit our website at
www.penguinputnam.com

The Library of Congress has catalogued
the Berkley Prime Crime hardcover edition as follows:

More Holmes for the holidays / edited by Martin H. Greenberg, Jon L.
   Lellenberg, & Carol-Lynn Waugh
        p.   cm.
     ISBN 0-425-17033-0
     1. Holmes, Sherlock (Fictitious character)—Fiction.   2. Detective
and mystery stories, American.   3. Detective and mystery stories,
English.   4. Private investigators—England—Fiction.   5. Christmas
stories, American.   6. Christmas stories, English.   I. Greenberg,
Martin Harry.   II. Lellenberg, John L.   III. Waugh, Carol-Lynn
Rössel.
PS648.D4M654   1999
818'.0108351—dc21   99-27229
                                                                          CIP

Berkley Prime Crime Books are published by
The Berkley Publishing Group, a division of Penguin Putnam Inc.,
375 Hudson Street, New York, New York 10014.

ACKNOWLEDGMENTS

CONTENTS

INTRODUCTION

Somewhere in the vaults of the bank of Cox and Co., at Charing Cross, there is a travel-worn and battered tin dispatch-box with my name, John H. Watson, M.D., Late Indian Army, painted upon the lid . . .

wrote Dr. Watson in "The Adventure of Thor Bridge," published in 1922.

It is crammed with papers, nearly all of which are records of cases to illustrate the curious problems which Mr. Sherlock Holmes had at various times to examine. Some, and not the least interesting, were complete failures, and as such will hardly bear narrating, since no final explanation is forthcoming. . . . Apart from these unfathomed cases, there are some which involve the secrets of private families to an extent which would mean consternation in many exalted quarters if it were thought possible that they might find their way into print. I need not say that such a breach of confidence is unthinkable, and that these records will be separated and destroyed now that my friend has time to turn his energies to the matter. There remain a considerable residue of cases of greater or less interest which I might have edited before had I not feared to give the public a surfeit which might react upon the reputation of the man whom above all others I revere.

This statement by Sherlock Holmes's collaborator and amanuensis has intrigued readers of his adventures for over seventy-five years, and not merely for Watson's tantalizing description of several of the cases that Holmes failed to solve—"that of Mr. James Phillimore," for instance, "who, stepping back into his own house to get his umbrella, was never more seen in this world," or of "Isadora Persano, the well-known journalist and duellist, who was found stark staring mad with a matchbox in front of him which contained a remarkable worm, said to be unknown to science." Many other writers, professionals and amateurs alike, have endeavored to make up for the continued withholding of Dr. Watson's marvelous, and seemingly bottomless, dispatch-box, and to give the public their own versions of these and other Unrelated Cases of Sherlock Holmes.

The stories in this volume are ones in that dispatch-box wrapped in leftover Christmas present wrapping paper, and tied up with green and red ribbon. They relate little problems in detection that came to Sherlock Holmes and Dr. Watson at Christmastime during the years they dwelt at 221B Baker Street, London. For Victorian Englishmen like Holmes and Watson, the holiday of Christmas celebrated the birth of Jesus Christ nearly two thousand winters before with lights, greenery, gifts that recalled the Magi who traveled to Bethlehem to pay homage to the infant Saviour, and a spirit of brotherhood and spiritual renewal. It was, as Sherlock Holmes remarked in "The Adventure of the Blue Carbuncle," the Season of Forgiveness, and in that tale by A. Conan Doyle, Holmes let a guilty man go free so long as an innocent one did not suffer—a Christmas gesture worthy of the great detective, who never confused Justice with Law whenever a difference between those two things occurred in the many cases he investigated.

The stories in this volume are also salutes to the world's first consulting detective by modern mystery and detective story writers, who have followed in the footsteps of Sir Arthur Conan Doyle, the creator of Holmes and Watson and so much else that entertained the Victorian and Edwardian Ages. They are Magi themselves, bearing gifts resembling as closely as possible—and yet not so slavishly as to rob them of their own authors' creative spark—the original tales that formed their own reading as boys and girls, when the Christmas season still possessed all its wonder and excitement for them. Whether their own preferred forms today of the genre Conan Doyle defined are mysteries in a contemporary vein, or police procedurals, or American hard-boiled detective stories, or the nostalgic British "cosies" that have emerged in recent years to fill the void left by Dorothy L. Sayers, Agatha Christie, and others, they have come together here under Conan Doyle's star to pay their respects to a colleague who a century ago revolutionized the detective story, held a worldwide audience spellbound and hungry for more for forty years, and left a literary legacy that continues to compel attention today. Some contributors to this volume are, in fact, less mystery writers than writers of fantasy or of nonfiction (albeit largely about the literature of mystery and detection), and at least one of them is an amateur magician of considerable ability.

But upon all of them Sherlock Holmes has worked his own magic, and these tributes are part of the result. To all of their authors, we are very grateful.

Jon L. Lellenberg

THE CHRISTMAS GIFT

Anne Perry

My friend Sherlock Holmes is not an emotional man. I have seen him excited by the chase when he knows the game is afoot, and I have seen him deeply angered by injustice. But I have no doubt whatever that the most moved I have seen him, beyond the ability or the desire for words to express, is by the music of the violin, when in the hands of a master.

Vassily Golkov is without question a violinist not only of such superb skill but of such subtle interpretation that I needed no deductive powers whatever to be perfectly certain that when he was giving a concert in London three days before the Christmas of 1894, nothing would prevent Holmes from attending. Even the most complex and intriguing crime would have had to await its turn in his order of priorities.

I was delighted that he should invite me to accompany him.

"Of course, my dear fellow," I said eagerly. "I should be most happy to come."

He looked at me with a slightly skeptical eye. He knows I am rather fonder of the piano than of stringed instruments. There is something in the soul of the violin which troubles me; perhaps it is the very similarity it has to the range of passion in the human voice. Nevertheless he did not argue but took my acceptance in good part. I rather think he meant it as some nature of gift to me, considering the season. He did not require company to gain the fullest possible pleasure from the music himself. Indeed I would have been surprised if he had uttered two words to me from the beginning of the concert to the end. And I would swear a year's income I should have received little answer had I interrupted his immersion in the glorious sound by speaking to him.

We took a hansom from Baker Street to the concert hall in the Strand and alighted onto the pavement in a sparkling frosty night with a thin rime of ice already forming over the cobbles. The air had a pleasant crispness to it and I felt in remarkably good spirits.

We were shown to our seats amid a crowd of people similarly buoyant in mood. The excitement of Christmas was everywhere apparent. I saw several women beautifully attired, their pale shoulders gleaming, slender necks adorned with jewels, bright hair shining under the blaze of chandeliers in the foyer. People called out to one another with greetings and compliments of the season, wishing each other happiness and good health.

Holmes sat down with a smile of expectancy in his keen face, his eyes already focused on the curtained stage, awaiting the appearance of Vassily Golkov.

A hush fell upon the audience as a gentleman came from the wings. It was not Golkov, and it took only a merest glance to recognise that he was in a state of extreme agitation, not to say embarrassment.

"Ladies and Gentlemen," he began unhappily. "It is with the profoundest regret, and apology to all of you, that I have to tell you that Mr. Golkov has been taken ill . . . quite suddenly . . . and will not be able to appear before you this evening. . . ."

A murmur of dismay ran through the gathered assembly, like a sighing of wind through the edge of a forest. It seemed they were too stunned to complain.

"I'm sorry!" the man on the stage repeated, his face very pink, as if he were somehow at fault. "I'm so sorry. Of course the management will . . ." The rest of his words were swallowed up in the noise of people rising to their feet and muttering their frustration.

I glanced at Holmes, sensing how acute would be his disappointment, not only for himself, but because he had treated me to the evening.

But far from mortification, I saw a look of puzzlement on his face, and he did not turn to leave, but grasped me by the cuff of my coat, and ordering me with him, started forward towards the stage.

"Where on earth are you going?" I protested. I had some fear that he was so determined to hear Golkov play that he imagined I might be able to help the poor man sufficiently to enable him still to fulfil his engagement. "I do not have my medical bag with me!" I protested, following him up the steps onto the stage and between the heavy curtains. All the lights were still on and it was instantly apparent that there was no one else present.

That did not deter Holmes at all. In half a dozen strides he was across the boards and into the corridor beyond, leaving me to follow him, or remain alone.

I charged after him and emerged from the stage door into the street in time to see a long-legged young man with a shock of wild, dark hair loping down the alley, with Holmes after him, shouting, "Come Watson!" without even turning to see if I were following.

I obeyed, compelled by curiosity. Who was the young man, and why were we pursuing him? We had come to hear one of the most gifted violinists in the world, and here we were running helter-skelter into the crowded street, watching startled men and women move out of our way as the young man hailed the first passing cab and leaped into it. Holmes, shouting and waving his arms, hailed another and flung open the door. Panting rather heavily, I scrambled up ahead of him as he called to the driver to follow the cab in front, and then threw himself in beside me.

"Who is that young man?" I gasped. "And why in heaven's name are we chasing him?"

"That is Vassily Golkov, of course," he replied, far less out of breath than I. "And he is no more ill than you are! In fact, my dear fellow, I would say rather less."

I resented his reference to my condition, and I did not reply until I could do so without seeming in the least out of composure. Meanwhile the hansom moved at a brisk pace through the icy streets, the horses' hooves clipping sharply.

"I understand your disappointment," I said at length. "But even if that was indeed Golkov, you can hardly chase him down and ask him to play for you! Even if he is not ill, he is obviously in some great distress."

"Obviously, Watson," he said tartly, staring forwards as if he would make out in the darkness and glittering street lamps where we were headed. "Does that not pique your curiosity? Do you not hunger to know what drives a genius like Golkov, dedicated to his art, a man who truly would 'fiddle while Rome burned,' to abandon his audience without warning, and career through the night in such a manner? We are going north, Watson, and I believe west!"

The cab was lurching around at an alarming speed. I confess I was concerned for our safety, and for that of the poor animal being thus driven.

"Whatever the reason, we have no business pursuing him!" I protested. "Even if we catch up with him, what can we possibly do?"

"Be reasonable, Watson!" Holmes protested with an injured tone to his voice. "How can I answer such a question until I know the cause for his flight? And for the lie to his audience who had paid a handsome sum to come out on a winter night to hear him play. Whatever is wrong, mark my words—it is serious."

We swung around a corner, throwing Holmes almost into my lap. He righted himself without a word, and as we passed close to a lamp I saw his face in the momentary light, lean, high cheek-boned, eyes staring ahead as keenly as those of a bird of prey who has sighted its quarry.

"I know where we are!" I cried in amazement. "The next cross-road is Baker Street! We are all but home!"

"You are right Watson!" he agreed. "Now do we stop here, or do . . ." His words were cut off by the sudden lurching of the hansom as it swayed around, went another twenty yards, and came to a halt.

" 'Ere you are, gents!" the driver said proudly. "Feller as yer wants is further up there ahead o' yer, 'ammerin' on somebody's door. Yer'd best 'urry, or 'e'll be let in an' yer'll 'a missed 'im."

Holmes scrambled out. "Thank you!" he said appreciatively. "You have done exceedingly well." And he handed him a coin without waiting for change.

I stepped out after him, the ice-sharp air stinging my face, and found myself not a dozen yards from Holmes's front door, upon which Vassily Golkov was flailing with his fists in a most desperate manner. Before I could express my amazement, the door opened and Mrs. Hudson's alarmed face was clearly visible.

"Who are you, young man?" she demanded. "And what do you think you are doing making a noise like that and disturbing decent folk? Can't you ring the doorbell, like everyone else?"

"I must see Sherlock Holmes!" Golkov replied, his voice rising in desperation. "It is of the greatest importance . . . please! I implore you, ask him if he will see me!"

Mrs. Hudson looked very doubtful. Even from where we stood I could see in the lamplight that she was perturbed. She had to have recalled that Holmes was out—she had wished us a good evening as we left—and yet the young man's distress had moved her to sympathy.

"Mr. Holmes is not in," she replied, shaking her head a little. "But if you . . ." She stopped as she saw Holmes starting across the street, his figure with its lean body and swift stride so easily recognisable. "Why, Mr. Holmes!" she cried in surprise. "Is something wrong, sir?"

I caught up just as the young violinist whirled around and his dark face lit with relief and a resurgence of hope.

"Mr. Holmes? Mr. Sherlock Holmes? Sir, I beg you, I have a most desperate need of your help! I am at the end of my wits, and I know of no other man who can save me."

Holmes could never have resisted such an appeal, both to his sense of honour, and his undoubted vanity. Coming from a young man with a sublime gift of musical genius it was doubly appealing.

"You had best come inside and tell me what it is that so troubles you," Holmes invited him. "This is my colleague, Dr. Watson. You may trust him absolutely." He did not wait for any answer, but assuming it in the affirmative, he thanked Mrs. Hudson with a glance, and went past her and up the stairs, leaving Golkov and myself to follow behind him.

As soon as Golkov was inside and I had closed the door, Holmes, having thrown off his overcoat, faced the young man, his features eager with anticipation.

Golkov did not need a second invitation. He did not even bother to shed his jacket, the only protection he had worn against the bitterness of the night. They looked oddly alike, these two men, although Holmes was perhaps fifteen years older. They had the same fierce leanness to them, the angular body filled with energy and the kind of grace which comes from the most excellent coordination of muscle and an intense sensitivity to balance, as if all the force of mind and will would be harnessed to one overriding purpose.

Golkov began immediately, his voice vibrant and made individual by a slight accent I was unable to place.

"I am of insignificant family, indeed I do not know my father—I regret my mother may well be able to add nothing to that. . . ."

Holmes's face darkened. He did not care for such personal confidences, and he found the young man's aspersion on his mother distasteful.

Golkov read his expression and understood it. "You think I speak disrespectfully. It is not so. I have the highest regard for my mother. Her beauty was more of a misfortune to her than a blessing. . . ."

Holmes coloured very faintly, the clearest sign of embarrassment I have seen in him. It is not an emotion familiar to him. Nor did he often leap to conclusions, even better-founded ones than this.

"I tell you," Golkov continued, "because such things are of importance to many people, including Hugo Carburton, the father of

Miss Helena Carburton, with whom I am most deeply in love. And until today, I had believed she also was with me, in spite of my reputation for having been . . ." He shrugged very slightly in a gesture of regret. . . . "a little generous with my favours in the past. I was young, and easily flattered. I do not think back on it with pride. My head was turned when so many pretty young ladies could not tell the difference between the music and the musician."

Holmes frowned. "I sympathise with you, Mr. Golkov, but I cannot assist you to raise yourself in Mr. Carburton's regard."

"No, no!" Golkov waved his hands. "Of course not! That is not why I have come. Something happened today which is of an entirely different nature, and for which you are my only hope. I am a stranger, a foreigner here in London, but even in Paris, or Rome, or Berlin your name is known, also that you are a lover of music, especially of the violin."

Holmes was mollified. I could see it in the softening of his expression, even though I believed he had not entirely forgiven Golkov for cancelling his concert without the least notice. Personal matters should not intrude upon the musician's professional obligation. The art should override even a broken heart, let alone the slight consideration of the dislike of one's lover's father.

Golkov was quite apparently labouring on the grip of some intense emotion. He could barely keep still, and his face was a picture of acute distress.

"This evening someone stole my violin!" he burst out. "My Stradivarius!" It was a cry of such pain it was as if he had lost a limb of his own body.

Holmes was truly appalled. The colour blanched from his cheeks and his body jerked to rigidity.

"This is terrible! Tell me everything, every circumstance to the tiniest detail. Omit nothing whatsoever."

I considered asking Mrs. Hudson to bring us tea. I could most certainly have used a cup myself, but I could see that neither Holmes nor Golkov were even aware of their physical surroundings, let alone requiring sustenance or comfort of such a practical nature, so I abandoned the idea.

"I have lodgings in Dudley Street," Golkov explained. "I keep the violin there, with me at all times."

Holmes nodded. "Of course."

"This afternoon, Helena came to see me. . . ."

"At what hour?" Holmes interrupted.

"Approximately half past four," Golkov replied. "She had been trying to soften her father's attitude towards me, without any success whatever. If anything, he seemed to be even more determined that we should not meet at all, much less that he would entertain the thought of permitting her to marry me."

Personally I found Carburton's feelings easy enough to understand. Golkov was one of the most brilliant violinists of the latter part of the century, but a flamboyant and somewhat questionable character to whom to give one's daughter in marriage. His art took him all over Europe, fêted and idolised by all manner of people. It was an uncertain life, and Helena Carburton might find herself miserable and in totally unfamiliar surroundings, among strangers, and entirely dependent upon a man who might turn out to be charming but completely irresponsible. However, of course, I did not say so.

"And the Stradivarius?" Holmes was ever on the point which mattered.

"In its case in the sitting room, where I had been practising," Golkov replied. "I went through to the small kitchen where I set the kettle on the hob and waited for it to boil. It was extremely cold and I wished to make Helena a cup of tea. It is something I always do. After a few moments she joined me."

"Naturally." Holmes moved his hands slightly in impatience for Golkov to reach the crux of the matter.

"We were there some ten minutes or less," Golkov continued. "The kettle boiled, I made the tea and we took it back to the sitting room and spoke some more about the same subject. She seemed determined to defy her father whatever the cost, and to marry me— in Paris, if that should be necessary."

"And then?" Holmes pressed.

Golkov's face darkened. "And then I bade her goodbye." His whole body tightened. "She kissed me," he said hoarsely, as if the memory of it were still on his lips. "And she left." He swallowed. "I returned to my violin. I opened the case. There was a violin there, but the instant I looked at it I knew it was not the Stradivarius. It was of moderate quality, a dead thing in comparison!"

Holmes was amazed. "She took it! But you would have seen her walk out with it! Did you leave the door unlatched while she was with you?"

"No!" Golkov denied hotly. "I turned the key in the lock when she was in, and again as she left. I am very sensible of the value of my violin, Mr. Holmes. Do you imagine I would have kept it so long, were I careless with it?"

"But it was there before Miss Carburton arrived, and the moment she had left, it was not there. I assume had she brought another violin with her, you would have mentioned it?"

"Of course. She had only a small reticule, sufficient for a hand-kerchief, no more. She is even obliged to walk to visit me, since her father has cut off her allowance as punishment."

Holmes's frown deepened. "Then while you were in the kitchen, she opened the door to someone," he deduced. "It seems the only explanation to answer the facts."

"That is not all," Golkov said wretchedly. "Within the half hour a boy came with a note for me. . . ."

"A ransom!" Holmes exclaimed. "You have the note?"

Wordlessly Golkov produced it and passed it into Holmes's outstretched hand.

Holmes read aloud for my benefit.

"Mr. Vassily Golkov, if you wish to see your Stradivarius violin again, you will pay to me the exact sum of money which is raised for the Babcock Orphanage at the concert to be given tomorrow evening.

"I require that you hand such money to me, at a time and place I shall name when I read in the newspapers that you have been charged with the theft. If you do not do so, I shall make matches to light my household fires out of your violin.

"Need I say that any attempt to involve the police, or a similar body, in this affair will bring the same conclusion?"

Holmes looked up, his face strained, his eyes wide.

"The man is a monster, I could say a barbarian, but that is to insult the savage races who destroy only because they do not understand. This creature knows and understands only too well, and yet will still destroy. But leave it to me, Mr. Golkov! Dr. Watson and I will conceive a plan. You must do exactly as I tell you. Will you trust me in this?"

"Of course! Of course!" Golkov said eagerly. "You see, I am in the divided stick, as you say! I cannot steal the money that belongs to the fatherless. What monster would do such a thing? And yet if I do not," he could barely speak, "then my beautiful violin, the voice of my soul, will be destroyed. . . ."

"Return tomorrow at two in the afternoon," Holmes commanded. "In the meanwhile Watson and I shall think, and deduce. Tomorrow I shall come to your rooms. Be there. Now return home and sleep. Tomorrow evening we have a concert to attend, and much to do before then."

"I shall sell everything I can," Golkov promised. "All the gifts I have received, everything I have with me, but even so it will do no good! It is not the money he wishes, but to ruin me!"

"Yes, yes," Holmes agreed. "So much I perceive. But by all means gather what you can. Now, my dear sir, leave us to think and to plan. Good night to you."

As soon as he had gone I spoke.

"Surely this is Hugo Carburton's plan to ensure that his daughter does not run away and marry Golkov! He will not allow the violin to be destroyed, and if he meets Carburton's plan to ransom it, then he will almost certainly be caught by the police, tried for the crime of theft, and imprisoned. Even if he could get away with it, what woman of the slightest moral decency would marry a man who would steal money from orphans, whatever the reason? And above all, he would have demonstrated exactly where his values lie! No young woman desires to be second in a man's affections, especially to a musical instrument." I rather fancied I had some understanding of women, perhaps more so than Holmes, who seldom, if ever, sought their acquaintance.

"That much is obvious, my dear fellow," he said dismissively. "Of course it is Carburton's plan. What is disturbing is that she appears to have been party to it. I do not wonder that poor Golkov is distressed. If she is indeed, then it seems she is determined to put him to some sort of test of his love for her, which I find despicable. I cannot see any answer to that which will not cause him the utmost disillusion. It would be a cruel and quite pointless exercise, sprung not in the least from love, but purely from vanity."

"Then you can hardly help him," I said, deeply disappointed. I am not sure what I had hoped, but certainly a better answer than this.

He looked at me sharply. "I am not beaten yet, Watson! I had thought you knew me better than that! Tomorrow I shall investigate the manner in which the indifferent instrument replaced the priceless one. Tonight I must address the issue of how we are to solve the problem of meeting Mr. Carburton's demands without spoiling young Golkov's honour or having him end his career in prison." His mouth pulled into a thin line. "I hardly feel like playing any music myself. I believe I play well, but compared with Golkov I am a squeaking door. I shall instead light my best pipe and smoke for some considerable time. Please do not disturb me. Good night Watson—sleep well, because I believe I shall need all your courage and resource tomorrow."

In the morning Holmes and I set out for Golkov's rooms in Dudley Street.

They were, as he had said, very gracious and well maintained. There was a porter in the cavernous hall who observed everyone coming and going and entered it in a book.

"Good morning, gentlemen," he said pleasantly, but making it quite apparent we should not pass him with explaining ourselves. He had an almost military bearing.

"Good morning," Holmes replied cheerfully. "We have called to see Mr. Vassily Golkov. Would you be so good as to direct us to his apartments?"

"I would, sir, when I have sent the lad up to see if Mr. Golkov is in, and receiving this morning. Who may he say is calling?"

"You will send up a boy?" Holmes said with some interest.

"That's right, sir."

Holmes nodded his approval. "While we wait for the boy to return, perhaps you would be good enough to answer a few questions for us. My name is Holmes, and this is my colleague Dr. Watson."

The porter's eyes widened. "Sherlock Holmes, sir?"

"The same."

"I don't know of any mystery here, sir, far less any crime!"

"There may not be one—yet," Holmes replied. "I am hoping we shall prevent it. Did anyone visit Mr. Golkov late yesterday afternoon?"

"Yes, Mr. Holmes, Miss Helena Carburton came at almost quarter to five, or a little earlier."

"You know her?"

"Indeed, sir. She has visited Mr. Golkov more than once. A very nice young lady, and seems very fond of him."

An expression of distaste flickered across Holmes's face, as if he had bitten into a lemon. "Can you please describe exactly . . ." he emphasised the word, ". . . what you saw on this occasion. Omit nothing."

The porter looked a little worried. "I hope no harm has come to her," he said anxiously. "A most charming young lady, and Mr. Golkov is quite devoted to her."

"As far as I know she is in excellent health," Holmes said impatiently. "Please describe her visit yesterday—precisely."

"Yes sir. Miss Carburton came in. . . ."

"How was she dressed, do you recall?"

"In a dark blue cape with a fur collar, sir. White. Very becoming, it was."

"Was she carrying anything?" Holmes asked keenly.

"No sir, except one of those tiny little bags ladies have. At least, the first time."

"The first time! She came twice?"

"Yes sir. Came back again about ten minutes later. She had a violin case the second time. The boy carried it up for her, and let her in, seeing as how the door was locked again and she said Mr. Golkov was in the kitchen and wouldn't hear her knock."

"A violin case!" Holmes seized the fact, but I could see in his expression that proof of what he most surely knew already gave him no satisfaction.

"Yes sir. I didn't see her leave the first time. It must have been when the boy was standing in for me. But I saw her leave the second time, about a quarter to six."

"With the violin case, or without?"

"Without, sir, just like she came the first time, with nothing but the little bag. The white muff and the bag. She said goodnight to me very polite, like usual."

Holmes frowned. "So she went up, came down when the boy was on duty, went up again with a violin case, again when the boy was on duty, and came down a final time?"

The man thought for a moment. "That's right, sir. I was gone for about ten minutes, for my break."

"And she came down and returned up again in that time?"

The boy returned from his errand to say that Mr. Golkov was not in.

"You were a long time," Holmes observed, regarding him critically.

"Up three flights o' steps," the boy defended himself. "Can't do it no quicker, sir. Sorry."

"Three flights!" Holmes seized on it. "Mr. Golkov lives at the top of the house?"

"Yes sir."

"How interesting! How very interesting. I begin to see the glimmering of an idea, Watson! I think there may be hope." He turned to the boy. "Now tell me, young man, when you saw Miss Carburton visit Mr. Golkov yesterday evening, what was she wearing? Please describe her as minutely as you can."

The boy glanced at the superior.

"Go on!" the porter urged. "This is Mr. Sherlock Holmes! You tell him anything you can."

The boy's eyes widened appreciatively. Apparently Holmes's fame had spread even this far.

"Yes sir!" He screwed up his face in concentration. "She were wearin' a dark blue cape wif a white fur collar, an' a skirt underneaf, an' very nice boots all shiny and very clean, like she never 'as ter walk across roads wot in't bin swept like. An' an 'at, o' course."

"Marvellous!" Holmes exclaimed. "There is hope, Watson. Indeed there is. Thank you, gentlemen. You have been of the utmost help." He flashed them a smile of gratitude, then turned to me. "Home, Watson, we need to make some enquiries about the Carburton family. I have great hope that we may solve this case to everyone's satisfaction—except that of Mr. Hugo Carburton, that is. Come—there is no time to be lost!"

Our investigations on that score did not take long. A simple enquiry of a gentleman well placed in society, for whom Holmes had done a considerable favour, elicited precisely what he had wished to hear.

Hugo Carburton was of an old and well respected family. His son had married the third daughter of a duke; his elder daughter, Miss Jeannie Carburton, was betrothed to the second son of an earl; but sadly his younger daughter had taken a fancy to a foreign violinist of questionable origin and unfortunate reputation with women.

"Placing the family honour in jeopardy?" Holmes exclaimed.

"Regrettably so," his friend agreed. "No doubt her father will be able to deter her, though she is a headstrong young woman. Allowed rather too much liberty since her mother died. Very sad. Still, for her sister's sake, I dare say she may be prevailed upon."

"Watson, I have a plan which may save everybody!" Holmes said when we had returned to Baker Street and were sitting beside the fire trying to warm ourselves from the cold and gloom of the weather outside. At least I was; he did not seem to be aware of it, so consumed was he with his enthusiasm.

"However, my dear fellow, I shall require your fullest participation—at some risk to yourself, I am afraid. Here is what I propose!"

Some of what happened later I know only because Holmes recounted it to me afterwards, when it was all over, but for the sake of clarity so you may understand the events in an order which makes some sense, I shall relate them to you in the sequence in which they occurred.

The concert to raise money for the children of the Babcock orphanage, so that they might have a Christmas of warmth and good food, was held in a large hall off Shaftesbury Avenue. A number of artists had offered to give their talents free of charge and it was something of a society occasion. I was not able to attend, because I was fulfilling my part of the plan. However Holmes was there in evening dress and cutting a conspicuous figure with his lean, tense body and face so fiercely alive with expectation. Vassily Golkov also was easily seen, his hair even wilder than usual and he was clothed in a green velvet jacket and flowing cravat, somewhat melodramatic in appearance. It was part of the scheme that they should both afterwards be remembered. Were Golkov not to be blamed for the theft, all we did would be in vain. That abominable piece of vandalism, the destruction of the Stradivarius, would still take place. I cannot think how a man who believed himself civilised would commit so wanton and destructive an act, whatever the provocation, short of the saving of a life.

Half of London society was showing its benevolence by attending. Everything was a swirl of colour beneath glittering lights. Women wore magnificent gowns and jewels. There was laughter and the buzz of conversation as people milled about and then began to pour into the auditorium to take their seats. It was the day before Christmas Eve and excitement and goodwill filled the air.

Outside in the foggy streets, the gas lamps burning like baleful moons, I was preparing to enact a very different scene. I was most uncomfortably cold, and, I confess, not a little apprehensive that something might go wrong. I might fail to execute my part successfully, and end up injured, or worse, in prison. I hope I am a brave man, but this thought required of me all the courage I possessed. There is something uniquely terrible about disgrace before your fellows, and the society to which you belong and owe your loyalties.

But I was determined not to let my friend down, or be less than he had thought of me. He had been most generous in his confidence in me, and not made little of my danger. The success of the venture turned as much upon my part as upon his.

The concert was magnificent. I should dearly liked to have heard it myself. I have a great fondness for music, especially of the romantic kind. There is little that is lovelier than a perfectly sung ballad. However I was shivering in the cold, awaiting my moment of adventure.

When the final curtain was brought down to a tumult of applause, Vassily Golkov disappeared backstage to congratulate some of his fellow artists, and then to pass on his good wishes to the management.

Holmes went first to the management, then when Golkov arrived, he excused himself and undertook the most dangerous part of the entire exercise. Using his oddly shaped keys, especially constructed for the purpose, he made his way into that private part of the manager's rooms where the proceeds of the evening were kept, opened the safe and took them, secreting them carefully upon his person.

As he emerged he skirted around the groups of people talking. He had the great gift of being able to alter his appearance simply by changing the stoop of his body and the way in which he moved. The extraordinary vitality which usually marked him seemed to drain away and he became a colourless person, such as you might see, and then instantly forget.

Then he straightened up and assumed his usual, striking posture and engaged the manager in conversation.

At the same moment Golkov slipped into the empty office and closed the door behind him.

As he spoke again to the manager, offering his admiration for the evening's achievements, Golkov took his leave.

Holmes asked how well the event had done, remembering the number of prominent people he had seen present.

The manager named a magnificent sum.

Holmes offered to add something to it himself, on behalf of a public figure who would prefer to remain anonymous.

The manager flushed with pleasure and conducted him to his office where he might write a receipt for the amount, and place it under lock and key.

Of course when he got there he saw immediately that the safe was open and empty, and the window gaped wide onto the low rooftop. The poor man was mortified. Very naturally, in his desperation he turned to Holmes. Was he not the greatest consulting detective in the world, and right at his elbow?

Naturally Holmes did not refuse. He spent what remained of the evening examining the office, asking searching questions of all present. The manager did not wish to make the loss public, hoping each moment that Holmes would discover the thief and all would be well.

But Holmes gravely advised him that the police should be called, and informed. It could no longer be hidden from the authorities.

With intense reluctance the manager complied.

Lestrade arrived on the scene, as lugubrious and self-important as always. He questioned everyone as to what they had seen and heard. By midnight for once he and Holmes were in agreement. There was only one conclusion the evidence supported. Golkov had been seen to enter the manager's office, but not to leave it. Obviously he had taken the money and left by the window while Holmes had been congratulating the manager on his success. There was no help for it but to make the matter public, and set up the hunt for Golkov, and the money.

The morning newspapers trumpeted; the story of Golkov was painted in the blackest colours. Not one person had a good word to say for him. The musician who had played with such skill as to be considered gifted of God, was suddenly a devil incarnate. The fact that we had once loved him and listened to him with such emotion, poured upon him such praise, made our rage now bite the more deeply.

"Good," Holmes said, pacing the floor of the sitting room in Baker Street. Several newspapers were scattered around, all of them carrying the tale of the robbery. "Good." However he looked anything but pleased. I did not like to ask him if his dark mood were a result of some flaw in our plan, or if it were merely the ugliness of the situation. I believed it to be to do with the criticism which he was shortly to bring upon himself when he initiated the next stage in the process. He is an intensely proud man. He would deny it, probably with considerable annoyance, but he does care what others think of him. He dismisses flattery, and yet I have seen how it pleases him when his gifts are truly valued, and something of his marvellous intelligence is glimpsed by others. I could only hazard a guess at what this performance would cost him, but to pretend I had no knowledge of it was all I could offer.

Golkov had accepted the terms Carburton had offered, and asked that the arrangement for the exchange should be delivered to us. Since Golkov was now inevitably a fugitive it was a natural enough arrangement.

The eagerly awaited message arrived at last. Holmes snatched it from Mrs. Hudson's fingers, barely thanking her for it, and tore it open. I noticed his hand was shaking.

"Come, Watson," he said grimly. "Now is the time to put it all to the test, win or lose. Within an hour or two we shall know." And without even glancing at me, he took his coat from the rack in the hall, jammed his hat on his head and strode down the stairs, leaving me to follow him.

It was a miserable day outside and bitterly cold. The sky was of a uniform greyness and the edge to the wind promised snow before the day was out. Still the streets were full of people in high, good spirits, and filled with the sounds of cheery wishes for the season

passing from one to another, the excited cries of children, the jingle
of harness as coaches and carriages passed by. The clatter of hooves
and the hiss of wheels on the wet road all but drowned out the sound
of a barrel organ playing a Christmas carol, and one or two voices
raised in song.

Holmes sprang forward off the kerb, his arm raised to hail a passing
hansom, risking being knocked down in his single-minded eagerness.

I grasped his arm and pulled him back, to his considerable annoyance. He shook me off, and shouted to the driver to take us to the
York Gate entrance of Regent's Park.

I scrambled up behind him, nearly losing my balance as the ve-
hicle lurched forward and gathered speed, weaving through the traffic
on all sides. Then followed a tense journey during which we did not
speak.

When we reached the park Holmes commanded me to remain in
the hansom and to wait for him, which I complied with only because
I appreciated that it must be so.

Holmes alighted, carrying with him a small bag in which was the
money from the concert. He strode away without once looking back-
ward. I confess I was sorely tempted to follow him regardless of his
command to the contrary, in case the blackguard should offer him
either resistance, or dishonesty.

I waited in an agony of apprehension, but it proved ill founded.
Within a few moments Holmes reappeared, carrying a violin case. He
leaped up into the hansom, calling out for the driver to return us to
Baker Street.

"Is it the Stradivarius?" I demanded, although I was certain from
the look on his face that it must be.

"Of course, Watson! Do you think I should have accepted it otherwise? He has no wish for the thing, nor for the money either, for

that matter. All he wants is to ruin Golkov. His purpose would be better served if Golkov has his precious instrument back again."

"It was Hugo Carburton?"

"Naturally . . . who else?"

I had known it, but it was still a satisfaction to me to hear it. I was finding the whole plan nerve-racking, and still afraid that the final part, upon which it all rested, might yet fail.

Again I was unable to accompany Holmes, although I knew exactly what he must do, and how dearly it would cost him. I paced the floor in Baker Street, as Holmes so often did himself, desperate, frustrated, my imagination racing, picturing what was taking place.

He told me afterwards, but with so little detail that I had to fill in from my knowledge of him, watching and reading his face as he spoke quietly, not meeting my eyes but staring downwards at his hands flexed, fingers rigid in his lap.

He left Baker Street and went to find Lestrade in his office.

"Well, good morning, Mr. Holmes," Lestrade said with some surprise. "What can I do for you today? If you've come to ask me if we've found Golkov yet, I'm afraid we haven't, but we will. He can't escape. He's too well known. He's a concert violinist. The day he steps on a stage, he'll be arrested."

"I'm perfectly aware of that!" Holmes snapped, then with an intense effort, changed his tone. "I am afraid we—I—may have come to a conclusion too rapidly."

"Oh no," Lestrade replied with confidence. "It's obvious he did it. No question, Mr. Holmes. You and I agreed, for once, and we were absolutely right. Only thing is, we haven't got the bounder! Now if you can help me in that, I'd be most grateful to you—and so would a hundred or more poor little orphans who've been robbed of their Christmas." He shook his head. "That's something I don't understand, Mr. Holmes, and that's for sure. Why would a man who's got fame and money go and steal from children?" His face screwed up in bewilderment. "Can you explain it? He's lost everything, all that respect people had for him, and when we catch him he'll end up in prison. Do you think he's a bit mad, maybe?"

"I think there's another explanation," Holmes replied, tight-lipped. "If you will be so good, Lestrade, let us follow the trail of Mr. Golkov after he left the concert hall last night."

"Can't see what good that'll do now!" Lestrade grumbled.

"Humour me!" Holmes said tartly. "If you will be so good . . ."

Lestrade conceded, perhaps for old friendship's sake. It was still clear in his expression that he thought it pointless.

Doggedly they set out again, beginning at the theatre back door where the roof was at its lowest pitch, and walking along the alley towards the street. Lestrade grumbled to himself with each step. Holmes bent forward, peering from one side to the other as if expecting any moment to see something of vital importance.

He came to the end of the alley and stopped. "Ah!" he said portentously.

"What?" Lestrade demanded. "I don't see anything! Just a narrow street. Hardly a soul here. Not even anybody to ask . . . if that was what you were hoping."

"You have missed the point, Lestrade, as usual!" Holmes retorted with unnecessary waspishness. "If you were fleeing the scene of a crime, and knew that your pursuers might be close behind you, which way would you go?"

Lestrade looked one way then the other.

"Quick!" Holmes cried. "They are behind you! Which way? Don't stand dithering, man!"

"That way!" Lestrade replied, somewhat stung. "There's nowhere to hide the other way, and up there is a main street where I could blend in with other folk, if I were lucky, and maybe catch a hansom. If I am Mr. Golkov, I've certainly got money enough. And," he added, "if I am Golkov I maybe don't know the back streets that well, and I don't need to get lost, or worse still, cornered!"

"Precisely!" Holmes agreed. "You are thinking, Lestrade. Excellent." And he set out towards Shaftesbury Avenue at a rapid stride, obliging Lestrade to caper along behind him to keep up.

Just around the corner there was a sandwich seller. I remember him only too well myself!

"My good man!" Holmes addressed him. "Were you here yesterday evening at half past ten, or thereabouts?" It was then mid afternoon.

"I was, sir," the man answered. "Sometimes the folk leaving the theatre fancy a bite. Do quite well then, I do."

"I'm glad to hear it. Did you see a young man come running down that alley, hair flying, velvet jacket on, looking as if he were pursued?"

"I did an' all! 'Ceptin' 'e were the one doin' the chasin'," the sandwich seller replied. "Arter the feller wot robbed the the-ayter, I reckon."

"What?" Lestrade demanded. "What are you saying?"

" 'E were a chasin' after the feller wot robbed them orphans," the man repeated patiently. "Big, rough-lookin' feller 'e were! Shoulders like an ox, 'at jammed down over 'is 'ead, moustache all bristling an' a big stick in his 'and like 'e'd bash someone's brains out wif it. I tell yer straight, gents, I'd a thought twice about chasin' arter 'im, in case I caught up wif 'im an' 'e did fer me."

25

Lestrade questioned the man closely, but he did not alter his story, because of course it was the truth.

"Well, I'll be blessed!" he said at last, staring at Holmes. "This alters everything! I blamed Golkov, poor devil! We've got to find out what happened to him, Holmes, and right away. Let us pray it is not too late."

Thus they followed the very distinct trail of one man chasing another for at least two miles until eventually the young man with the flying hair and the velvet jacket was seen to catch up with the older ruffian and there ensued a terrible battle in which the younger man was beaten about the head and left all but senseless on the cobbles of a stable yard, but not before he had belaboured his prey and sent him off only too grateful to escape both his attention, and that of the crowd which had begun to gather.

"Damn it!" Lestrade swore furiously. The apparent injustice of it outraged his sensibilities. "He nearly had him, Mr. Holmes!"

"So it would seem," Holmes conceded.

"Never mind 'seem'!" Lestrade retorted. "Golkov wasn't your thief at all! You were wrong, Mr. Holmes. First time I can recall that ever happening."

"No, it isn't," Holmes contradicted him, I think merely for the sake of argument. He could not endure to be gracious about it.

Lestrade did not labour the point. "Now we must find what happened to poor Golkov. Somebody took him in. Who?" He looked around at the small gathering of old men, boys and a washerwoman who had given their various pieces of the story.

"Ol' Gertie," one of the men replied. "Pick up any stray, she will, an' feed 'em, like as not." He pointed helpfully to a narrow doorway, the top half of which had once been glassed, but was now covered over with sacking.

In the room beyond Holmes and Lestrade found a very impatient Golkov, pretending to brave a severe headache and to be sufficiently newly recovered of his senses to be unaware of his surroundings.

"Well, young man, a fine dance you've led us!" Lestrade said cheerfully, immensely relieved to see him not seriously the worse for his adventure. "Mr. Holmes here thought as you'd run off with the money from the concert!" He could not resist saying it one more time. "In all the newspapers, it is! Never mind. We'll put that right."

Golkov stared at Holmes. Lestrade could not possibly have imagined the reason for the passion in his face.

"So it was!" Holmes said grimly. "Read by Mr. Hugo Carburton, who made several decisions regarding your future relations with his family because of it." He managed a look of sufficient clarity that Golkov understood his meaning. However he recalled Lestrade's presence just in time, and refrained from expressing his joy, or his gratitude.

Golkov turned to Lestrade. "I have the money! I got it from the villain before he ran off." And he produced the bag of money which he himself had provided by selling everything he could to raise it. It may not have been precisely the same amount, but it would have been within a few guineas. It was to be hoped that the theatre manager would not count it, and the guardians of the orphanage would be far too grateful to think of such a thing.

Holmes, Lestrade and Golkov went back to Scotland Yard, where Golkov was finally relieved, both of the money, and the accusation of having stolen it. Holmes bore the good-natured teasing with as much fortitude as he could muster. Golkov was the hero of the hour.

Holmes returned to Baker Street and found me stiff and tired, nursing a brandy before the fire.

"Well?" I demanded.

"Very satisfactory," he replied, then seeing my hunched shoulders and remembering my contribution, he softened somewhat. "Thank you."

"It cannot be entirely satisfactory," I argued. "Golkov may have both his reputation and his violin back, but nothing can redeem Miss Carburton's part in it all."

Holmes looked smug. "I think it was understandable, in her situation, Watson."

"Well I don't!" I said hotly. "I find it contemptible."

"She is in love with an earl's son, and very well aware of the realities of society," he replied.

"What?" I was dumbfounded. It made no sense at all.

Holmes smiled. "Miss Jeannie Carburton, Watson. The clean boots, remember? The second visit up the stairs, which required the boy to unlock the door for her? Planned and carried out with some skill, but I dare say she is less proud of herself now."

"Oh! Oh yes, I see." I confess I was too thankful for Golkov's sake not to smile at it.

Later that evening Holmes and I visited Golkov in his rooms. He could hardly contain his gratitude, and I was doubly delighted to see Miss Helena Carburton there also. She proved to be a most charming and courageous young woman, willing to risk her father's wrath and abandon all the comfort of his position in order to be with the man she loved.

"I can never thank you enough for what you have done for me!" Golkov said, his admiration for Holmes lighting his face till his eyes were like a child's who has seen the magic of Christmas and understood it for the first time. "You have sacrificed your reputation for infallibility, in order to save my honour, and my violin! You are a truly noble man. . . ." He put his arm around Miss Carburton and she also gazed at Holmes with the utmost respect; indeed her regard for him seemed second only to her feeling for Golkov.

Holmes basked in it for a moment, savouring its pleasure, then turned to me.

"Of course I could not have done it without Watson!"

Golkov blushed. "Of course! Dr. Watson, I do apologize for my ingratitude. Had you not been prepared to play the villain, at such risk to yourself—I was terrified those men who rescued me were going to beat you severely. . . ."

I tried to be gracious, feeling my bruises as tactfully as I could.

"Not at all," I murmured. "Always glad to serve in the cause of justice." But I was not displeased with the look of intense admiration with which Miss Carburton regarded me, her eyes shining.

"We can never thank you enough!" Golkov repeated, a faint flush of embarrassment on his thin cheeks. "I cannot even offer to reward you financially yet. It took all I had to replace the concert money. . . ."

Miss Carburton blushed with shame for her father, but did not speak.

Golkov's arm tightened around her.

". . . but I shall, as soon as I can earn enough," he promised.

Holmes shrugged and brushed it aside. "I do not wish for money, Mr. Golkov. I have sufficient for my needs. But there is another reward you could give me . . . for one day . . ."

"One day?" Golkov was confused. Then suddenly he perceived . . . and the blood drained from his face, his eyes wide.

Holmes would not say it, he could not bring himself to ask.

Slowly Golkov turned and walked across the room, picked up the violin case and came back, carrying it in his arms like a child . . . the beloved Stradivarius. Without a word he gave it to Holmes and stepped back.

"One day," Holmes promised. "Christmas Day. I shall return it to you the day after."

Golkov bowed. "For no other man on earth," he said softly. "But you, Mr. Holmes, have earned it."

Lestrade, beaming all over his face, presented the money to the orphanage. I spent a solitary Christmas by the fireside, eating Mrs. Hudson's most excellent cake, while from the next room drifted the soul-searing music of a man playing the most beautiful instrument on earth and charming out of its strings all that he could not and dared not say in words.

THE FOUR WISE MEN

Peter Lovesey

One December morning in the year 1895, Sherlock Holmes tossed aside *The Times* and said to me with some abruptness, "Stop dithering, Watson. It's your duty to go down to Somerset for Christmas, regardless of the plans you made."

I stared at him in astonishment. I had spoken not a syllable of the matter that was exercising me.

He amazed me even more by adding, "An old soldier's loyalty to his senior officer is a commitment for life. He needs your support and you are not the man to withhold it."

"Holmes," said I, when I found my voice again, "your feats of deduction are well known to me, but to discover that you are also a mind reader is truly a revelation, not to say unnerving."

He made a dismissive gesture with his long, limp hand. "My dear fellow, I can think of few things I should less enjoy than peering into the minds of my fellow creatures. My advice to you is based on observation alone." As if to provoke me further, he stopped speaking, thrust his unlit pipe in his mouth and looked out of the window at the traffic passing along Baker Street.

I waited. It became obvious that he proposed to say nothing more unless I pursued the matter.

I was loth to give him the satisfaction, but at length my curiosity prevailed. "I hesitate to trespass on your time. . . ."

"Then don't."

Some minutes passed before I steeled myself to begin again. I do believe he, too, was finding the silence intolerable, though he would never have admitted as much.

"I thought I knew your methods, Holmes. In this matter, I confess myself mystified."

He continued to stare out of the window.

"I would appreciate some explanation."

He sighed heavily. "There are times, Watson, when I despair of you. You are blind to your own behaviour. When I told you to stop dithering, it was after you had removed that letter from its envelope for the third time and perused it with much frowning. By now you know the contents. You can only be re-reading it to see if you can think of some half-decent way of avoiding Christmas in Somersetshire."

"How on earth do you know about Somerset?"

"The Taunton postmark."

"Ha!" I chuckled at my own naivety, and I should not have done so, for Holmes took it as dismissive of his brilliance. Recovering my tact, I continued, "But the other things. Your statement—which I have to declare is accurate—that my presence is required by an old army colleague."

"I said your senior officer."

"And you are right, by Jove. Have you been reading my correspondence?"

He emitted a sound of impatience. "How could I? It hasn't been out of your possession since the moment you tore open the envelope. The explanation will, of course, disappoint you, as these things do."

"I'm sure it will not."

With a show of reluctance, he enlightened me. "The festive season is approaching. We're all aware of that. A time of invitations."

"You made an inspired guess?"

Now a look of extreme disfavour clouded the great detective's features. "I do not guess."

"I said 'inspired.'"

"It does not lessen the insult. Guessing is the province of charlatans. I make deductions. I was about to point out that when you first perused the letter you turned to look over my shoulder at the front page of *The Times*, which has nothing to interest you except the date."

"So I did!"

"Today's date told you how close we are to Christmas, how many days are left. You're an active fellow, with much to attend to in the coming days. You had to calculate the time at your disposal."

"Absolutely true."

"An invitation to the country for Christmas. Need I say more?"

"Please do." His statements had the force of logic, as always. "What mystifies me most is how you divined that the invitation comes from one of my regiment—and his senior rank."

"Oh, that," he said, knocking his pipe against the window ledge and producing a cloud of ash. "It's training, Watson."

"Training in the deductive method?"

"Not my training. Yours. In the army. The drilling every soldier undergoes. What did you do when you met a superior officer?"

"Saluted. But I didn't salute just now."

"No, no, but when you saw who the letter was from, your free hand snapped to your side with the fingers lightly clenched, the thumb pointing down the seam below your trouser pocket in the military fashion. Highly indicative."

"Good Lord," I said. "Am I so transparent?"

"Quite the reverse."

"Opaque?"

He looked away and I believe there was a gleam of amusement in his eye. "You have made your decision, I see. You will go to Taunton. Loyalty demands it, even though duty no longer applies."

I took the letter from its envelope once more. Holmes had delivered his advice, and I saw the sense of it, but I felt that a more considered opinion might be forthcoming. The invitation was, indeed, from my old Commanding Officer in the Fifth Northumberland Fusiliers, Colonel Sloane, M. C., a hero of the Afghan campaign. I offered to read it aloud.

My Dear Watson, (it began)

Some years have passed since we were last in contact, but your admirable strengths impress me still. I always regarded you as utterly dependable.

"True," Holmes generously interposed.

I never expected to ask for your support after we retired from Her Majesty's Service, but a strange contingency has arisen here in the village of Bullpen, near Taunton, where I reside.

"Would you repeat that?" Holmes requested.

"Bullpen, near Taunton. May I continue?"

He nodded. I had all his attention now.

I can forgive you if you have never heard of the Bullpen Nativity Service, but it has some celebrity in these parts. Each year on the Sunday preceding Christmas it is the custom for the villagers to take part in a masque and procession to the church, where our Nativity Service takes place. We take turns to play the parts of the characters in the age-old story, and this year I have the honour to be Balthazar, one of the Three Kings.

"Wise Men," Holmes interjected again.

"It says 'Kings.'"

"Kings are not mentioned in any of the Gospel accounts."

"Really?"

"The figure of three is not specified either, for that matter," said he, displaying a hitherto unrevealed acquaintance with the New Testament.

I resumed reading:

It is a role of some responsibility, for by tradition Balthazar carries the Star. I should explain that the Star is a representation in silver and precious stones of the Star in the East, of Biblical renown. It is about the size of a dinner plate and is carried high, mounted on a seven-foot pole, so that the impression is given that we Kings—and, indeed, the shepherds—are being guided towards Bethlehem. The star is of mediaeval workmanship, beautifully constructed of Welsh silver and set with seven rubies. It is kept in the strong room of the United Bank in Taunton. Without exaggeration it is one of the most valuable mediaeval treasures in England, rivalling even the Crown Jewels in workmanship and beauty. Last summer, it was put on exhibition at the British Museum, and insured for twenty thousand pounds. My task—my honour—is to collect the star from the bank, travel with it in a closed carriage to my home, the manor house, where the principal actors assemble to put on their robes and the procession through the street to the church begins. I carry the Star aloft on the stave, keeping it in my possession until the moment during the service when it is placed over the crib. The responsibility then passes for a brief time to Joseph, who returns it to me after the service.

"Ha!" said Holmes with animation. "He wishes you to be his Joseph."

I nodded.

"And you will go." As if the matter no longer held any interest, he reached for his scrapbook and opened it. "Have you seen my paste bottle?"

"Behind you on the mantelpiece."

"And scissors?"

"Where you left them, in the top pocket of your dressing gown."

"So I did. There's an item of passing interest on page three about the theft in Paris of a necklace that belonged to Marie Antoinette. It has features that lead me to suspect my old adversary Georges Du Broc is active again."

"Du Broc?" I repeated. "You've never spoken of Du Broc before."

"The Jackdaw. A chirpy little fellow half your size. The most brazen thief in Europe."

"He is unknown to me."

"Be thankful, then. He'd have the shirt off your back without your

36

noticing. Have I not mentioned the case of the Tsarina's ankle chain?"

"Not to me," said I. "I should have remembered a case like that, I'm certain."

"How discreet I have become," mused Holmes.

He exasperated me by saying no more of Du Broc, the Tsarina, or the ankle chain. But he was good enough to announce, "I shall attend the Bullpen Nativity Service."

We took the train together from Paddington on the Saturday before Christmas. A dusting of snow in London became quite an Arctic scene as we steamed towards the West Country. I still hoped to return to London by Christmas Eve, but my confidence ebbed when I saw the snowflakes getting larger by the minute. At Bristol, we changed to the Exeter and Plymouth line.

"I doubt if they'll cancel it," said Holmes, reading my thoughts with ease (he *was* capable of it, I swear). "A tradition that has lasted five hundred years isn't going to be ended by a few inches of snow."

"Perhaps they'll dispense with the street procession and go straight to the church."

"My dear fellow, Joseph and Mary travelled scores of miles over mountains and across deserts from Nazareth to Bethlehem through the most inclement conditions and you complain at the prospect of a ten-minute walk in the snow."

I turned aside and faced the window.

We were greeted at Taunton by Colonel Sloane himself, little changed from the gallant officer I had last seen in Kabul, six feet tall, with a fine, erect bearing and a cropped iron-grey moustache. He walked with a marked limp, the result of a stray bullet that had shattered his left kneecap. I had patched him up myself, and he always maintained that I saved the leg from amputation.

I introduced Holmes.

"I have heard of you, of course, Mr Holmes," said the colonel. "What brings a man of your reputation to our humble village?"

"A bird I seek," Holmes answered cryptically.

This was news to me. I had never heard my illustrious friend discussing ornithology.

"Most of them migrated months ago," said Sloane. "You'll see a few sparrows and chaffinches, no doubt. A robin or two."

Holmes appeared uninterested. He makes no concession to the social graces.

Colonel Sloane had come for us in a four-wheeler. His former batman, Ruff, a strapping fellow I faintly recalled from Kabul, stepped forward to assist with our luggage. I gathered that the colonel lived as a bachelor in Bullpen Manor House and was looked up to as the squire.

With Ruff at the reins, we were smoothly conveyed through the lanes towards the village. It was like riding on a sleigh, for the hooves and wheels made little sound on the snow.

The colonel wasted no time in explaining my duties. "You will have gathered that I put the highest priority on securing the safety of the Bullpen Star. I have engaged two sergeants of the Taunton police to act as bodyguards. My batman is big enough to handle most emergencies, but I see this as a full-scale military operation, which is why I detailed you to be Joseph. I shall hand the Star to you at the appropriate time in the church."

"When is that?"

"You will be standing beside the crib with Mary and the Angels. You are not in the procession."

I could not resist a triumphant glance at Holmes, who gazed back stonily.

"You may stand easy during the service," the Colonel continued, "but mentally you will be at attention, if you understand me. The procession will march up the aisle with me at the front."

"*March?*" said Holmes.

"With me at the front holding the Star," Sloane reiterated, "and the two policemen, disguised as shepherds, in close attendance. The congregation will be singing a carol, 'Once in Royal David's City.' As the 'Amen' is sung, I shall take two paces forward to the crib. The Rector will say the words, 'It came and stood over where the young child was'—whereupon I shall hand you the staff on which the Star is mounted. You will grasp it firmly with both hands."

"Military fashion," murmured Holmes.

My companion's irony was threatening to discompose the colonel. I gave him a sharp glance of disapproval.

"This is of the utmost importance, Watson," Colonel Sloane stressed. "Do not let go of that staff until the service is over and I take it from you. No one else must be in possession of the Star at any time. Is that understood?"

"Absolutely, sir."

"Do you still have your service revolver?"

The question somewhat surprised me.

"Not with me."

"No matter. I have guns. I shall see that you are armed."

"In church?"

"The enemy are no respecters of the Lord's house."

"The enemy? Who do you mean precisely?"

"The criminal class, Watson. They will rob us of the Star if we give them the opportunity."

Holmes raised an eyebrow.

"Are you expecting an ambush, Colonel?"

"Deplorably, there is the possibility," Sloane answered gravely. "Did I mention that the Star was loaned to the British Museum for several months in the summer? Thousands of visitors saw it. The newspapers wrote of it. The *Illustrated London News* and the *Graphic* printed line engravings of it. More of the public know of its existence than ever before. Our simple Nativity Service was fully described. Isn't it a tailor-made opportunity for the wickedly disposed to attempt a grand larceny?"

"You may well be right," Holmes was fair enough to concur. "You are wise to be alert."

The guest room of the Feathers Inn had been booked for us. Bullpen was a modest-sized village of about two hundred souls, of whom a fair proportion crowded into the public bar that night. We joined them. In the course of the evening we met Andrew Hall, the farmer who was to play Melchior in the masque, a massively built individual with the reddish, leathery complexion of one who makes his living in all weathers.

"We take it by turns," Farmer Hall told us, speaking of the casting of the players. "I were a simple shepherd two year back. Now I'm carrying the gold."

"Real gold?" I enquired.

"Lord, no. Don't get ideas, just because our Star is valuable. 'Tis only a box of trinkets I carry."

"Who plays the other Wise Man, Gaspar?" Holmes asked.

"The frankincense man? Our landlord, Jeb Wiggs."

"You're all well known in the village—you, Wiggs and the colonel?"

"That's a fact, sir. Parts are played by villagers, according to tradition."

I was beginning to feel uneasy about my role as Joseph, but Farmer Hall reassured me by saying, "Them's the walking parts I'm speaking of, kings and shepherds. It's they the crowds come to see and it's they that gets handed mince pies and mulled wine along the route. We don't mind who plays Joseph and Mary—stuck in the church for upwards of two hours. They're non-imbibing parts. We got a Joseph from London this year, old army friend of the colonel."

I was about to make myself known when Holmes spoke up first: "And what of Mary? Who plays Mary?"

"Any young girl of sixteen, provided she has a pious expression and a spotless reputation. This year 'tis young Alison Pugh, the church warden's youngest."

"And the infant Jesus?"

"A china doll."

"Does anyone else take part?" Holmes asked, at pains to get the entire cast list.

"The angels. Girls who wanted the part of Mary and had to be overlooked for various reasons. There are only two this year. The Dawson sisters. Winsome little things. Just a mite too winsome, I reckon."

We spoke no more of the Dawson sisters. By the end of the evening we had a useful understanding of the entire arrangements. At five the next evening, the players in the procession would assemble at the manor house.

"I shall follow the procession," Holmes declared before we retired.

"Are you sure you wouldn't care to dress up as a shepherd?" I asked. "You enjoy going in disguise."

"Dressing up is not disguise," said he witheringly.

So it was that by five the following afternoon I found myself standing berobed in a "manger" in Bullpen Church, ankle-deep in straw that scratched my feet distractingly through the sandals. Had I been in the procession, I should have been allowed to wear my own shoes, but as a non-moving player I earned no concession. At my side in virginal blue, seated on a bale, was young Alison, in the role of Mary. She kept her eyes downcast and said little. The Dawson sisters, playing the angels, were more sociable. Cicely, the older of the two, golden-haired and extremely pretty, invited me more than once to adjust the angle of her wings, which involved unbuttoning her bodice a little way at the back and retying the satin straps over her shoulders. But when her parents joined the congregation and sat in the front pew, she needed no more adjustments.

The animals around us were constructed by a local carpenter, flat wooden figures of full size that the angels were at some risk of knocking over with their wings. In fact, a donkey fell against me when the organist startled us by launching suddenly into "The First Noel."

The service was beginning, but my thoughts were outside, on the snow-covered street. The procession must already have left the manor house with Colonel Sloane at its head, proudly carrying the Bullpen Star, its rubies glittering in the light of scores of flaming torches. I hoped the Colonel was not being too literal about the "march" and setting a pace out of keeping with the occasion. As a spectacle, it should have been stately and devout, like an Epiphany procession I once saw in one of the Latin countries.

We reached the last verse of the carol and the rector made his way up the aisle to receive the procession at the west door. The gas was turned so low that we could barely see the words in the hymn books, and the dimness contributed to the charmed atmosphere, the air of anticipation.

A draught of cold December air gusted through the church when the door was opened. The organist started a *diminuendo* rendering of "Once in Royal David's City," with just the trebles in the choir singing, and I do not mind admitting I was moved almost to tears. Hastily I reminded myself that I was on duty for the colonel and ought to be at full alert.

The procession entered the church. With deep satisfaction I saw the Star above the heads, gleaming proudly in the unbroken tradition of five centuries or more. The lights were turned up gradually and the silver fairly shone as it was borne up the aisle.

My role in the service was about to begin. Along the aisle I saw Balthazar gripping the staff with the Star aloft, dressed in a robe of glittering fabric with an ermine collar that would not have looked out of place at a coronation. He sported a crown, of course, fashioned in the eastern style; and a black beard that gave him a splendid Oriental appearance, so his limp did not take anything away from the effect.

Beside him, the two policemen dressed as shepherds were moving with the heavy tread of officers on duty, but this was noticeable only to me, with the advantage of knowing who they were. I spotted my drinking companions of the night before, as sumptuously arrayed as the colonel, playing Gaspar and Melchior with great conviction.

The carol drew to a close and the "Amen" was sung. The rector spoke his few words about the star standing over the stable. Balthazar stepped forward like a colour-sergeant about to hand over the regimental standard. His lush black beard quite covered three-quarters of his face, but our eyes met briefly and I believe I conveyed confidence. I put out my hands to receive the precious Star and it was handed across. Resolutely I gripped the staff with both hands.

The Three Kings—or Wise Men, as Holmes would have it—by turns presented Mary with their offerings of gold, frankincense and myrhh. Having stepped back, they knelt, allowing the shepherds to come forward. When everyone was kneeling I had a clear view of the congregation and I was pleased to observe that Holmes had found a seat at the end of one of the pews. It would do him no harm to have a good view of me at the centre of proceedings, loyally carrying out my duty, just as the colonel had instructed. For once in his life, I reflected, Mr. Sherlock Holmes was obliged to play second fiddle.

There followed more verses from St. Matthew and then the Rector, an elderly man with a fine crop of white hair and a rather monotonous voice, said, "Let us pray." I had better explain that I am not in the habit of praying standing up and with my eyes open. On this occasion (may I be forgiven), I made an exception. Primed for any occurrence, I looked steadily ahead, whilst every other head was bowed. I was resolved not to relax my vigilance for a second, even though it was difficult to conceive of anything untoward happening whilst we were at our devotions.

I was mistaken.

There was an interruption, and the offender, of all people, was Holmes!

I spotted a movement along the aisle and to my mortification saw him crawling rapidly and with uncanny stealth, Indian-fashion, over the flagstones and the monumental brasses in my direction, or at least towards the kneeling shepherds and Wise Men in front of the crib. When he was near enough to touch their robes, he dipped even closer to the floor like a ferret.

That it was Holmes, I had not the slightest doubt, or I would have raised the alarm there and then. I knew the man. I knew what he was wearing, the Inverness cape and the brown suit and the goloshes. No one but my Baker Street companion could move with such remarkable agility.

Aghast, I held onto the Star, craning to see what he was doing. He appeared to strike a match.

"And now let us pray for the health and happiness at Christmas of Her Majesty the Queen," intoned the Rector.

Holmes blew out the match, turned, and was back in his pew before the "Amen." There was the merest wisp of smoke indicating where he had been. Some of his fellow worshippers must have been aware of some movement close to them, and there were a few glances his way, but by then he was joining lustily in "God Rest Ye Merry Gentlemen, Let Nothing You Dismay."

The Grace was spoken and the service ended. The organ soared in a Christmas anthem and people began to file out. Naturally, I remained staunchly at my post. In all the movement I lost sight of the Three Wise Men, and I must say I felt a trifle neglected. The colonel had promised to relieve me of the treasured Star at the first opportunity.

One of the angels (the winsome Cicely, in fact) asked me if I was going to the vestry to change out of my costume. I shook my head.

She said without much maidenly coyness that she was tired of being an angel and hoped I would help her remove her wings.

Nor without regret, I said I must guard the Star until the colonel came. To Cicely, this was unreasonable. She responded with a toss of her pretty curls.

I remained at my post. Almost everyone had filed out, leaving two church wardens collecting hymn books, and me, still in my costume. My feet itched from the straw and my legs ached from standing up for so long. I am bound to record, self-pitying as it must appear, that I felt neglected. Presently Cicely Dawson and her sister came from the vestry dressed in their own clothes and strutted past and out of the church without even wishing me goodnight.

I could understand the colonel forgetting about me, but how could he have neglected to remember the Star he had been at such pains to protect?

Then a voice echoed through the church. "Come, Watson, time is short!"

It was Holmes. He, at least, had remembered me. He was standing in the doorway.

"I can't leave," I called back. "I'm guarding the Star."

"That thing on the pole?" he said, striding up the aisle towards me. "Paste and nickel-plate. That isn't the Bullpen Star! The Star is well on its way to Taunton by now. If we hurry we may yet save it."

"No," I insisted. "This is the Star and those are my orders."

To my horror he reacted by grabbing the staff above my handhold and shaking it violently. The Star, loosened from the shaft, fell, hit the flagstones and shattered into three pieces.

"Does solid silver break like that?" he demanded, eyes blazing.

I stared at the fragments in amazement. He was manifestly right. The plaster of Paris was laid bare. I had spent the evening guarding a fake replica of the medieval treasure.

"Where's the Colonel?" I asked hoarsely. "We must inform him at once."

"No time, Watson, no time. Do you have that gun he gave you?"

"Under my robe."

"Capital. I've borrowed Farmer Hall's dogcart. We must be in Taunton before the next train leaves for Bristol."

"I'm not dressed."

"Nonsense."

Without a notion as to the reason, I presently found myself seated beside Holmes exposed to the elements on a light cart behind a black gelding that fairly raced through the night. Fortunately the snow had stopped in the last hour. A full moon and a clear sky made the going possible. I was chilled to the marrow in my biblical apparel, yet eager for information.

"Who exactly are we pursuing, Holmes?"

"The thief," he said, through bared teeth.

An appalling thought struck me. "Not Colonel Sloane?"

"No. Sloane isn't our man."

"But what happened to him? He promised to see me after the service."

"He's at home, at the manor house. Could be dead, but I think not." He cracked the whip, urging the horse on.

"Good Lord!"

"Trussed up, more likely. He never left home."

"How can that be so? I saw him in the church. He handed me the Star."

"No, Watson. That wasn't your colonel. That was the thief."

"Are you sure?" I asked in disbelief. "He was limping like the colonel."

"Naturally he was. The robbery was planned to the last detail. Almost the last, anyway," Holmes added on a note of self-congratulation that I picked up even with the wind rushing in my ears.

I hazarded a guess. "Was he limping on the wrong side?"

"Ha! Nothing so obvious," said he.

"Wearing a built-up shoe? I saw you creeping up the aisle behind him and lighting a match."

"No, Watson. His shoes were a perfect pair. That was the detail I went to some trouble to ascertain. Whilst Balthazar knelt in prayer, I examined his heels. The heel of a lame man always shows wear on the edge of the shoe that takes most weight. This pair of heels was evenly worn. So the wearer was not lame. Whoa!"

We were going too fast, and the wheels skidded towards a hedge. Holmes pulled on the reins in time to avert a disaster.

"Deucedly clever," I said. "But you must have had your suspicions already."

"I knew if the Star was to be stolen, it would be well-planned. The weak point in the Colonel's arrangements was when he had brought the Star from the bank to his house. He needed to change into his costume. He wouldn't want the bodyguards in his bedroom watching him dress."

"Lord, no."

"But he wanted the Star in his possession at all times, so he took it in with him."

"And that was when the thief struck?"

"Yes. He was hidden in the room, waiting. I hope he didn't injure the colonel seriously. My guess is that he tied and gagged him."

"If that was what happened, why didn't this scoundrel—whoever he may be—escape with the Star across the fields at once?"

"Too risky. The bodyguards were outside the bedroom waiting. The hue and cry would have been raised within minutes. His plan was more ingenious. Under Balthazar's robes and behind the black beard, he was well disguised. He'd gone to the trouble of making that cheap, but convincing, replica of the Star. He made the substitution, tucked the real Star under his robes and went out to lead the procession."

"What nerve!"

"He's audacious, I grant you."

"And resourceful. How did he know what the Star looked like, to manufacture the fake replacement? Of course!" I found myself answering my own question. "He saw it for himself in London last summer, and used the illustrations in the press as blueprints. Diabolical."

"And at the end of the service," said Holmes, "he walked quietly away, dismissed the bodyguards, slipped off Balthazar's robes behind the church wall—where I found them a few minutes too late—and helped himself to one of the carriages lined up in the lane."

"And escaped!"

"Just so."

Our dogcart slithered over the snow for some minutes more. The lights of Taunton were showing across the fields.

"Holmes."

"Yes?"

"How shall we recognize the thief?"

His answer was cryptic. "He'll be waiting at the railway station—if we're in time." He whipped up the horse again.

The streets of Taunton, being more used by traffic than the country lanes, glistened black under the street lamps and our wheels clattered over the cobbles as we raced the last minutes through the town and into the station yard, where several carriages were waiting.

"Take out the gun and be ready to use it," Holmes ordered. He sprang down from the dogcart and strode into the booking hall, his cape billowing. At such times, in pursuit of wrong-doing, he was like a hound, fearless and unstoppable.

I followed as well as I was able, hampered by my New Testament robes. I wondered how well I could use a revolver these days. Of one thing I was certain: my heart had not forgotten how to thump as it always did in battle.

"Has the last train left for Bristol?" Holmes demanded of the ticket collector.

"Due in two minutes, sir," came the answer.

We hurried onto the "Up" platform, which appeared deserted, save for an elderly couple.

"He's hiding up," said Holmes.

"The waiting rooms?" said I.

"We don't have the time to check. He'll have to make a dash for the train when it comes in. Take up a position halfway along and to the right. I'll be up here."

"Shall I use the gun?"

"Wing him, if you have to."

The sound of the approaching express carried down the line before the engine came into view. My throat was dry and my legs felt like jelly. I'm sure Holmes, at the other end of the platform, was as steady and primed as a hunting lion. I looked about me, at the waiting rooms and cloakrooms of different classes from which the thief might emerge.

The rasp of the locomotive increased. It would be in sight now, snorting pink steam and sparks into the night sky, but my eyes were on the doors nearest to me, expecting a figure to dart out any minute and dash for the train.

Somebody did emerge from the ladies' waiting room, but it was a young woman carrying a child. I saw nobody else.

The train steamed in and came to a halt. Several people opened doors and got out, bringing confusion on the platform. I couldn't possibly use my gun.

"Watson!"

I turned, hearing the shout from Holmes.

"Behind you, man! The end of the platform!"

I swung about, in time to see a tall, male figure in the act of opening a compartment door near the front, away from all the station buildings. He must have left it to the last moment to climb over the paling that extended along the platform. I gave chase. When I got to the compartment and swung open the door, no one was inside. He had gone straight through, opened the door on the other side and jumped onto the line, dashing along the rails. I followed, shouting to him to halt.

The man turned, saw me, a horrified look in his eye, and redoubled his running.

As I tried gamely to catch up, a movement at his side caused him to veer off course. He was powerless to evade the tackle. Holmes felled him with a grab that was as good as anything I ever saw on a football field.

I hastened towards them, gun at the ready, but Holmes, a master of *baritsu*, the Japanese system of wrestling, already had his man in a stranglehold. And there in the snow, between the railway lines, lay the precious Bullpen Star, thankfully undamaged.

"You see who this scoundrel is?" said Holmes.

In the poor light I had some difficulty recognizing the fellow, particularly as most of his face was pressed into the snow. However, I hazarded a guess. "Is it the Jackdaw, Georges Du Broc, the most brazen thief in Europe?"

"No, Watson, it is not," said Holmes on a petulant note. "I told you Du Broc is a short man. He couldn't possibly impersonate Colonel Sloane, who is quite six feet in height. This is Ruff, the Colonel's own batman."

"Oh, my hat!" I exclaimed in horror.

"Only a servant," Holmes charitably pointed out.

The shock I felt was nothing to the colonel's when he was apprised of the news. He had known Ruff for twenty years and the man had given no hint of dishonesty.

"Yes, but when did he become your civilian employee?" enquired Holmes, over a late glass of claret in the manor house.

The Colonel had by this time recovered from being trussed and gagged, and lying in his bedroom, just as Holmes had deduced.

"About eight months ago. He turned up one afternoon. I was delighted to see him again, the first time in years."

"By which time you were already chosen for the part of Balthazar in the masque, I presume?"

"That is true," the Colonel admitted. "The service has to be arranged a long time in advance."

"And it was in the press?"

"Yes."

"So he learned of the opportunity and insinuated himself into your employment." Holmes flapped his long hand as if that answered all questions.

"You're an amazing detective, Mr Holmes."

"If you insist."

"But one thing still puzzles me," the Colonel went on.

"What is that?"

"You said when you arrived that you had come in search of a bird."

"Yes, indeed."

"Did you find it?"

"Certainly. You may not be aware, Colonel, that there is a member of the sandpiper family known as a ruff."

"Oh."

Not one of us had thought of that.

We returned to London by an early train next morning. The landscape was still seasonally white, without any overnight snowfall. The prospect of Christmas at home cheered my spirits no end after the shocks of the night before.

Holmes, too, was in festive mood, and appeared to have acquired a present in his short stay in Somersetshire, for there was a large, interesting parcel on the luggage-rack above his head.

With Holmes in a buoyant mood, I taxed him on a matter that had not been explained to my satisfaction.

"Now that we're alone, old friend, will you admit that it was pure chance that the thief's name happened to be that of a variety of sandpiper?"

He laughed. "Total coincidence, Watson."

"Then your remark to the Colonel—the one about seeking a bird—was the merest eyewash."

He gave me a long, disdainful look. "Is anything I ever say eyewash? Of course I was seeking a bird in the country. And I found one." He pointed upwards to the parcel on the luggage rack. "Thanks to Farmer Hall, who you will remember as Melchior, the Wise Man, we shall have a twenty-pound goose for Christmas luncheon."

I shook my head in admiration. "Truly, Holmes, there was a fourth Wise Man this year, and he is sitting opposite me."

ELEEMOSYNARY, MY DEAR WATSON

Barbara Paul

For once it was I rather than Holmes who was complaining about the season. I don't know what there is about the word "holiday" that makes the average Englishman think all the common-sense rules of eating and drinking have been temporarily suspended. I'd just returned from treating another case of over-indulgence and was not in the best of moods.

Holmes was amused. "Come now, Watson, surely you know these periods of Bacchanalian excess serve a purpose. They're what enable men to continue in their tedious, uneventful lives for the rest of the year. The occasional vacation from normalcy can be a benefit."

"It's all very well for you to philosophize," I grumbled. "You're not the one who has to go out in the cold and the snow to treat nothing more serious than a severe case of dyspepsia."

"The cold and the snow? Why, the snow stopped falling hours ago, and I daresay you were wrapped up warmly enough in your hackney cab. Come, Watson, this disgruntlement is not like you. You mustn't sit there and brood. Let us go take tea in Portman Street. You need to be out and about."

"I've *been* out and about. I just got back."

"From visiting a sickbed. But tomorrow is Christmas Eve. A time for rejoicing!"

"I don't *want* to rejoice."

"Of course you do. A brisk walk to Portman Street will do you worlds of good. Besides, I have a craving for nut cake with raspberry sauce. Come, Watson, let us be off!"

So because Holmes wanted the taste of raspberries in his mouth, I put back on the outdoor apparel I'd just taken off. We informed Mrs. Hudson we'd not be home for tea and began our walk.

We had gone no farther than Berkeley Square before I realized Holmes was right; I was feeling better already. The air was crisp and invigorating, the sun was sparkling on the snow, a small group of boys was singing carols, the smiling faces of the people we passed reflected the good will of the season, and I began to think of raspberries. I felt a spring come back into my step.

Holmes noticed. "Well, well. I see my prescription is working."

At least he had the courtesy not to say *Physician, heal thyself.* We were about to turn into Portman Street when I happened to glance at the carolers. "I say, Holmes, look at this!"

The carolers were all Chinese. Seven boys of twelve or thirteen celebrating a religion that surely was not their own. The incongruous sight of those young Asians warbling "The Holly and the Ivy" had drawn a small crowd. "Their ancestors must be turning in their graves," I remarked. "I wonder if their parents know what they're doing."

"Their parents may have sent them," Holmes said. "Boys that age do not naturally sing in harmony, no matter what their racial ancestry. These singers have been trained to do so."

"Trained? But for what purpose?"

"Here comes your answer now."

The carol had ended and a Chinese lad approached us, tin cup in hand. After a quick glance at Holmes, he spoke to me. "A penny for the orphans, guv?"

I fished in my pockets for a coin, but Holmes said, "What orphans would those be, young man?"

"The Lime'ouse Charitable 'ome for Boys," he answered cheerily. "We alluns live there." He waved an arm at the other carolers.

"You're quite a distance from home. Why not sing your carols in Limehouse?"

"Oi, guv. There ain't no money in Lime'ouse."

Holmes dropped a coin into his cup. "Impeccably reasoned. Tell me, who is the director of the Limehouse Charitable Home for Boys?"

"Reverend Burns. It useter be Reverend Dawson, but 'e got sick and died."

I added my own coin to his cup. "A Christian institution, then."

"Oh, yes, sir. We're alluns good Christians, we are." He flashed us a grin and moved off to solicit the other onlookers.

"And there, Watson," Holmes said, "you have as good an example of Cockney English as you're ever likely to hear. That young Oriental lad was born within sounds of the Bow Bells, I warrant you. I wonder how many others there are like him."

I was about to reply when a shout rang out. We turned to see a man of middle age, blood running down the side of his face and his shirt torn, staggering out of a shop door that said Jas. Lombard & Son. Holmes was halfway across the square before I was able to react.

"Three of them!" the man gasped and almost fell.

Holmes put an arm about him to support him. "Three men? They did this to you?"

"They robbed me! They took everything!"

I started to examine his wound but he waved me away. "I'm a physician," I said. "Let me help you."

"Lord Edgar," he gasped. "See to Lord Edgar Blanchard!"

I hastened into the shop. A slight man in his thirties lay on the floor, moaning. I helped him sit up, noticing that the left side of his face and mouth was an angry red; he had been struck hard. "It was the same ones," he said thickly.

"Don't try to talk," I said and found a chair for him. The place was a jeweler's establishment, with a display case against each of the two side walls and a round table covered with black velvet centered between them. Lord Edgar Blanchard sat at the table and cradled his head in his hands.

Holmes came in, still supporting the man who'd shouted for help—the proprietor, I assumed. And so he was; he said his name was James Lombard and he had been showing Lord Edgar a necklace for Lady Blanchard when three men entered and robbed them. His injury was only a scalp wound and a little pressure in the right places stopped the bleeding; I bound up his head with my pocket hand-kerchief.

"A police constable will be here shortly," Holmes said. "I sent one of the onlookers to find one. Tell me, Mr. Lombard, do you keep spirits on the premises?"

He did. Lombard poured himself and Lord Edgar a brandy; Holmes and I declined. Both men gradually began to regain their composure, and the proprietor said, "I thank you, gentlemen, for your assistance. May I know your names?"

"I am Sherlock Holmes," said my companion, "and this is Dr. Watson."

Both men looked up. "Mr. Holmes!" Lombard exclaimed. "Well, sir, it seems I have desperate need of your services. I entreat you for your help. Will you undertake the return of my goods to me? They took everything I own."

"Yet your display cases are undamaged and their contents intact," Holmes pointed out.

"Paste, Mr. Holmes. Replicas of the real pieces that I kept locked in my safe." He opened one of the cases and took out a delicate necklace fashioned of what looked like emeralds to my eye; an excellent reproduction. Lombard spread the necklace on the velvet-topped table. "I was showing the authentic necklace to Lord Edgar when those three men came in."

"I've seen them before," Lord Edgar said. "Those same three men."

Just then the door burst open and a police constable stepped in followed by an agitated young man with dark circles under his eyes. "Father!" the latter cried. "What has happened? You are injured?" He turned to the man at the table. "And Lord Edgar? You have been hurt too?" The young man then started a wailing and moaning that made me want to cover my ears until his father spoke to him sharply. He was still more boy than man.

"This is my son, Wilfred Lombard," the jeweler said. "He was delivering a pearl tiepin when this unfortunate incident occurred." To his son, he said, "My injuries are negligible. I fear Lord Edgar has got the worst of it."

Lord Edgar shook his head. "Don't concern yourself, Mr. Lombard. As soon as I feel more steady, I will be on my way."

"But . . . but what happened?" Wilfred repeated. "You were robbed? Why did they hurt you?"

"They had no reason to," Lord Edgar said sharply. "Neither your father nor I offered resistance. But they began raining blows upon us as soon as they came in—and they did so without saying a word."

"But . . . but that's dreadful! How could this have happened?"

I looked at the boy sharply; there was a tinge of hysteria in his voice. Holmes heard it too. He said to Lombard, "Perhaps a spot of that brandy to steady your son's nerves?"

The jeweler gave Wilfred a splash of the brandy in a small snifter; the son's hands were shaking as he took it. "You are not seriously injured?" His father assured him he was not.

The police constable spoke for the first time. "Well, now, sir. Just what did happen here?" Coming from him, the question was practical and free of nerves.

It was Lord Edgar who answered him. He had commissioned an emerald necklace from James Lombard; it was to be his Christmas gift to his wife, Lady Blanchard. The jeweler made up several designs in paste, and Lord Edgar had selected one. He'd requested the necklace not be delivered, to retain the element of surprise. The finished necklace had been promised for today, and Mr. Lombard was showing it to him when the three men came in. They attacked without uttering a word. "I fear I lost consciousness at that point," Lord Edgar said.

Lombard continued the story. They'd hit him a glancing blow on the head with a metal bar—more a tap, really, just enough to start the blood flowing. And then they forced him into the rear chamber of his establishment. One man had pointed to the safe while the other threatened him with the metal bar.

"Where was the third man?" Holmes asked.

"In the front with Lord Edgar," the jeweler said. Lombard had protested he didn't have the key to the safe; one of the men had ripped the jeweler's shirt and pulled out the chain around his neck holding the key. Lombard had resisted no further and opened the safe. They emptied the contents into a burlap bag they'd brought with them. Then one of the men had driven his fist deep into the jeweler's midsection; Lombard was on his knees gasping for breath when the thieves left. As soon as he was able, he'd struggled to his feet and gone out to shout for help.

"And they never spoke the entire time they were here?" I asked.

"Not a word, Dr. Watson."

Holmes was examining the door. "The lock has been forced," he said. "Do you always keep your door locked when you are showing authentic jewels?"

"Always."

The constable didn't look at the door. "What did these three men look like, sir?"

"They were dressed in black," Lord Edgar said. "Their hats were pulled low and their mufflers concealed most of the face. Only their eyes were visible."

"And yet, Lord Edgar," Holmes interposed quickly, "you yourself said you had seen these men before."

He sighed. "This is the second time I have been present at a robbery. The other was a silversmith's establishment in Chancery Lane. Lady Blanchard and I were there when three men broke in. That time we were not harmed, although the proprietor was treated roughly."

"But if only their eyes were visible?"

"They were Oriental eyes, Mr. Holmes. The same eyes both

times. The man who struck me recognized me from the previous robbery. They were the same three men."

Holmes said, "Three men dressed in black, only their eyes showing, breaking into a jeweler's establishment in late afternoon—surely someone must have observed them. Watson, be so good as to step outside and summon the Chinese lad who solicited us for a charitable donation. It's possible he or one of his fellows knows who these miscreants are."

I did as he asked, but the carolers were gone. A workman I spoke to said they'd scarpered when the ruckus broke out.

Holmes took the news in stride, but the constable said he'd just look for witnesses himself before reporting in. When he'd left, young Wilfred spoke up. "Guards. We must hire guards, Father."

"There is nothing left to guard now," his father answered testily.

Holmes made his decision. "Very well, Mr. Lombard, I will undertake a search for your stolen goods. If you would be so good as to prepare a list of what was taken—"

"Later, Holmes," I interrupted. "Mr. Lombard should return home and rest for a few hours." His color was not good.

"I do feel the need," the jeweler admitted. "I will send the list to you this evening."

"Do not trouble yourself," Holmes said. "If you will give me your address, I will come get it. Lord Edgar, did they take Lady Blanchard's necklace as well?"

"They did. Now I have no gift for Christmas."

Lombard wrote down his address for Holmes and sent Wilfred out to find a hackney. Holmes and I escorted Lord Edgar to his carriage; and it was fortunate we did so as he came near to collapsing in the street. I insisted we see him home; the man was displaying all the symptoms of concussion.

The Blanchard residence was in King's Cross—not a large building but a graceful one. The servant who opened the door gasped when she saw two strangers supporting the master of the house and ran to tell her mistress. Lady Blanchard turned white when she saw her injured husband but remained steady and soon we had him settled in bed, where he immediately fell asleep. I gestured toward the hallway; with a worried glance at her husband, Lady Blanchard followed us out.

I introduced myself and Holmes, and said, "Sleep is the best medicine Lord Edgar can have. I believe he struck his head when he fell. You must keep him as quiet as you possibly can."

"He had a fall? How did this happen?"

Holmes said, "I fear it is even more unpleasant than that, Lady Blanchard." He told her what had happened at the jeweler's establishment, and she pressed a hand to her mouth to keep from crying out. Holmes went on, "Do you recall a similar incident at a silversmith's in Chancery Lane?"

"Yes!" she exclaimed. "Three men robbed the silversmith while we were there. But we were not harmed."

"Lord Edgar says they were the same three men today."

She looked surprised. "But how could he know? Their faces were covered by scarves."

"He says they had Oriental eyes."

Her own eyes narrowed in thought. "Yes, I do recall his saying so at the time. But I'm sorry, Mr. Holmes—I did not notice."

I repeated that Lord Edgar must be kept quiet and we left her to nurse her husband back to health. Outside, the daylight had gone and a light rain had begun to fall; the streets would be icy for Christmas Eve. We turned up our collars and started looking for a hackney.

"We have missed our tea, Watson," Holmes said. "Let us see if

Mrs. Hudson can give us an early supper before we call on Lombard."

"Why not just have him send the list of stolen goods?"

"I wish another word with him. Tonight is the best time for that, after he has recovered from the shocks of the afternoon."

When we reached Baker Street, we found that Mrs. Hudson could indeed provide us with an early meal, which we consumed at a leisurely pace. It was after nine in the evening when we set out for Lombard's home in Knightsbridge.

The jeweler himself was looking much better than the last time we saw him. His color had returned and his breathing was regular. He offered us a sherry and handed Holmes the list of stolen jewelry.

Holmes read through the list and slipped it in his pocket. "Your son was most distressed this afternoon. I hope he has recovered from his shock?"

Lombard's face darkened. "I do not know."

"He is not at home?"

"He is not." Lombard offered no explanation.

Holmes persisted. "I would like to speak to your son. Do you know when he will return?"

"I do not. I have not seen Wilfred since I was robbed this afternoon."

How very strange. I asked, "Nothing unfortunate has occurred, I hope?"

Lombard jumped from his chair and began to pace. He struggled for a moment before deciding to confide in us. "It pains me to admit it, gentlemen, but I am deeply disappointed in my son. He is a wastrel and a weakling. Perhaps you noticed how little brandy I gave him this afternoon? In moments of anxiety—and Wilfred has many such moments—his reaction is always the same. He reaches for the nearest bottle."

"And I recommended you give him the brandy," Holmes said quickly. "I do beg your pardon, Mr. Lombard."

"You had no way of knowing, Mr. Holmes. Even now I am trying to rescue Wilfred from a life of dissolution." Lombard stopped pacing and braced himself against the mantelpiece, staring down at the fire. "He was sent down from Oxford for drunkenness. I thought if I myself prepared him to take over the business, gave him a goal to work toward, taught him to live within his income . . ." He shook his head. "It made no difference."

"Are there just the two of you in the business?"

"Yes, I let a good assistant go to make room for Wilfred. But he's out there now somewhere, carousing with the lowlife whose company he prefers. He spends most of his time in Limehouse, with the sailors and the smugglers and the thieves and the ladies of the night. I sometimes fear for his life."

As well he might. Holmes asked, "Do you know the names of any of the places he frequents?"

"I know one—The Glorious Lotus. Are you going to find him, Mr. Holmes?"

"I am going to look for him, Mr. Lombard. But do not raise your hopes too high. Limehouse guards its secrets well." And with that, we left him.

Limehouse could be a model for Hell. The skies glow red with reflected light from the factory furnaces that blast forth day and night. The buildings are so covered with grime that merely to brush up against a wall is sufficient to ruin a greatcoat. The stench from the paper mills is overpowering. The basin that the area surrounds is filled with floating things that one would not care to examine too closely. And the denizens of that dreadful place openly inspect every stranger with an eye to doing him harm; I think only the fact that there were two of us kept us from being attacked and robbed in the streets.

Even the police constables walked the streets in pairs in that part of London; two were even then strolling in our direction. "Ah, Watson," said Holmes, "here come two men who undoubtedly know the area well." He approached them and asked not about The Glorious Lotus but the Limehouse Charitable Home for Boys.

Both constables shook their heads. "There's no such place, sir," one of them said. "There's St. Anne's, but no orphanage. No orphanage in Limehouse at all."

"No institution of any kind headed by the Reverend Mr. Burns . . . who succeeded the Reverend Mr. Dawson as director?"

"Not in this parish. This lot here ain't much for church. Someone's been telling you a story, sir."

"As I suspected," Holmes said. "Thank you, Constable, you have been most helpful."

The two policemen went on their way. "I thought you were going to ask about The Glorious Lotus," I said.

"The Glorious Lotus? Oh, that's down the street to our left."

It was a dive of the most disreputable sort; there was certainly nothing either glorious or flowerlike about it. Young Wilfred Lombard was not to be found, however. A few well-placed inquiries and a half-crown piece elicited the information that he had recently departed for Mr. Chu's.

I trailed Holmes back out to the street and asked, "Where and what is Mr. Chu's?"

"Two streets away. It is an opium den, Watson."

I stopped; he knew the place. "Holmes," I said.

"Hurry, Watson! There may still be time to stop him!"

There was nothing to do but follow, although I was filled with dread at the thought of Holmes in one of those places even on a rescue mission. We reached a blackened building indistinguishable from its neighbors.

Holmes stopped at the door. "They know me as Lewis here," he said. "Watson, I must ask you to say nothing once we go inside. Do not protest against anything you see or hear. And keep your face impassive at all times—you must not express disapproval in any way whatsoever."

I understood. We went in; I had trouble seeing at first, the place was kept so dark. But Holmes didn't hesitate; he made his way straight to a mountainous Chinaman reclining on some sort of divan and addressed him courteously as Mr. Chu.

The Chinaman took his time answering, and then said, "Mr. Lewis. It has been a long time since you last visited Chu's house."

"Too long, Mr. Chu. But as you see, I have brought a friend with me this evening. We would like a private alcove, if one is available."

"One is available." Money changed hands. From a lacquered storage chest, Mr. Chu produced two opium pipes and handed them to us; I kept a blank face as I accepted the noxious object. The pipe was made of black horn and had a sort of funnel cup resting on the top about two-thirds of the way between the mouthpiece and the other end.

"There were to be three in our party," Holmes was saying, "but the third was not at The Glorious Lotus where we were to meet. If he comes in, Mr. Chu, would you be so good as to direct him to the private alcove?"

"What does he look like?"

"About twenty-two or -three, light brown hair. He has dark shadows under his eyes."

The Chinaman made a noise I think was laughter. "Your young friend could not wait," he said. "You may find him by the far wall."

My eyes had adjusted to the dim lighting by then, and I could see the room was filled with bunk beds three tiers high. Almost every bunk was occupied; as we moved among them I could not help but stare at those empty faces, the slack mouths, the unseeing eyes. The sluggishness of motion among those who could still move at all. What demons drive men that make them choose oblivion over life? I did not then nor do I now understand that impetus to slow but inevitable self-destruction.

Young Wilfred Lombard had not yet been in that den of corruption sufficiently long to have succumbed to a drug stupor; he recognized us immediately. Holmes stopped him from speaking, saying he was known by a different name here, and invited Wilfred to join us in our private alcove. I was sickened by the look of smug gratification that appeared on the young man's face; our presence in that vile place excused his own weakness.

Holmes led us to an adjoining room of small partitioned-off spaces with only curtains covering the entries; nevertheless our alcove would afford some modicum of privacy. The sole source of illumination was a lantern suspended from the wall.

The first thing Holmes did was take away Wilfred's opium pipe. "No more for you, my lad," he said in a low voice. "I want you lucid and thinking."

Wilfred protested, to no avail. I took all three pipes and looked for a place to put them. There were no bunks in the alcove, only filthy mats on the floor. I tossed the pipes into a corner.

Holmes and Wilfred sat on the mats, but I remained standing.

"And now, young man," Holmes said, "we'll have the truth, and we'll have all of it. Who were the men who robbed your father this afternoon?"

Wilfred looked as surprised as I felt. "How would I know who they were, Mr. Holmes? I was not even there when the robbery took place!"

"Come, come—let's have an end to prevaricating. The thieves knew to bring a tool to force the lock. They knew the display cases contained only paste reproductions and passed them by. They even knew your father wore the key to the safe on a chain around his neck—*under his shirt*, Wilfred, where it could not be seen. How did they know these matters? Only you or your father could have told them, and I hope you are not so foolish as to claim your father arranged to have himself robbed. You and only you gave the thieves the details they needed. Come, Wilfred, the game is up. Salvage what you can. We may still recover what your father lost."

Wilfred began to weep. "They were supposed to take only Lady Blanchard's necklace," he said softly between sobs. "They were not supposed to rob my father of everything! He gave me his word my father would not be hurt."

"Or Lord Edgar?" I asked.

"No one was to be hurt! He gave me his word!"

Holmes's face was in shadow but the contempt in his voice was unmistakable. "You are not only a dishonest man and a faithless son, you are also naïve beyond belief. You put your trust in thieves? Again, what are their names?"

"I know only one of them. His name is Hu Wei-Yung." Wilfred took a moment to catch his breath. "I told him of Lord Edgar's appointment at four o'clock to claim the necklace. And I delayed delivering a pearl stickpin to Mayfair in order to be away when he arrived—he said nothing of bringing two others with him. Hu Wei-Yung was to break in, take the necklace, and leave. That's all. Instead, he beat my father and took everything he owned." His voice was tinged with self-pity. "He betrayed me. When he stole my father's livelihood, he stole mine as well."

I turned my back in disgust.

Holmes asked what their plans were for after the robbery. "We were to meet at The Glorious Lotus at eight o'clock," Wilfred replied. "But he failed to keep the appointment."

"And that surprised you? Where can we find this Hu Wei-Yung?"

"I don't know, Mr. Holmes! I never knew where he lived—I've seen him only in public places."

The lantern flickered. "Then we need spend no more time here. Come along—we're taking you home to your father."

"Mr. Holmes, must you tell him my part in this?"

"Not if you tell him yourself. Which is better, that he learn the truth from you or from a consulting detective he met only this afternoon? Be a man, Wilfred! Face up to what you have done. Throw yourself on your father's mercy and beg his forgiveness." Wilfred began to moan. Holmes stood up and said to me in a low voice, "Watson, take close hold of his arm. I don't trust this young scoundrel not to run away."

I took Wilfred's arm and pulled him to his feet. "It's Christmas time, Wilfred," I said. "You can exploit your father's charitable instincts if you're clever enough."

"Tsk, Watson." But Holmes smiled as he said it. We left our alcove and made our way through the main room with the triple bunks. Holmes paused before the mountainous Chinaman.

"Mr. Chu," he said, "I fear I neglected to pay you when we first came in."

Money changed hands again; Mr. Chu accepted the folded bills and waited. "I am desirous of making the acquaintance of one Hu Wei-Yung," Holmes added.

Mr. Chu's eyes flickered downward as he thumbed through the bills Holmes had handed him. "Do you make donations to the Salvation Army, Mr. Lewis? There is an abandoned mission house on Northey Street that may be of interest to you."

"Ah. Truly abandoned?"

"Tonight, yes. Tomorrow night . . . perhaps not."

"I see. Then I bid you good night, Mr. Chu."

The Chinaman nodded expressionlessly. "Until we meet again, Mr. . . . . Lewis," he said.

It was close to two AM when we returned to Baker Street after delivering Wilfred Lombard to his father, so I slept later than usual on the morning of Christmas Eve. Holmes was up and dressed when Mrs. Hudson brought our breakfast; I put on a dressing gown and joined him. My companion was pensive that morning and not inclined to talk, a condition that suited me admirably as I was slow in coming fully awake.

After we'd finished eating, I dressed and returned to our sitting room to find Holmes looking down through the window at the street. "I do believe I'm looking at the carriage in which we returned Lord Edgar to his home yesterday. Watson, did you not say he must remain quiet? Wait—it is Lady Blanchard who alights. Something is amiss."

He was standing by the door and holding it open before she reached the top of the stairs. "Mr. Holmes!" she exclaimed. "I desperately need your help!"

I've heard those words uttered a hundred times in those rooms, but they still have the power to strike a chill in my heart. Holmes insisted that Lady Blanchard be seated and take time to compose herself.

She sat down, but she couldn't wait. "Edgar has been kidnapped! He was taken even as I watched! I could not prevent them!"

"Oh, dear lady!" I exclaimed. "Are you hurt?"

"No, Dr. Watson. They simply brushed me aside as they would an insect."

Holmes asked, "They broke into your house?"

"No, they took him on the street. They threw him into the back of a wagon and drove away."

"Lord Edgar was on the street?" I said. "He should not have left his bed!"

"I'm aware of that, Dr. Watson. Edgar woke up this morning feeling much better except for a severe headache. He dressed and claimed a walk in the brisk December air would clear his head. I pleaded with him not to go, but he would not listen. I insisted on going with him, of course, but we'd no sooner stepped out of the house than those men set upon us."

"Holmes," I said, "a man suffering concussion who is handled roughly—"

"I know, Watson," he said shortly. "Lady Blanchard, please describe the men who took your husband."

"They looked exactly like the three men who robbed the silversmith in Chancery Lane. Dressed in black, scarves covering their faces. And this time I did look at their eyes, Mr. Holmes. They were Oriental eyes."

"The same three that robbed Lombard?" I asked.

"Assuredly," Holmes agreed. "Lord Edgar said one of the men remembered him from the Chancery Lane job. And Wilfred no doubt had told them his name—discretion is not Wilfred's strong point."

Lady Blanchard looked puzzled. "Wilfred?"

"Wilfred is Mr. Lombard's son, who, alas, instigated the robbery. Tell me, how long ago was Lord Edgar taken?"

"Ah, it must be two hours now. I have been with the police—but I fear they have no idea of how to find Edgar. So I came to you."

"So you have not been home since he was kidnapped? Lady Blanchard, it is quite possible your husband was taken for ransom and a message naming the amount will be sent to you. You must return to King's Cross immediately. Do you have any cash in the house?"

Her eyes were wide. "I have money for household expenses."

"That won't be sufficient. Where does Lord Edgar keep an account?"

"At the Bank of England."

"Watson, your coat! We must make haste to Threadneedle Street."

Holmes sought out a bank official for whom he had once done a service, and Lady Blanchard's needs were attended to swiftly and efficiently. I almost fell as we were coming out of the bank; last night's drizzle of rain had frozen over and the walks were icy. Holmes saw Lady Blanchard into her carriage and instructed the coachman not to stop for anything until they had reached King's Cross.

I watched the carriage until it was out of sight. "Do you believe it was indeed for ransom that Lord Edgar was taken?"

"Let us pray that is the case," Holmes answered. "But if Lord Edgar realized that the thief remembered him, could the thief not realize that Lord Edgar recognized him as well?"

"Then—"

"Then Lord Edgar may be in the greatest peril of his life."

Theft, kidnapping, a son's betrayal, and now possibly murder—

what a hideous way to observe the season. The normalcy of the scene around us was a heartless mockery of those unhappy events. The sun glittered brightly on the ice, holly wreaths tied up with bright ribbon adorned the lamp poles and many of the business establishments within sight, strangers wished one another happy Christmas as they passed, the sound of caroling drifted from down the street.

Holmes and I had the thought at the same time. I said, "Could it possibly be . . . ?"

"Let us find out."

We made our way as quickly as we could along the icy walk to the next street corner—and there stood our seven carolers from the fictional Limehouse Charitable Home for Boys. They were attracting the same kind of attention as yesterday in Berkeley Square; a group of passersby had stopped to listen to these young Chinese boys singing of Christmas. Even a police constable stopped, enjoying the scene.

And then something strange happened. The carolers broke off their rendering of "The Holly and the Ivy"—stopping in mid-phrase, in fact—and began to sing, loudly, "God Rest Ye Merry, Gentlemen."

"Constable!" Holmes shouted above the singing. "Blow your whistle! Summon help! A robbery is taking place even now!" To me he added, "The carolers, Watson! They act as lookout for the robbers—whom they have just warned of a police constable on the scene!"

The carolers scattered at the sound of the police whistle, each running off in a different direction; Holmes took off after the nearest one. He looked like a great black scarecrow slipping and sliding across the ice, his long arms flailing to help keep his balance. But the boy he was pursuing fared no better, and Holmes was able to nab his prey, whom he held in a tight grip. It was not the same boy who had solicited us for donations; this boy was younger.

When I caught up with them, Holmes was saying, "Answer me! Where is the robbery taking place?"

The boy answered in a high sing-song using words I did not know.

"And don't pretend you can't speak English! You have a choice, you young rascal. You can tell me which establishment is being robbed, or you can live your life in an English prison. Well? Which shall it be?"

The boy was frightened. He swallowed hard and said, "Telegraph office."

The telegraph office—which would have more money in the till than usual because of all the Christmas greetings being sent this day. Holmes released the boy and gave him not so much as a glance as he ran away. "Constable!" Holmes called. "The telegraph office!"

"Oi!" someone cried out. "It's the telegraph office!"

Two other constables had appeared in answer to the summons. We made a strange procession as we slid our way to the building under siege—the three constables in the lead, followed by Holmes and myself, and we in turn followed by a number of onlookers who'd joined the chase, all of us doing a bizarre little dance to keep ourselves upright on the icy walk.

The constables rushed into the telegraph office and a great uproar broke out. Two of the black-garbed thieves erupted through the door; the crowd immediately captured one of them, and the constables came out dragging another. But the third man was getting away.

"After him!" Holmes cried and set off in pursuit.

But this time he was not able to run down his quarry. Holmes stepped on a particularly treacherous piece of ice that ended the chase. Down on one knee, he called out, "Hu Wei-Yung!"

The fleeing man stopped, turned, and raised a fist which he shook at Holmes. Then he rounded a corner and made good his escape.

Limehouse was only slightly less menacing in the daylight. The main difference was that now I could see the ramshackle slums more clearly, not that that was an advantage. We were there to locate the abandoned Salvation Army mission house on Northey Street Mr. Chu had told us about.

"I strongly doubt we'll find Lord Edgar there," Holmes said. "Mr. Chu's information about the mission house was delivered before the kidnapping took place. Most likely the house on Northey Street is where Hu Wei-Yung will meet his fence to dispose of Lombard's jewels, and he won't want Lord Edgar on the premises at the same time. But we must search nevertheless. Besides, we want to be there before the villain arrives and we want to be well-hidden."

"It would have helped if Mr. Chu had provided us with an exact hour."

"We can't ask for miracles, Watson."

We found the house on Northey Street, a wooden two-storey affair in a state of serious disrepair; I could barely read the faded lettering that spelled out SALVATION ARMY on the painted sign. We'd each brought a lantern, and Holmes carried a pry bar. The main entrance was fastened with a new padlock. "We don't touch that," Holmes said.

Around to the rear of the building we found an exterior staircase; it looked fragile enough to collapse if so much as a bird lighted on it. But Holmes would hear no objection, so up we went, frequently stepping over empty space where treads were missing.

At the top of the stairway we found a door and another padlock, only this one was old and rusty. "*That* we touch," Holmes said. He got to work with his pry bar and soon had the door open. Inside was pitch black; we lighted our lanterns.

And found ourselves standing on the brink of an enormous gaping hole where the floor had fallen in. Holmes edged forward as far as he could and held his lantern over the hole. "Excellent," he said.

We made our way cautiously around the hole to a door in the wall opposite to where we'd come in. It opened onto a landing at the top of a flight of stairs, and directly opposite was another door. That door opened to an empty room, not so much as a box or a scrap of paper to be seen. We did not test the floor.

The flight of stairs leading down was in better condition than the exterior stairway, since it had not been exposed to the elements. Downstairs we found a kitchen, a small scullery, and a storage room cramped into a small space together; the kitchen door led to another room, the largest in the house. The large room showed signs not of occupancy but of recent presence. We found a table with candles and matches on it, and five wooden chairs were grouped haphazardly around it.

"This is where they will meet," Holmes said. "Look upward, Watson."

I raised my eyes; we were standing directly under the hole in the floor above. "Umm."

"And that is where we will be, seeing but not seen. If luck is with us, Hu Wei-Yung will arrive first and we can put an end to this business before his cohorts get here."

"Let me see if I understand you," I said. "We are to teeter precariously on the brink of a dangerous hole for who knows how many hours, awaiting the arrival of a villain we are in no way certain will even appear in this place at all—all on the word of a Chinese criminal opium-seller who profits from the misery of others?"

"Yes, that is approximately right," Holmes said. "Although in the country of Mr. Chu's origin, selling opium is not a criminal activity. Mr. Chu has provided me with reliable information in the past and I have no reason to doubt him now. Come, let us take up our posts."

We went back up the stairs and into the room missing most of its floor. After a bit we selected spots that with luck would not collapse under our weight and settled in to begin our vigil.

"Holmes, there is something that has been puzzling me," I said. "Lady Blanchard was with her husband when he was kidnapped. Why did those brutes not take her instead of him? They did not know Lord Edgar was suffering from concussion, and surely a woman would be less able to resist than a man."

"That is the Englishman's point of view," Holmes replied. "But to the Oriental mind, women are servants. There is no profit in kidnapping a servant."

At a word from Holmes, we both extinguished our lanterns. The resulting blackness was disorienting. It was only six o'clock, but not a glimmer of light showed anywhere; all the windows had been boarded up from the inside. I heard a faint rustling sound: rats.

"I say, Holmes, I have spent jollier Christmas Eves."

"And so you shall again, old chap. But now we must maintain silence. We don't know when Hu Wei-Yung will arrive."

If he arrived. I made myself as comfortable as I could and prepared to wait.

It was difficult to judge the passage of time under those conditions, but after what seemed like an hour, I felt my muscles beginning to stiffen. I shifted my weight slightly and could hear Holmes doing the same.

Approximately another two hours passed, and to my dismay I found myself nodding off. I fought against it, but the darkness and the silence defeated me. I fell asleep with my chin resting on my chest . . .

. . . only to awaken with a cry to a loud clamor in my ears. As I became more alert, I realized I was hearing bells. Church bells.

"It is Christmas Day," said Holmes.

Christmas bells, that rang at midnight all over London. We had been waiting for six hours. I listened until the last of the bells died out and said, "How much longer must we remain here?"

"All night, if necessary. We don't—*hist!*"

I'd heard it too—a sound from below.

Silence for a moment, then we heard a chair scrape on the floor. The scritch of a match was followed by a tiny flame as a candle was lighted, then another, and another—twelve candles in all. We could see only the top of the Chinaman's head as he placed six candles at one end of the table and six at the other.

The man whose face we'd not yet seen placed a burlap bag on the table between the two rows of candles. He sat down and reached into the bag without looking; what he pulled out was a diamond brooch. He turned it this way and that, prisms of color shooting out as the various facets caught the candlelight.

"He is alone," Holmes murmured—and jumped.

"Holmes!" I cried, and tried to rise. My cramped muscles delayed me; but when I did manage to get to my feet, I peered into the hole. I could see neither man, although the sounds of a struggle going on outside the circle of candlelight were unmistakable.

I lighted my lantern and made as much haste as I could in working my way around the hole. Out the door to the landing, down the stairway, through the kitchen to the large room—where I found the Chinaman slumped in a chair, his hands tied behind his back.

Holmes was replacing some candles that had been knocked over in the struggle.

"Ah, there you are, Watson," he said with maddening nonchalance. "Meet Hu Wei-Yung, thief and kidnapper."

I threw up my arms. "Holmes, sometimes I think you must be out of your mind!"

"Quite possibly." He leaned in so close to his prisoner that their noses were only inches apart. "Hu Wei-Yung also turns children into criminals. He teaches them Christmas carols and instructs them in what lies to tell if they are ever questioned."

I took my first good look at Hu Wei-Yung—and was disappointed, he was so ordinary looking. He was younger than I thought he'd be. With the exception of those Oriental eyes, there was nothing distinguishing about his features at all. He didn't *look* evil; he didn't look *anything*. I examined his bound hands.

"And of course you just happened to have a piece of rope in your coat pocket," I said to Holmes.

"No." He sounded surprised. "I brought it with me for this purpose."

Of course he did. I sighed and said, "What now?"

"Now Hu Wei-Yung is going to tell us where Lord Edgar is."

The young Chinaman's lips tightened. "I tell you nothing. Your English lord dies where he is."

"In which case you will most certainly die on the gallows," Holmes said. He picked up the burlap bag from where it had fallen on the floor and upended it over the table; the jewels came tumbling out. Holmes ran his long fingers through the gems and lifted out a necklace that was the authentic version of the paste model Lombard had shown us the day before. "Lady Blanchard's necklace," Holmes said and slipped it into a pocket. "That goes to her. The rest goes back to the man you stole it from. You gain nothing, Hu Wei-Yung. Not one farthing have you profited from this theft or kidnapping. So why let Lord Edgar die? What do you accomplish?"

The man's voice was thick. "You do not understand."

"Do you understand?" Holmes countered. "If Lord Edgar dies, you die. You are committing suicide if you do not take us to him. Do you want to die?"

"No!"

"Then show us where he is, man! Quickly!"

"I cannot! If I take you to him . . ."

"Yes?"

"If I show you where I hid him, I lose face." His head drooped.

Holmes was silent for a moment. "And death is preferable to losing face," he murmured. "I see." He folded his arms and closed his eyes, thinking. "What if there were a way to release Lord Edgar without losing face?"

"That is not possible."

Holmes opened his eyes. "Is it not? Consider. What if I offered you the lives of all your Christmas carolers in exchange for the life of only one Englishman? Would that not be considered an honorable arrangement?"

"You arrest the boys?"

"If Lord Edgar dies, everyone even remotely connected to his death will be tried, convicted, and hanged. Including the boys. Would not sacrificing yourself to save the boys be considered an honorable act? You not only save face, you gain respect."

Hu Wei-Yung looked hopeful for a moment, but then his head sagged again. "But no one will know of my sacrifice."

"On the contrary, everyone will know—once I tell Mr. Chu how you put the boys' well-being above your own."

His head snapped up. "You will tell Mr. Chu?"

"If you lead us to Lord Edgar. You have my word on it."

The Chinaman wanted to believe him but still hesitated. I spoke up. "Sherlock Holmes has given you his word. And he never breaks his word."

He looked at Holmes. "Your honor is in your word?"

"It is. The boys will not be touched if Lord Edgar lives. I promise you that."

The two of them exchanged a long look, and then Hu Wei-Yung bobbed his head, once. "I take you to him."

"A wise choice. Where is he?"

"On a canal barge. We put him in a storage locker."

"Regent's Canal? That leads from Limehouse Basin?"

He said yes. We left the Salvation Army's abandoned mission house and headed east. I led the way with my lantern; Holmes's was still upstairs in the house but we didn't want to take the time to fetch it.

It was a good half hour's walk before we reached the tow path alongside the canal. Even in the dead of winter the canal water was odorous. I thought of the effect on a man with a concussion of that nauseating smell combined with the constant motion of the water and picked up the pace.

Holmes said, "Was your purpose to hold Lord Edgar for ransom?"

That had been the plan, originally. "But with my companions locked away behind bars, it is too difficult for one man alone."

"So you were just going to leave him there to die?"

Hu Wei-Yung said nothing.

We walked another ten minutes before he said, "Here." The barge was moored under a narrow bridge that spanned a break in the tow path. We stepped aboard and gathered around the storage locker;

an air hole had been drilled in the lid. Holmes broke it open with his pry bar.

Lord Edgar lay curled inside. He was not moving. Holmes stepped back to allow me to examine him; I lay my hand at the base of his neck and detected a faint pulse. "He's alive, but unconscious. We must get him to hospital immediately."

"You will keep your word?" Hu Wei-Yung asked.

"I will," said Holmes.

So Lady Blanchard got both her husband and her necklace back for Christmas, a day she spent in a chair by Lord Edgar's hospital bed. His condition was serious but not critical, and in time he would recover from his ordeal. I wondered if Lady Blanchard would ever be able to wear the necklace without remembering that it had almost cost her her husband's life.

The other part of our story did not end so happily. James Lombard was overcome when we returned his goods to him. "You have restored my livelihood to me, Mr. Holmes! I had nothing, and now I have everything again. You have given me back my life."

"And Wilfred?" Holmes asked.

A cloud passed over Lombard's face, his joy in the return of his jewels forgotten. "I have disowned Wilfred. He is no longer my son."

Not unexpected, but nonetheless a sad thing to hear. Holmes said, "Yet his concern for you was genuine when he first learned you had been beaten."

"Oh, yes, Wilfred is always sorry afterward. Sincerely sorry."

"It took courage to admit his part in the robbery to you."

"He did not do even that. I discovered him packing some clothing—he was planning to run away without a word to me. I forced the truth from him. What you've seen, Mr. Holmes, is only the most recent chapter in a story that has been going on a long, long time. Wilfred has always been a liar and a thief, from the days he was a small boy. When his mother lay dying, he crept into her room and took all her jewelry. When he was found out, all he had to say was that she wouldn't be wearing it again. Wilfred understood when I took him into my business that this was to be his last chance. He has had one opportunity after another to reform, but the truth is he does not wish to reform. He is what he is. But he is no son of mine."

There was nothing more to be said. We took our leave.

Back in Baker Street, Holmes threw himself into his armchair without removing his coat. "I have saved Lombard's jewels, but I have lost him a son."

"Nonsense, Holmes. Wilfred lost himself long ago."

"Nevertheless, if I had not insisted that Wilfred confess his role in the robbery—"

"You would not only have deceived your client but also made it possible for Wilfred to betray his father again."

"Oh, I daresay you are right, Watson. But there should have been some solution other than the one at which Lombard ultimately arrived."

"Perhaps. But Lombard is only half the story—you have prevented a death this day. Surely that is more rewarding than unmasking a killer! This has to be one of your most successful cases, unquestionably."

"As you no doubt will claim in your scribblings." He stretched out a long arm and picked up his largest pipe.

My heart sank. Whenever Holmes reached for that particular pipe, it invariably meant he would spend hour after hour smoking and thinking. Or smoking and fretting. Mrs. Hudson was preparing a

Christmas goose, but it would be several hours before it was ready. More than anything I wanted to spend those hours sleeping, but I did not relish the thought of coming back to a sitting room so thick with tobacco fumes I would be unable to taste the goose.

There was only one thing to be done.

"Come, Holmes—this self-blame is not like you. You mustn't sit there and brood. Let us go take a stroll in Regent's Park. You need to be out and about."

"I've *been* out and about. I just got back."

"From visiting an unhappy man. But today is Christmas. A time for rejoicing!"

"I don't *want* to rejoice."

"Of course you do. A brisk walk in Regent's Park will do you worlds of good. Besides, I have a desire to hear some real carolers, ones who sing for the joy of the season rather than for some nefarious purpose. Come, Holmes, let us be off!"

"Oh, very well, since you're so set on it. Although I fail to see why we cannot sit here quietly until Mrs. Hudson brings us that plump goose she is cooking."

"Because I worry you may be growing stale. Sit quietly, indeed!" He stared at me in disbelief.

For once, I had the last word.

THE ADVENTURE OF THE GREATEST GIFT

Loren D. Estleman

"You know, Watson," remarked Sherlock Holmes, "that I am not a religious man. Neither, however, am I a blasphemous one, and I trust I won't offend one of your fine sentiments when I wish that the Great Miracle could be repeated in the case of the late lamented Professor Moriarty. I do miss him these foul evenings."

The date, according to the notes I have before me, was the twenty-third of December, 1901. The fog that evening was particularly dense and yellow, and to attempt to peer out through the windows in Holmes's little sitting room in the digs we used to share yielded results no more satisfactory than looking into a filthy mirror. Beneath that Stygian mass, the fresh snowfall of the morning, which had carried such promise of an immaculate yuletide, had turned as brown as the Thames and clung to hoof and boot alike in sodden clumps, exactly as if the Great Grimpen Mire of evil memory had spread

beyond Devonshire to fill the streets of London. The heavens themselves, it seemed, had joined us in mourning the loss of our queen,
dead these eleven months.

I was concerned by my friend's remark, not because it stung my
faith, but for the evidence it gave of the depth of his depression.
Weeks had passed since he had last been engaged upon one of the
thorny problems that challenged his intellect and distracted him from
the unsavory pursuits that endangered his health, and to whose sinister charms he was never wholly immune no matter how long he
stayed away from them. Indeed, although the ugly brown bottle and
well-worn morocco case containing Holmes's needle had gone sufficiently untouched for an industrious spider to have erected a web
between them and the corner of the mantelpiece, that gossamer
strand posed no barrier to inactivity and *ennui*, which were the only
things on this earth that Holmes feared. He feared them no more
than I dreaded their artificial remedy.

"I should think there are dark enough hearts abroad in a city this
size without resuscitating Moriarty," said I, "even in the present season." I hoped by this to begin a debate that might stimulate him
until such time as his thoughts turned in a more wholesome direction.

"Dark enough, perhaps. But black is an exceedingly dull colour
without the scarlet stain of imagination. Even the agony columns
have nothing more original to offer than the common run of spouse
beatings, lost Gladstones, and stray children. It's enough to make
one cancel all his subscriptions." He waved a slim white hand towards the mountainous rubble of crumpled newspapers that had ac-
cumulated around the basket chair in which he sat coiled like Dr.
Roylott's adder. The hand went on to scoop up his charred brier,
which he filled with shag from its receptacle of the moment, a plaster
cast of the skull of the murderer Burke, currently on display at Scot-

land Yard. The top had been hinged to tip back for convenient storage.

"You once ventured the opinion that your absence from London for any length of time encouraged boldness in the criminal classes. Perhaps you should consider a trip to Paris."

He smiled without mirth. "Good old Watson. You were less transparent when you urged me as my physician to go on holiday, without resorting to subterfuge. I should be just as bored there as here, with the added exasperation of all those cream sauces. No, I shall stay here and await the diversion of a good poisoning."

I should have argued the point further had not someone chose that moment to ring at the street door.

"Hark!" exclaimed Holmes, shaking out the match with which he had been about to light his pipe. "There is a merry bell, and there to answer it the stately tread of our esteemed Mrs. Hudson. She may bring us glad tidings yet."

Within moments his prediction was confirmed, as I swung open the door to the landlady's polite tap. "A delivery for Mr. Holmes, Doctor," said she. "I gave the fellow tuppence."

I handed her that sum and accepted a cylindrical package, wrapped in ordinary brown paper and bound with string.

"Who delivered it, pray?" asked Holmes, who had unwound himself from his chair with a panther's quickness at the first touch of her knuckles against the door. He stood behind me crackling with energy, the indolent lounger vanished.

"A commissionaire, sir. He said the package was waiting for him when he reported for duty and no one seems to know who left it."

"Did you believe him?"

That good Scotswoman drew herself up to her not inconsiderable height. "I'd sooner question the character of the prime minister than a veteran."

"The king himself could not have said it better," Holmes said, when we were alone once again. "What do you make of it, old fellow?"

"It's a package."

"Pawky elf!" He snatched it from my hands and carried it over to the gas lamp, where he studied the object thoroughly from end to end and all around. It was less than five inches in length, with a diameter of some two and one-half inches, and weighed rather less than a common box of matches. "No return address or postmark, just 'Sherlock Holmes, Esq.' and the address, written in block." He sniffed it. "Petroleum-based ink, obtainable in any stationery shop for less than a shilling." He shook it. It made no noise.

"Careful, Holmes! It may be an explosive device."

"If so, it cannot contain enough powder to snuff out a candle. I examined quite thoroughly the weight and volume of the various volatile compounds in my monograph on demolitions." Absorbed in the package, he fished a hand inside a pocket, appeared to realize tardily that he was wearing his dressing gown, and charged to the deal table where he kept his chemical apparatus and instruments. He used a surgeon's scalpel to slit the wrapping from end to end.

The gaily decorated cardboard canister that emerged brought an expression of chagrin to his face that nearly made me smile. The red-and-gold lettering described an undulating pattern across the adhesive label, spelling out EDISON GOLD-MOULDED RECORD.

"It's a wax recording cylinder!" I cried.

"That is obvious. Its significance is somewhat more obscure."

"Perhaps someone knows you're a lover of music. An anonymous admirer."

"Perhaps." He removed the lid and peered inside. Then he tipped the contents out onto the table. The glistening roll of hardened wax rotated to a stop against the base of his microscope.

"Nothing else inside," Holmes reported, groping at the canister's interior with the ends of his fingers. "The cardboard doesn't appear to have been tampered with. I doubt any messages are hidden between the layers." He set it down and lifted the cylinder, submitting it to the same scrutiny.

"Play it," said I. "Perhaps it's a recorded message."

"My conclusion precisely. I will make a detective of you yet." He carried the cylinder to the parlor phonograph, slid it into place, worked the crank, and applied the needle. A second or two of hoarse scratching issued from the horn, then the sweet strain of strings, accompanied by the singing of an accomplished male tenor:

> *After the ball is over,*
> *After the break of morn,*
> *After the dancers' leaving,*
> *After the stars are gone.*
> *Many a heart is aching,*
> *If you could read them all;*
> *Many the hopes that have vanished,*
> *After the ball.*

The refrain was repeated, after which the recording scratched into silence. I could make nothing of it, but Holmes was galvanized. He charged towards the basket chair, and there on his knees sorted feverishly through the wrecked newspapers, snapping open the sections and raking them with his eyes, disposing of each as it disappointed him and seizing upon the next. At length he shot to his feet, folding one over.

"Hullo, Watson! Listen to this."

He read:

> All of London society is expected to gather at Balderwood House, home of Sir John Whitsunday, M.P., and his wife Alice, where on the 23rd a ball will be held to honour their guest, the Marquis DuBlac, of Paris and Bordeaux, France. The Marquis is popular in this country, as his efforts on behalf of the French Republic to cement peaceful relations between his homeland and England are well known.

" 'After the Ball' is a popular song in America," said I. "How can you be certain the recording refers to this event?"

"You must agree that this recording arriving on the night of this affair is an unlikely coincidence. Use your imagination: 'Many a heart is aching'; 'Many the hopes that have vanished.' What cataclysm might we expect to cause these tragic considerations?"

I frowned. "War?"

"Bravo! The friendship between DuBlac and our government is a slim barricade against the centuries-old differences that have plunged England and France time and again into bloodshed. Certain foreign powers would have much to gain by eliminating so well-known a French dignitary on British soil."

"Good heavens! Are you suggesting he may be assassinated at that ball?"

"There is no time to discuss the matter. How soon can you be dressed for a gala evening?"

"Ten minutes from here to my house, and twenty minutes to change." I snatched my coat and hat off the peg.

"I shall be there with a hansom in thirty minutes. Do not forget to add a revolver to your ensemble. A well-armed man is dressed for any occasion."

"How are we to get in without an invitation?"

His eyes were bright. "I am Sherlock Holmes. My presence is always welcome among the law-abiding."

Balderwood House had been built under Charles I upon the foundations of a monastery burned during the Reformation. In those days it had occupied a country plot far from the bustle of Medieval London, but in the ensuing three centuries the city had spread to encompass its walls; a twenty-minute hansom ride deposited us at the gate, which stood open for the convenience of the evening's guests. Notwithstanding the gay occasion, the dour fog, and beneath it the stark fact of a nation bereaved, cast over the estate a sombre, even baleful aspect. The candles burning in the windows created the impression that one were under the hostile scrutiny of a many-eyed beast from pagan mythology.

The butler, a cherubic enough fellow, bald of head and pink of cheek, frowned decorously at Holmes's admission that we had not been invited, but accepted our cards and asked us to wait in the entryway. Moments later we were joined among the room's baronial trappings by a handsome woman in her middle years, attired in a black evening dress of dutiful mourning and a minimum of jewels, who introduced herself as Alice Whitsunday, wife of Sir John.

"And which of you is Mr. Holmes?" asked she, looking from one of us to the other. "You do us a great honour, along with embarrassment that we omitted you from the list of our guests."

Holmes accepted the well-bred rebuke with equal grace. "I am Holmes, dear madam, and by that admission the man who must apologize for this breach of protocol. This is Dr. Watson, my friend and confidant. It is my belief that someone intends to do your party a great deal more mischief than mine."

"My stars! A theft?" Her hand flew to her busom.

"No, madam. A murder."

She paled suddenly, and I stepped forward. However, she was an estimable lady, and instead of swooning tugged at a bellpull. Instantly the butler appeared.

"Gregory, please fetch Sir John."

The servant withdrew. Within a short space of time the doors to what once must have been the Great Hall slid open, emitting music, sounds of merriment, and the lord of the manor, who drew the doors shut behind him and stood looking down at his two unwanted visitors from his astonishing height. He was a full head taller than my friend, but weighed not a copper more; beneath a shock of startling white hair the very bones of his face protruded beneath his bluish pallor like stones in a shallow pool. The black satin mourning band sewn to the sleeve of his evening coat was not darker than his gaze.

"What is this outrage?" he demanded coldly.

Holmes wasted no time in niceties. "My name is Sherlock Holmes. It has come to my attention that your guest of honour, the Marquis DuBlac, is in grave danger. He may not leave this house alive."

"Indeed. Where did you obtain this information?"

"There is no time, Sir John. Is there a room where we can be alone with the Marquis?"

Parliament has never been known for swift action. I was impressed, therefore, when this esteemed member directed us immediately to a room at the top of the stairs and joined us there within five minutes, accompanied by the Frenchman. The room was Sir John's study, spacious and scholarly, with books on all sides and claret and cigars on a table opposite his desk, an uncommonly fine one of carved mahogany.

"A very great pleasure, Monsieur 'Olmes. Your services to my country are known in every corner of the Republic."

The Marquis was a small man as was common to his race, with a large head adorned by a neatly pointed moustache. A red satin sash described a violent diagonal across his starched shirtfront, with the golden starburst of the *Legion d'Honneur* appended to his right breast. He bowed deeply.

"I hope to do it one more this night, on behalf of both our home-lands," replied Holmes. He proceeded to tell both the Marquis and our host, in the sparest possible terms, the circumstances that had led us to this meeting.

"And what do you propose to do?" asked the honoured guest when the detective had finished.

"Nothing, your excellency."

"Nothing?" The Marquis's great brow creased.

"Nothing?" Patches of unhealthy colour appeared upon Sir John's hollow cheeks.

"Nothing," confirmed Holmes.

"Holmes!" Even I, who knew never to expect anything but the unexpected where my companion's methods were concerned, was astounded.

"Then I trust you will have no objection to my sending Gregory out to fetch the police." Sir John reached for the bellpull beside the desk.

Holmes held up an admonitory hand. "Forgive me for assuming too much, Sir John. There is no reason to expect a busy M.P. to be familiar with the lyrics to a popular American song. I call your attention to the first stanza." Whereupon he astonished us all further by singing, in a pleasant tenor:

> *After the ball is over,*
> *After the break of morn,*
> *After the dancers' leaving . . .*

"The message is clear," he said, abandoning the rest of the composition. "Our assassin will not strike before the end of the evening. If we disrupt the entertainment with an aggressive investigation, we will put him on alert, and merely postpone the inevitable until another time when we are less prepared. Whoever our unknown benefactor is—we shall assume he is a traitor in the enemy camp—we must not waste the clue he has sent us by behaving rashly."

Our host withdrew his hand from the bellpull. "Do you mean to suggest that we go on with the ball as if we knew nothing?"

"That is the impression we must leave. In reality, of course, we will be wary. Is there a location from where Dr. Watson and I can observe the activity in the ballroom without calling attention to ourselves?"

"There is a landing on this floor where you can stand between the staircases and look down. There will likely be other guests there," added Sir John apologetically.

"All the better for us to lose ourselves in the crowd. *Au revoir*, your excellency," Holmes executed a smart bow in the Frenchman's direction. "I pray that you will be able to enjoy your fête without fear for your safety."

"I do not see how it could be otherwise, with the great Sherlock

'Olmes as my protector." The Marquis responded in kind and took his leave.

Following him, Sir John Whitsunday paused at the door to peer down at my friend. "I should warn you that if it turns out my guest's trust is misplaced, you will have to answer to all of Europe."

The ballroom had been refurbished in the grand Victorian manner, with a high vaulted ceiling and twin staircases swooping down from a balustraded landing, where we stood among a group of gentlemen elders who had sought refuge from the energetic activity on the floor to smoke cigars and pontificate upon the situation in South Africa. To one who recalled the bright hues and laughter of happier times, it was a sobering experience to observe the subdued fashions of the dancers moving decorously to restrained music from an orchestra clad in black from neck to heels. Even the wreaths and coloured glass ornaments that decorated the hall were understated to a degree which seemed funereal.

Holmes, I saw, was in no such reverie. In spite of his own assurance that nothing would happen for several hours, his hatchetlike profile and intense gaze as he gripped the marble railing made him resemble a bird of prey. I slid my hand into my coat pocket and found comfort in the cool touch of my old service revolver, veteran of so many adventures.

I directed my attention to the Marquis, who stood drinking wine and chatting with the Whitsundays beneath a huge full-length portrait of our late Queen, suitably framed in black crepe. When that proved uninvolving, I endeavoured for some time to pick out the villain or villains who had infiltrated the gathering. It seemed that this swarthy fellow standing by the refreshments table fit the bill, but then that nervous dancer drew my suspicions regarding the source of his unease. Such diversions are contagious; at the end of an hour I had decided that everyone present, with the exceptions of my friend and I, our hosts, and of course the Marquis himself, was capable of assassination.

I became particularly interested in a stout, red-faced guest who shared our landing, whose vehemence against the French government for criticizing our stand against the Boers rose shrilly above the music—loudly enough, in fact, to draw annoyed glances from the floor below. Holmes was sanguine when I directed his attention to the tirade.

"That is Lord Sutworth," said he. "He's been in the House of Peers since Gladstone was a boy. In any case I have eliminated the men on this landing. Their tailoring will not admit the accessory of an air rifle or a crossbow. The range is too great for any accuracy with a revolver."

"Perhaps we should move closer to the Marquis. 'After the break of morn' may be a ruse to divert us from the actual timetable."

"I considered that. The floor is too crowded for the killer to make good his escape. He will wait until the guests thin out."

I resolved thenceforth to withhold my opinions, which were clearly an irritation to my companion.

Sometime later I suppressed a yawn and withdrew my hand from my weapon to reach for my watch. Holmes's sudden grip upon my arm arrested the movement. Belatedly I became aware of the tune the orchestra was playing.

" 'After the Ball!' " I whispered.

"I've been a fool, Watson! The clue was not in the lyrics, but in the song itself. It is a signal for action!"

"But the killer's escape—"

"No time!" And with that he was gone from my side, flying down the stairs with his tails fluttering behind.

I strained to catch up, drawing my revolver and shouldering aside a number of guests who were climbing the steps to escape the heat and noise of the ballroom. A middle-aged woman in black taffeta shrieked when she spied my weapon.

Holmes was halfway across the floor, shoving men and women sprawling in his anxiety to reach the guest of honour, by the time I quit the stairs. I hastened in his wake, dodging and leaping over the hunched forms of outraged dancers attempting to regain their feet. I overheard a Scotsman declare in an angry, burring baritone that this was what one might expect now that Edward was on the throne.

Now the refreshments table was the only thing separating Sherlock Holmes from the endangered Marquis. He seized it in both hands and flung it over. It was a twelve-foot trestle, and it went down in a flurry of white linen, flashing silver, and shattering crystal as Holmes vaulted on over, bound for the shocked trio of DuBlac, Sir John, and Alice Whitsunday.

I am not as athletic as my friend. I paused before the ruined table, and was immediately grateful that I had; for as I glanced up, I had a sudden vision of Queen Victoria *moving*, with the same stately dignity with which she had comported herself in life. Instantly I realized this was a misapprehension, and that the great seven-foot portrait that hung behind the Marquis and his hosts was swinging outward as on a pivot. Beyond it was the dark rectangle of an open passage, and inside that rectangle, standing poised within easy striking distance with a dagger of the French dignitary was—

Mycroft Holmes!

I was drawing aim upon that figure with my revolver, and recognized the generous proportions and lofty brow of Sherlock Holmes's older brother just in time to withdraw my finger from the trigger. The detective, however, was too close to react, and threw his arms around the man in the passage in a flying leap that carried them both to the floor inside the opening.

"Hold, Sherlock!" Mycroft exclaimed, disentangling himself from his sibling. "When will you learn to use your head before your feet?"

Ten minutes later, Holmes and I were seated in our host's commodious study with Sir John, the Marquis DuBlac, and Mycroft, who had corrected his dishevelment and occupied the largest armchair with cigar in hand and a glass of claret on the table at his elbow.

"All your questions will be answered in the fullness of time," said he. "Impatience always was your great weakness, Sherlock. First, tell us how you guessed at the presence of a secret passage behind the painting."

"I haven't guessed since we were children," Holmes replied. "When the orchestra began playing 'After the Ball' and I realized the die was cast, a passage was the only possibility that offered both access to the intended victim and escape afterwards. The antiquity of Balderwood House suggested the probability that such a passage existed."

"Admirable!" cried the Marquis. "Unfortunately, our society includes a number of deranged individuals for whom the prospect of flight holds no importance."

"The wax recording cylinder that was delivered to my door and the whole business of the song pointed to a subtle and devious mind. A fanatic did not answer."

"Such men have been known to employ fanatics," Mycroft reminded him.

"The prize was too large, and deranged men are often unpredictable. Skilled labour demands a steady hand."

Sir John sat back and crossed his long legs, exhibiting calm for the first time. "He is brilliant, as well as cool under fire. Gentlemen, I withdraw my objections. I feared that he was an invention of fiction, but his performance tonight convinces me he is the man for us."

"I was never in doubt." The Frenchman's eyes twinkled. "Dr. Watson's accounts of his friend's adventures are very popular in my country. I am privileged to have witnessed his genius and daring firsthand."

"I felt sure you would see it that way," put in Mycroft. "I was not so certain of Sir John, and so remained neutral."

Here Holmes displayed the impatience that his brother deplored. "The time has come to tell me the purpose of this charade. You haven't the ambition, Mycroft, for practical jokes, which in any case would be unseemly in the shadow of our recent loss."

Mycroft pulled at his cigar. "That loss has led to a most unstable situation upon the continent. For some time now the great powers have feared unrest, but could not come to an agreement as to who should be entrusted with investigating its source. Until now." He drew a folded sheet of paper from inside his coat and handed it to his brother.

Holmes unfolded the exquisite stationery and read. The text was all but obscured by the presence of royal seals. "What is the purpose of this?" he asked at length.

Mycroft said, "It is a letter signed and sealed by all the crowned heads of Europe and Great Britain, presenting the bearer with authority to go anywhere and interrogate anyone with the absolute co-operation of the local constabulary. Your mission will be to investigate any and all rumors of subversive activity and to report your conclusions to an international tribunal headquartered in Berne, Switzerland. You will answer to no one government; which means, of course, that you will answer to them all. I should warn you before you accept this post that it will leave you little time for quiet contemplation. It will never be boring."

"I begin to understand," said Holmes. "Tonight was an audition of sorts."

His brother nodded. "I must claim credit for the sham's details. I'm inordinately proud of the business with the wax cylinder. It was an early Christmas present from an American dignitary, which I decided to put to good use. I was somewhat concerned when Sir John reported that you did not expect anything to happen until the ball was concluded, but I must compliment you upon the swiftness of your actions the moment you realized you'd erred. Flexibility and reflex are crucial. Do you accept the post?"

"I can do no other in the name of peace. I'm grateful you chose me."

"You should thank Dr. Watson. He visited me last week in my offices at Whitehall, reminded me sternly that England was wasting its greatest natural resource and challenged me to put you to work on its behalf. I confess that because I am related to you I lacked the objectivity to have considered you for this assignment. It was good luck all round that he should have approached me when he did."

Holmes looked at me with the first signs of astonishment I had ever seen upon his face. I hastened to reassure him that he had not lost his keen powers of observation.

"I knew nothing of the test," said I. "Mycroft said only that he would take up my suggestion with the foreign secretary. I was convinced tonight's mystery was legitimate."

"A great adventure!" the Marquis exclaimed.

"It is more than that." Holmes was still looking at me. "It is a great gift."

At that moment the clock on Sir John Whitsunday's mantelpiece chimed midnight, announcing that Christmas Eve was upon us. "Happy Christmas, Holmes," said I.

My friend made no reply.

My doorbell rang on Christmas morning while I was breakfasting with my wife.

"Oh, dear." She set down her cup. "I hope that isn't a patient, today of all days."

I arose from the table resignedly. "Perhaps it is just Mrs. Ablewhite's annual case of the sniffles."

A fat commissionaire stood upon the doorstep, his great bulging middle barely contained by his brass buttons. An enormous pair of snow-white moustaches obscured most of his florid face. "Package for Dr. Watson," said he.

I signed the receipt and accepted the parcel, which was no larger than a tin of tobacco and wrapped in bright silver paper. Curious to see which of my patients had sent me a gift, I unwrapped it there upon the threshold.

It was a box containing Sherlock Holmes's needle in its morocco leather case and his bottle of cocaine.

"Happy Christmas, Watson," came a familiar voice from behind the commissionaire's moustaches. "I shan't be needing it again this century."

THE CASE OF THE RAJAH'S EMERALD

Carolyn Wheat

It was said of the late Ebenezer Scrooge that he knew how to
keep Christmas well, if any man alive possessed the knowledge.
His former reputation, that of the miser who greeted the festive
season with a curmudgeonly "bah, humbug," had fallen to another
prominent citizen of London, who stood in the doorway of my surgery stamping snow off his boots and loudly declaiming that Christmas was the dreariest holiday in the entire calendar year.

From the point of view of crime, that is.

"It is not," Sherlock Holmes explained, handing me his furred cap
and greatcoat, "that I fail to appreciate the sentiment of the season,
my dear Watson. Indeed, as a man and a citizen," he added, un-
winding the long woolen muffler from his neck and tossing it onto
the nearest chair, "I applaud the milk of human kindness that succors
us all at this most holy time of the year. It is solely," he continued,
striding toward the fire with his hands outstretched to receive its

warmth, "in my capacity as the world's first consulting detective that I deplore the general falling-off of crime that attends the birth of our Saviour. Even the common burglar fears to commit his crimes at this most—"

I seldom interrupted my friend, but his words forced a protest from my lips. "But surely, Holmes, you do not wish for—"

He answered my rudeness with an interruption of his own. Holding his slender hands in a placating gesture, he replied, "Surely not, Watson. I do not require a murder to restore my sagging spirits. Nor do I clamour for a plot to rob the Bank of England or a conspiracy to steal Whitehall's most closely-guarded secrets."

His hooded eyes seemed to contain the tiniest glint of amusement as he said, "A simple problem will do, something delightfully puzzling without being attended by blood and misery, snakes and blackmail. Something along the lines of that blue carbuncle we had for Christmas last year."

I could not but smile at the reference. That evidentiary bird had led Holmes to the most notorious jewel-thief in England. Indeed, the discovery of that marvellous jewel in the crop of a dead fowl had been the best Christmas present Holmes could have received, far better than the German microscope I gave him as a token of the season.

How was I to provide my friend with that delightful, puzzling, yet not murderous case he so longed to solve?

The answer presented itself at the door of my surgery less than a week later. Taking a leaf from Holmes's book, I summed up my visitor as a man in his forties, who had once suffered quite badly from poliomyelitis and even now depended upon a cane. He had a pale complexion and large, burning eyes in a thin face, a man, I was certain, who felt things far too deeply and lived on his nerves. Even before I examined him, I had resolved to prescribe more sleep and less coffee.

This intention dissolved into thin air when I discovered that my visitor had not come as a patient. He handed me a card, and I studied it as Holmes might have done, attempting to glean all I could from its features. Cream-colored stock, raised letters in a plain font, a proper card for a professional man, and, indeed, the card proclaimed its bearer to be such, for the legend, TIMOTHY CRATCHIT, SOLICITOR, 32 LITTLE QUEEN STREET, LONDON, WC1 was embossed thereon.

Oddly enough, I felt I ought to know the name although I had had few dealings with the legal profession, save for the formalities that surrounded the strange death of my wife's father. Perhaps this inquiry was related to that sad business?

It was not. Mr. Cratchit, at my invitation, seated himself in the chair closest to the fire and availed himself of a cup of tea into which I poured a restorative tot of brandy, for the wind outside was bitter that early December afternoon.

"Dr. Watson, I have come to consult you on a matter so delicate, so important and yet so fantastic, that I find myself at a loss as to how to begin my tale. It is, you may imagine," he said with a smile that lit his thin face, "an unusual position for me to be in. As a solicitor, I am of necessity a man of facts, sir, a man of details and subordinate clauses. A man who does not, as it were, see spirits."

"You see spirits?" I had decided Mr. Cratchit had better abstain from spirits as well as coffee, if he were to regain his health.

"Only one spirit, in point of fact," my visitor replied with that same enigmatic yet engaging smile. "The Spirit of Christmas Past."

"You're Tiny Tim!" I exclaimed, all but jumping from my chair. Surely my wife, my lovely Mary, would be enchanted to meet the living embodiment of that Christmas tale all England delighted in repeating at this happy time of year.

A faint blush marked the solicitor's thin cheek. "I was," he admitted. "I was Tiny Tim, and my benefactor, my second father, was Ebenezer Scrooge. It is on his behalf that I seek your counsel, Dr. Watson."

"But Mr. Scrooge is dead," I blurted. All London had mourned the passing of the great humanitarian; the procession that followed his hearse to the cemetery was of legendary length and the flowers that banked his coffin reminded those in attendance of Covent Garden in spring.

"Oh, yes, Mr. Scrooge is dead. This must be distinctly understood, or nothing wonderful can come of the story I am about to relate."

"Mr. Cratchit," I said, leaning forward in my chair, "I hesitate to stop your account before it begins, but may I ask whether this is a problem that could benefit from the services of my friend, Sherlock Holmes?"

"Why, I suppose it may be," Cratchit replied. "I came to you, truth be told, for your Army connexions. But it seems plain as day, now that you mention it, that Mr. Holmes is the very man to plumb this matter to its depths and bring it to a satisfactory conclusion for all concerned."

"Then may I impose upon your patience and send for Holmes? Or perhaps you would prefer to meet him at his rooms in Baker Street?"

It was decided that we would take a hansom cab to Baker Street, but not before I contrived to invite Mary into the consulting room to introduce her to our visitor. She was properly impressed, and only raised a blush on Cratchit's thin, sensitive face three times with her references to Tiny Tim and how he had grown.

I was afraid she would say them, and say them she did. As I assisted Cratchit into the cab, she called out from the doorway, "God bless us, every one."

Cratchit sighed. "I applaud the sentiment," he confessed, "but I also wish I did not have to hear the words quite so often."

"Rest assured," I said, "that you will not hear them from Holmes. He is as much enamoured of the Christmas spirit as was your late benefactor prior to his transformation. Indeed, you may even hear that immortal phrase 'bah, humbug' from his lips."

My companion laughed. "It would be most refreshing," he admitted. "A draught of tart lemonade to counterbalance all the treacle."

There was but a dusting of snow left in the city, and that was rapidly turning mud brown and ash gray. The fairy castle look of new-fallen flakes lasted but a short time in the metropolis, not unlike the spirit of the season itself, which had an evanescent quality certain to vanish altogether by the Feast of Stephen.

As the cab jounced along the mud-rutted street, I thought with some satisfaction of the Christmas gift I should shortly present to my friend. Timothy Cratchit, Solicitor, was the perfect client for the holiday, although I could not for the life of me imagine what problem had brought him to my door, and what it had to do with my old Army career.

I was enlightened soon enough. Mrs. Hudson met us at the door and ushered us into the sitting room I once shared with my detective friend, who sat at his ease before the fire, perusing a cheap newspaper.

As was his wont, he came to the point at once, after inviting us to sit and light our cigars.

"And now, Mr. Cratchit, pray tell us what brings you here. I know nothing of your problem save that it involves the estate of your late benefactor and that certain individuals have appeared from the Far East to claim the inheritance."

"Come, Holmes," I protested. "This is too much. How can you profess to know these particulars before Mr. Cratchit has begun his account of the matter?"

"You know my methods, Watson." He ticked off his points upon slender, ink-stained fingers. "First, Mr. Cratchit began his errand with you instead of me. This argues either a medical or an Army matter; since you arrived without your medical case, I am inclined toward the Army. Second, when Mr. Cratchit hung his greatcoat in the hallway, I noted the corner of a document in one of the pockets. It bore the crest of the Oriental Club, which caters exclusively to those employed by the British East India Company. I deduced two separate visitors from the East, one connected with the military and the other with the civil service. This newspaper told the rest of the tale."

"Has word of this affair reached the newspapers?" Cratchit's tone was one of agitation. "I would not have had them notified for all the world."

"Do not fear on that account, sir," Holmes replied with an enigmatic smile. "I doubt that many Londoners receive the *Lahore Civil and Military Gazette*. My copy arrived on the East Indiaman *Star of Rajput* only yesterday." He puffed on his pipe, sending a cloud of smoke into the already frowsty room. "As the estate of the late Mr. Scrooge is the subject of a protracted inquiry in Chancery, I concluded that someone from the Far East has appeared to assert an interest in the matter. Am I correct, Mr. Cratchit?"

"Yes." Cratchit's answering smile held a tinge of wry humour. "If I had but one claimant to present to the Lord Chancellor as the heir to the Scrooge fortune, I should not be here at this moment. One would be a sufficiency."

"But two claimants are—" Holmes invited.

"One too many, Mr. Holmes."

I leaned back in my accustomed Morris chair, basking in the glow of the fire, and feeling a sense of peace and tranquillity such as I had not enjoyed for a long while. I loved my wife, and I was more than ever contented with my wedded existence, yet some part of me yearned always for the masculine comforts of Baker Street, and the stimulating company of my friend Holmes. I never felt so alive as I did when engaged in one of his cases.

"This excellent newspaper," Holmes said, pointing to the cheaply printed thing, "contains a most enlightening item in its police reports. It appears that the widow and son of the late Frederick Scrooge were robbed while awaiting the departure of the *Star of Rajput*. No valuables were taken, save documents which were intended to prove the heir's identity before the Chancery Court."

"Indeed, Mr. Holmes. I am presented with two claimants, neither of whom possesses a complete set of papers, each of whom charges the other with theft and maintains that he is the true heir. One is a liar and a fraud; the other is the true son of my late benefactor's nephew, but I—well, sir, I'm blowed if I know which is which!"

The thin cheeks colored with intense emotion as the solicitor continued. "You must believe me, Mr. Holmes," he said with solemn-faced earnestness, "when I assure you that neither I nor anyone in my family has the slightest claim upon the Scrooge estate. It is my sole and dearest wish to administer the estate as Mr. Scrooge intended, and to carry out to the letter every clause and codicil of his will."

"And what, precisely, does that will provide, sir?" Holmes puffed on his pipe, sending a cloud of foul-smelling tobacco into the close air of the parlor. "Or should I ask, rather, for whom does that will provide?"

"Ah, there's the heart of it, right enough, Mr. Holmes. You have struck straight at the marrow of the matter and dug out its meat. Whom does the will benefit? *Cui bono*, as the ancients would have it?"

"You are well-educated, sir," Holmes remarked.

"All that I am," the solicitor replied with becoming humility, "I owe to my generous benefactor. But for him, I should not even be alive to breathe the air of London on this day. But," he said, "I stray from my theme, and yet, sir, I do not, for everything good that Mr. Ebenezer Scrooge did for me he did three and four times over for his own nephew, Mr. Fred, and what, I ask you, sir, could be more natural?"

"Then I take it Mr. Fred Scrooge—for I believe the young man took his uncle's surname so as to keep that fine old English name alive—I take it Fred Scrooge was the elder Scrooge's chief heir?"

"He was, Mr. Holmes. As was only right and natural, he being the only living blood relative Mr. Ebenezer Scrooge possessed. Mr. Fred," he went on, his face clouding, "was widowed young. His lovely wife, whom I looked upon as a second mother, was taken ill and died, without issue, meaning that there were no children, Mr. Holmes."

"I believe Mr. Fred Scrooge decided to pursue the firm's business in the Far East after his wife's death," Holmes remarked. It was always astonishing to me how many details of London life Holmes knew, without seeming to take an interest in anything outside of his test tubes and cigar ashes. "I take it the present situation arises from that decision in some manner."

"You are correct, Mr. Holmes. While in India, Mr. Fred met a young woman. He was no longer young himself, being approximately the age I am now, but he fell in love with this lady and married her in Calcutta. Naturally, old Mr. Scrooge was too infirm to make the trip, so Mr. Fred was unattended by any of his family at the service. He planned to return to England with his bride, but she was confined almost at once and gave birth to a child, a son."

"Was old Mr. Scrooge still alive at this time?"

"Yes, sir, very much so. Hale and hearty in spite of his years. He looked forward very much to entertaining Mr. Fred and his new family, but somehow or other every visit that was planned failed to materialize. Either the boy or the wife or Mr. Fred himself became ill, or there was too much press of business, or the war had broken out again and no passenger ships were sailing. For whatever reason, Mr. Ebenezer died without ever seeing his grand-nephew."

"I note that you do not refer to Mr. Fred Scrooge's wife or son by name, Mr. Cratchit."

"Ah, you note at once that which it has taken me several years to realize, Mr. Holmes. My own correspondence with Mr. Fred was confined to legal matters, for the most part, although he always asked after my own family most cordially. He said little regarding his own family life, and I, out of delicacy, forebore to ask. Only lately have I come to realize how little I actually know about Mr. Fred's wife and child."

"And to what, pray, does that circumstance point?" Holmes steepled his fingers and spoke softly, inviting me to engage in his favourite pastime of deduction.

"Plain as a pikestaff, Holmes." I puffed on my pipe. "Marriage beneath his station. I saw it any number of times in my brief Army service. A young lieutenant, fresh from England, set upon by the daughter of a low-ranked soldier and married before he knew his way about. Trapped for life in a marriage of unequals."

"There is no hint of such a thing in Mr. Fred's letters," Cratchit protested. He reached inside his coat pocket and pulled out a bundle of letters tied with ribbon. Handing them to Holmes, he said, "You will note several references to the boy's health and his education at St. James's Academy in Lahore. I urge special attention to the second letter, which informs Mr. Ebenezer of the marriage."

Holmes undid the ribbon and opened the letters, reading with such quickness I was certain he could not possibly absorb the contents, yet within a minute his eyes left the paper and stared at Cratchit with astonishment. "It says here," he recited, "that Fred Scrooge acquired a 'most precious emerald' from a local maharajah. The newspaper makes no mention of stolen jewels, but I take it you are concerned that the rightful heir has not only been stripped of the proof of his identity, but of a valuable gem."

"Indeed, Mr. Holmes. I had expected to know Mr. Fred's heir not only because he would show proof of his birth, but because he would bring this emerald as a pledge." The solicitor reached into his pocket yet again and this time withdrew a telegram, sent from India.

ARRIVING STAR OF RAJPUT STOP IN COMPANY OF EMERALD STOP PLEASE
TO MEET SHIP. A. SCROOGE

"So we know the boy's name begins with the letter A," I remarked unnecessarily.

"If this telegram was sent by the genuine Mr. Scrooge, that is," Cratchit corrected.

Holmes returned to his interrogation. "I take it the elder Mr. Scrooge never met his nephew's wife or child."

"Correct, Mr. Holmes. Some nineteen years passed, and then Mr. Fred himself died without ever returning to his native land. Enteric fever," Cratchit added and I groaned, for I had barely escaped with my life from that debilitating disease, the curse of our Eastern possessions.

"Where are these two claimants now?" Holmes asked, his eyes alight with the joys of the hunt.

"One is in residence at the Army and Navy Club," Cratchit replied, "and the other, as you already deduced, is staying at the Oriental Club. I have appointments with each, and I hope Dr. Watson will accompany me to the Army and Navy Club, for his knowledge of a certain orderly is bound to be of enormous assistance."

My heart leapt within my breast. "Murray?" I said with great excitement. "The man who brought me to the base hospital at Peshawar?"

"That is what he claims, in any case," Cratchit said with an enigmatic smile.

"Let us go at once." Holmes jumped from his chair in his usual manner of accepting a case, which is to say, he pounced upon it like a cat upon a fat mouse, not giving it time to get away. "We shall unmask the impostor and toast the true heir by the end of this day."

"I pray you are correct, Mr. Holmes," Cratchit said. "It is a poor solicitor who does not know his own client."

Holmes wrapped his muffler around his neck, threw his cloak over his shoulders and was out the door hailing a cab before Cratchit and I managed to extricate ourselves from our chairs.

The solicitor reached for his stick and leaned heavily upon it as he rose; it seemed to me his leg grew more infirm with the passage of the day, and he limped rather badly as we made our way to the hansom cab Holmes had secured for our journey. But then, my own hip gave a twinge of pain as I hoisted myself into the cab. As we bounced along Baker Street toward St. James's Square, I found myself grateful that this case was unlikely to involve physical violence, for poor Holmes was assisted, not as he should have been, by men of strength and agility, but by two cripples.

Perhaps it was the lowering clouds, promising snow before morning, and the bitter damp cold that turned my thoughts so bleak. Perhaps it was the forcible reminder of my injury and illness in the East, but something in me curdled and shrank as we drove toward the Army and Navy Club, as if all joy had left the festive season even as its most tender representative sat beside me in the cab, rubbing his leg and gazing out the window with an expression of muted pain upon his thin visage.

The front entrance to the Army and Navy Club boasts an ornate grand staircase of white marble, graced with elaborate brass railings and featuring a huge painting of half-clad nymphs. We turned to the left and entered the coffee room, which was furnished with dark, oversized chairs and smelled of leather and smoke.

A hand on my arm stopped my progess toward the fire.

"Do you recognize anyone in this room, Doctor?" Cratchit whispered in my ear.

I gazed around the room; soldiers old and young, mustachioed and clean-shaven, sat in chairs and smoked. They read books or newspapers, or chatted in quiet tones. They were all, so far as I could tell, complete strangers.

"Should I recognize anyone?"

"I should think," Holmes said sotto-voce, "that you might have cause to remember the man who saved your life."

I looked about, but did not see anyone I knew.

"I—it was a few years ago," I mumbled, ashamed of myself. "I was injured and, though I did not know it at the time, I was ill as well. No doubt his features failed to impress themselves upon me."

"Or perhaps, Watson," Holmes said, his lips barely moving, "the man you knew as Murray is not in this room, and someone else has taken his name and identity."

"And if Murray is not the genuine article," I finished, "then this supposed Mr. Scrooge must be a bald-faced impostor as well." Anger swept through me; how could any man stoop so low as to impersonate a true hero?

"Not necessarily, Watson," Holmes admonished. Without waiting for a signal from Cratchit, he strode to the corner of the room and presented himself to a young man with hair of burnished gold, who sat at his ease, his long legs outstretched in a most uncivil manner.

"Mr. Scrooge, I presume?"

The young man looked down his nose at Holmes without bothering to rise from his chair. "You do, sir, you do."

"And this, I take it, is Sergeant Murray, about whom my friend Dr. Watson has told me so much."

The sallow little man in the chair opposite started at the name, and looked about him as if for a place of safety. He was a stranger to me, for the Murray I remembered had been tall and broad of shoulder, dark-haired and bushy-eyebrowed.

"I—I never said I was that Murray," he stammered. "Indeed, Mr. Holmes, I am a different Murray entirely. No connexion whatever to Dr. Watson."

"But that is not what you told this impressionable young lad, now, is it?"

The impressionable young lad stared long and hard at his companion. "So, you are not the man you purport to be? You dared take another and a better man's identity for your own unscrupulous ends? Get away from me, and do not return."

The sallow little man rose from his chair and said, "I'll go, Mr. Scrooge-I-don't-think. But before you call others impostors, it might be well to examine your own conscience."

He walked away with an oddly touching air of dignity, leaving us with the young man, who remembered his manners sufficiently to invite us to sit and to order coffee and sandwiches.

Questions were put by both Holmes and Cratchit, answered with some show of sullenness by the young man. Documents were taken from an oilskin pouch and examined in great detail by Cratchit as to legal particulars and by Holmes, who produced a large magnifying glass for the purpose.

I myself had no doubt of the young man's falseness, but I could not see how Holmes was to prove the matter. The documents in the oilskin pouch appeared genuine enough; as the only man present who had been to India, I vouched for the official seals and stamps and proclaimed the paper to be Indian-made.

"Perhaps," Cratchit said in a tentative voice, "this young man is the genuine article and he speaks truth when he says he was taken in by the man pretending to be Murray."

"I think not, Mr. Cratchit. Observe this line of the birth certificate." He pointed to the space where the name of the child was listed as Andrew Ebenezer Scrooge.

"See here," he went on, holding the paper up to the light. It was translucent at just that place where the name had been written in bold India ink, opaque throughout the rest of the document.

"Erasure, Mr. Cratchit. Someone has bleached away the actual name and substituted this one. As India ink, which is carbon-based, does not alter with age, the ink itself is consistent throughout the document. But the worn patch gives the game away. Someone changed this name."

The young man's ruddy face paled. "You—you won't call the authorities on me, will you? It was all Murray's idea. He stole the papers and said if I played my part well I should have half the swag. I—I've never been to India in my life."

"Of that," Holmes replied, "I never had the slightest doubt."

"But why?" I knotted my brow. "Why alter the document? Why not just claim the name already on the birth certificate?"

"An excellent question, Watson. As to that, I have my own ideas. Just a glimmer at present, but I shall soon put the matter to the test."

As we made our way out of the Army and Navy Club, Holmes stopped at the front desk and requested a telegram to be sent to the India Office. He instructed the bearer to return a response to us in care of the Oriental Club, where we would soon encounter the second claimant to the Scrooge estate.

As we climbed into a cab, I noted the presence of lowering clouds and predicted snow before nightfall. The prospect oddly cheered me, as a reminder of the holiday which was about to begin. Messy muddy streets and damp wool notwithstanding, there is something about snow at Christmas which brings out the child in the hardest of hearts.

"The second young man calling himself Mr. Scrooge," Cratchit explained, "is accompanied by a Mr. and Mrs. Micawber. You will find them to be—well, sir, perhaps I had better let you find them as you will find them, for you will find them soon enough."

The famous Wyatt drawing room at the Oriental Club was a welcoming sort of place, very much in the style of the Regency, with high, arched windows and bas-relief acanthus leaves on the ceiling. It was light, airy, and open, all of which might have been delightful on a sunny spring day, but it felt a bit too close to the elements on this squally afternoon. One fireplace tried in vain to give the room sufficient warmth for the few people sitting in overstuffed chairs.

Cratchit limped across the Turkish carpet, making his way to the corner of the room in which sat a tall young man in a blue serge coat and embroidered waistcoat, such as one seldom saw in conservatively dressed London circles. Next to him sat a thin woman of indeterminate age and indeterminate hair color and faded eyes, a woman of whom it must be said that she was a shadow of her former self, even if one had never set eyes upon that former self. No one could have been born so colorless, so apparently devoid of personality.

The man I took to be her husband was as plump and jolly as a Toby jug, bald as an egg with but a fringe of curly hair tickling his neck. His collar was high and his necktie rather fussy in the old style that matched the room itself, for he looked like a Regency dandy who had eaten and drunk far too well in that long-ago hedonistic time and grown old without growing into adulthood.

"Mr. Scrooge, I presume," Holmes said, repeating his earlier address. The young man rose and proffered his hand in a most frank and friendly manner. Micawber, too, rose and beamed as if he had arranged the meeting for the sole benefit of everyone concerned and thus had the prerogatives of a host. Indeed, he called for best brandy all around, a hospitable gesture that only lost a bit of lustre by his adding, "Put the bottle on Mr. Scrooge's account, if you please."

Brandy was poured, sampled, and praised. Cigars were lit and pipes tamped and one or two pleasantries attempted, but the business at hand asserted itself at last and Holmes said, in his blunt way, "I take it you are here to claim your inheritance, Mr. Scrooge? What proof of your bona fides do you present?"

The boy smiled and pointed to a box of Benares metalwork on

the table. "I brought this box from Calcutta, Mr. Holmes. Fortunately the thief who stole my birth certificate failed to acquire this. It contains letters from my great-uncle to my late father. I have not opened it, sir, wishing to preserve the documents in a pristine condition for the Lord Chancellor."

He reached into his waistcoat pocket and produced a small brass key, which he handed to Holmes with a ceremonial flourish. "I pray you, Mr. Holmes, open the box in the presence of these witnesses and receive the proof of my identity as the son of Fred Scrooge."

The young man lifted a glass of brandy to his lips as Holmes fitted the delicate key into its lock and turned it. The box opened, and Holmes gently lifted the lid. Inside lay a packet of letters, not unlike the ones Cratchit had shown us at Baker Street, but tied with a black ribbon instead of red.

Holmes withdrew the letters with care. He loosed the ribbon and lay the first envelope on the table, then reached into his pocket for his fingerprint kit. I smiled, having seen him do this magic before; Cratchit's eyes were round with interest, and the young man began to look decidedly queasy.

Holmes dusted powder on the envelope, blew upon the powder, and then used his tweezers to lift the envelope to the light. The thin Indian paper brought out the prints wonderfully; a film of silver nitrate powder remained, showing the whorls and ridges made by various fingers that had touched the envelope.

Before anyone could react, Holmes swooped down upon the brandy snifter the young man had used. He dusted it for prints as well, examined both snifter and envelope with his magnifying glass, and said, "You lied to me. You said you had not touched these letters, and yet I find your fingerprints upon them. Why, if you are the genuine heir to the Scrooge fortune, would you feel the need to dissemble?"

"I—I didn't want you to confuse me with the thief who stole my birth certificate," the young man said. "I thought if you knew I'd handled the letters, you'd condemn me as a fraud."

The skeptical look in Cratchit's eye told me this argument was unlikely to sway the Chancery Court upon whom all depended. But Holmes had clearly made up his mind that this second claimant was no more genuine than the first, and the receipt of a telegram from the India Office seemed to confirm some hidden deduction he'd made without telling either Cratchit or me what he was thinking.

As we left the Oriental Club, Cratchit's face was a study in consternation. "Mr. Holmes," he said, "I must congratulate you on your excellent deductions. However, I cannot say I am entirely satisfied with the results; I began this day with too many claimants, and I end it with none. I am not entirely convinced that I have emerged better off than before."

"The day, Mr. Cratchit," Holmes replied, gazing at the lowering sun struggling to peer from the clouds, "is not yet over. We have one more stop on our tour of London."

He maintained secrecy by taking the cab driver aside and stating his destination in low tones. I helped Cratchit into the cab and he kindly gave me his arm in the same capacity; soon we found ourselves rattling along the Thames, the salt tang of the sea filling our nostrils.

Masts filled the sky, a veritable floating forest at the edge of London. We passed Cheapside; I began to have an inkling of our destination: the East India Company docks at the Isle of Dogs, where the huge East India men docked upon their return from the exotic East.

"But, Holmes," I protested, "the *Star of Rajput* docked yesterday; there will hardly be anyone left aboard."

"We are not meeting the *Star of Rajput*," Holmes replied. "The ship we seek is the *Argosy*, which arrived less than an hour ago. Passengers will still be emerging."

"Of course," Cratchit exclaimed. "The telegram you received from the India Office. The robbery forced young Mr. Scrooge to board a later ship."

"Precisely. If we wait just here," he said, jumping with maddening agility from the cab, "we are bound to spot them."

"Them?"

"Young Mr. Scrooge and his mother," Holmes replied, "and their travelling companion, whose acquaintance I am most anxious to make."

Although the afternoon chill had deepened, and the damp river air made my leg ache, I gazed long and hard at every young man who stepped off the ship. Even the deckhands I examined with a close eye, for since I was certain the Scrooge widow was of low birth, the young man might be anyone at all. But no matter how promising a young man appeared, Holmes waved him away with an enigmatic smile.

At last one more stepped onto the gangplank, accompanied by an Indian woman in a bright green *saree*. The young man was of slight build and scholarly mein, wearing spectacles stronger than my own, though he was scarcely into his majority.

"Ah, he has brought his *ayah*," I said, referring to the Indian woman, undoubtedly the nurse who had raised him. "And the boy who follows—an Indian servant, no doubt." The young man in question was dressed in white cotton leggings and a bright silk tunic; a turban topped his head.

Holmes stepped toward the bespectacled young man, thrust out a welcoming hand, and, to my complete astonishment, addressed him as "Mr. Kipling, I presume."

"The same, sir." The young man thrust a hand in Holmes's direction and said, "But how do you come to know me?"

"I have had the pleasure of reading your excellent stories in the *Lahore Gazette*," Holmes said. "Welcome to England, Mr. Kipling. I am Sherlock Holmes, this gentleman is Dr. John Watson, and the third is Mr. Timothy Cratchit. Pray introduce us to your companions."

The eyes behind the thick spectacles glittered with intelligence. "I suspect, Mr. Holmes, that you know their names already."

"Only the surname, I assure you."

Wild surmise filled my breast. I had thought of a misalliance, but this—

The heir to the Ebenezer Scrooge estate was—

A half-Indian boy.

The woman in the emerald-green *saree* folded her hands in front of her in an attitude almost of prayer, bowed slightly, and said, "*Namaste*."

I answered her in kind, although I had not heard the greeting in many a year. The boy did the same, but his bright black eyes darted about the docks, as if he intended to learn and understand everything about this new place at once.

"Are there no elephants, Kipling Sahib, to do the heavy work?"

"There are no elephants, Adri. England is a poor country and cannot afford elephants."

The boy laughed. "You chaff me, Kipling Sahib. England is the greatest country on the earth, and the most scientific. Take a *dekko* at that if you do not believe me."

He pointed to the steam engine which operated the machinery hoisting heavy cargo off the ship. "Machines instead of elephants. My father would be most pleased to see this."

As our party made its way along the slippery dock toward the public houses, Kipling explained that Adri's grandfather was the Maharajah of Rampur, and his mother, Panna, was the Rajandini, or princess, of that small principality. He added that the name Panna meant "emerald" in Hindi and I burst into laughter.

"I must say, Holmes," I said as I followed the graceful Indian princess, "I believe the jewel the maharajah gave Mr. Fred Scrooge was even more precious than advertised. No wonder the thieves never managed to find the emerald they coveted."

Holmes led our party to a respectable-looking public house—no mean feat in that quarter of London—called the Mermaid Inn. We asked for a private room, and Holmes gave orders for an Indian tea, which consisted of strong darjeeling accompanied by Indian delicacies such as I hadn't sampled since my Army days. Wrapped turnovers called *samosas* and vegetable fritters known as *pakoras*, to be dipped into tamarind sauce and eaten with chutney.

I could hardly take my eyes off the Widow Scrooge. She was a mature woman, with dusky skin and gigantic doe eyes, long black hair and a straight Aryan nose. She glittered in the gaslight; gold earrings winked and danced, her arms were bedezined with gold bangles, she wore a gold ring in her nose, and the bright green silk of her dress was shot through with gold thread. She smelled of exotic spices and her laugh was like the tinkling of tiny bells. I was put in mind of a sailors' song about the dark-eyed Indian maiden who waited on the coast of Malabar.

She wore far more colour and jewelry than the boldest of English-women, and the effect ought to have been gaudy, but against cinnamon-colored skin, the bright green and gold appeared not only perfectly natural but the height of beauty.

"Kipling Sahib has been most gracious to me and my son," she said, in English so perfect it took my breath away. There was but the slightest sing-song lilt to her speech, but otherwise, she might have been bred in Mayfair.

She noticed my surprise and smiled. "My father is a very great admirer of all things English. He was most pleased when I married an English husband, for he wanted more than anything to have a grandson who understood the English ways of science."

The boy looked at me shyly and spoke for the first time since we had left the dock. "Are you truly a *hakim*? An English *hakim*, not our poor Indian excuse for a doctor?"

I knew the term, and I knew that in India it meant anything from a certified medical man to a fakir dispensing herbs to the gullible. But the boy said the word with such respect and longing that I understood at once.

"You want to be a doctor."

"With all my heart, Hakim Watson," he replied. "This is why I come at last to the country of my father. It is my wish to study at the Royal College of Surgeons and to return to my own country as a man of science."

"It is, of course," his mother said with a half-apologetic smile, "a great offense against caste. It is not for such as he to dirty his hands with the diseases of others. No other Rajah in all India would countenance such a thing. But my father has read the works of Mr. Darwin and thinks very highly of science, so he consents."

"This explains the alteration of the name, Holmes," I said with excitement, for I felt unduly pleased with myself for making the deduction. "The genuine birth certificate listed the boy's name as

Adri Ebenezer Scrooge, and that rascal who stole it changed the name to Andrew so that an Englishman could play the part."

"Excellent, Watson. Excellent indeed."

Kipling removed a cigar from his pocket and inquired of the rajandini if she would permit us to smoke. "On one condition," she replied with a smile, and having been to India, I knew what that would be. Cratchit looked on with astonishment as the lady herself bit the end off a cigar and allowed Kipling to light it for her.

If an Englishwoman had dared to do such a thing, we should all have been forcibly ejected from the pub, but the waiter who brought our tea only smiled, having seen Eastern women from Ceylon to Kuala Lumpur smoke fat cheroots.

"Our proof of identity is gone," the rajandini said with simple dignity. "I do not know how it will stand with the court of Chancery. I care little for the money of my late husband, but I would like my son to know his father's country and to attend school here according to his wishes."

"If only there had been an emerald," I said, then hastened to amend my remark. "Not that you are not as beautiful and precious as an emerald, but if there had truly been such a jewel, your possessing it would constitute some proof of your identity."

The spicy appetizers were wonderfully warming on the cold afternoon, spreading heat throughout our chilled bodies. We drank ale with our dumplings, and the rajandini opened an embroidered bag filled with walnuts, offering them all around the table.

I supposed it was an Indian custom, but I declined to take one. Cratchit lifted one from the bag, but made no move to open it.

"I do entreat you, gentlemen, to sample my walnuts," she said again, offering her silk bag to the company once again. I was becoming annoyed at her persistence, but Kipling joined in, a sly smile on his face.

"You must take one, Mr. Holmes. I suspect you will never have had such a walnut as this in all your days on earth."

Holmes reached in and selected a nut. I did the same, as did Cratchit.

They were ordinary nuts. No special flavor, no spices, no particular distinguishing features.

Then the rajandini picked one from the bag and opened it. She displayed the half-shell as if it were an oyster and there, inside the shell itself, sat the largest, shiniest emerald I have ever seen.

"It is an old trick," Kipling explained. "There is much thievery in India, and everyone who has precious jewels must take care to hide them at all times. The rascals who stole Adri's letters had no idea where to look for the emerald."

"You were lucky they weren't hungry, or they might have taken the nuts to eat. What would have happened then?"

"I should not have liked to be in their shoes if they stole the emerald, gentlemen," Kipling replied. "For the female of the species is more deadly than the male."

Our holiday dinner that year was most memorable, for we sat at the Cratchits' table eating roast goose and plum pudding with none other than the original Tiny Tim and his large, blooming family. The Rajandini of Rampur cooked channa dal and saffron rice with her own hands, and Adri Ebenezer Scrooge quizzed every member of the company about every facet of life in England until Kipling declared him to be the most curious creature alive, as curious as the Elephant's Child.

And that is how Holmes and I became among the first in England to hear that wise and wonderful tale.

THE CHRISTMAS CONSPIRACY

Edward D. Hoch

It was Mrs. Hudson who'd persuaded me to dress up as Father Christmas and distribute a few toys to the neighborhood children. I felt just a bit foolish toting my sack into her front parlor on that Christmas Eve Sunday of 1899, emitting a jolly "Ho Ho Ho" as I brought forth the gifts.

"Look here, children!" she announced enthusiastically. "It's Father Christmas!"

My sack was quickly emptied and I was out of there in ten minutes. That was when I decided to drop in on my old friend Sherlock Holmes on the floor above. It had been weeks since I'd seen him and I wondered if I could astound him with my costume.

But he barely glanced up from his paper as I entered, saying simply, "I'm glad you dropped by, Watson. I have a little problem here which might interest you."

"I assume Mrs. Hudson told you I was coming tonight," I muttered, deflated by his casual reaction to my entrance.

"Not at all, old friend. But do you think I could have listened to your tread upon the stairs for all these years and failed to recognize it? I see Mrs. Hudson has recruited you in her latest mission to spread a bit of Christmas cheer. I could hear the commotion all the way up here."

I was busy pulling the false beard from my chin. "They're a noisy bunch at holiday time," I agreed. "Now what is this little problem that's so important as to concern you on Christmas Eve?"

"We have a new century beginning in just eight days," said Holmes. "It is a time for all manner of skullduggery."

"Her Majesty's government is of the opinion the twentieth Century does not officially begin for another year," I pointed out.

He shrugged. "Let them think what they will. In America this has been a decade known as the Gay Nineties. It certainly began in 1890, not 1891, and it will end next Sunday midnight."

"I quite agree."

"But now to business. I was visited yesterday by a charming young lady named Elvira Ascott. She has been married just one year and now her husband is off in South Africa fighting the Boers. Her parents are deceased and she has no one to advise her on financial matters. Now an offer has been made on a piece of land she inherited from her family. The offer is good only until the end of the year, at which time it will be withdrawn."

"That's hardly your line of work, Holmes," I pointed out.

"But a gentleman has come forward to help her in the matter, free of charge. His name is Jules Blackthorn and he claims to be a solicitor. However she called unexpectedly at his office a few days ago and found it was only a convenience address where he received mail.

He did not even have a desk there. That was when she consulted me."

"And what have you learned about this man Blackthorn?"

Holmes leaned back and lit his pipe. "Very little, except to confirm her suspicion that he is not a solicitor. She suspects a plot of some sort to steal her property while her husband is away."

"Is this property especially valuable?" I asked.

"It does not seem so, which adds to the mystery. The land is a flood plain near the mouth of the Thames, often under water when there are storms with onshore winds. The man offering to buy the property is a fellow named Edgar Dobson, the owner of an adjoining estate. As it happens, Dobson holds a Christmas party at his home each year and has invited Mrs. Ascott to attend. Blackthorn has offered to escort her in her husband's absence, but she doesn't trust him. She has asked me to accompany her instead."

"You, Holmes, at a Christmas party?" It was difficult to picture in my mind.

"She fears Dobson may pressure her to conclude the sale while she is at the party. Since she is a client, I feel I must protect her interests. If you are free tomorrow I'd like you to accompany us as well."

"Surely you jest!"

"Not at all. Mrs. Ascott resides in London. We will be taking an afternoon train to Rochester, where Dobson's carriage will meet us. His home is in Cliffe, overlooking St. Mary's Marshes. Could you join us?"

My wife was spending the holiday with an elderly aunt in Reading, and there was no real reason why I could not accompany Holmes. "But I have not been invited," I pointed out.

"Let me worry about that."

There was a decided chill in the air on Christmas Day, despite the unaccustomed sunshine, when I met Holmes and Elvira Ascott at Victoria Station shortly after noon. Mrs. Ascott proved to be a handsome young woman in her early thirties, wearing a long gray coat over her dress. Her brown hair was gathered attractively beneath a stylish black hat. One look told me she was a woman of the upper classes.

"Mr. Holmes tells me you are his closest confidant," she said as the train pulled out of the station for the hour-long journey to Rochester.

"We have shared many adventures together," I agreed.

"You may be as frank and open with Watson as you have been with me," said Holmes.

"Then you know of my distress. I met my husband, William, last year when we appeared together in an amateur theatrical production. Now he is half a world away fighting for the Empire." She took a photograph from her purse and showed it to us. A handsome young man, standing tall in an army officer's uniform, had his right arm around her in a protective gesture while his other arm was stretched out straight, pointing a revolver at some unseen menace. "Isn't he handsome?"

"Indeed so!" Holmes agreed. "You make a handsome couple. But a Christmas party seems like an awkward setting for the signing of an important contract."

"Mr. Dobson only wants me to initial it tonight as a show of good faith. The actual signing will take place on Wednesday at his solicitor's office."

"And Jules Blackthorn is urging you to do this?"

"He is, and I fear he may appear at the party tonight. Mr. Dobson insists that the land must be deeded to him before the new year or there will be no deal. Of course this gives me no time to contact my husband in South Africa."

"Is the land held jointly?" I asked.

"No, it is from my family."

"But your husband would inherit it if you died."

"Actually, no. As I said, it is land from my family. I have made provisions for it to pass to my sister's children in America. William has no connection with it at all. It's only that I value his opinion and would have sought it had time allowed. Instead I was forced to rely upon the good offices of Mr. Jules Blackthorn."

"Which proved to be no good at all," Holmes observed.

Our train was passing through the countryside around Bexley, about halfway to our destination. There were patches of snow there, a reminder that winter had set in. "How did you happen to contact Mr. Blackthorn?" I asked.

"He contacted me. He sought me out at the theater early last week, on the very day Edgar Dobson made his offer for my land. It was at a production of the new *Nutcracker* ballet. Have you seen it?"

I noticed a smirk on Holmes's face as I admitted I had not.

"It is a wonderful show for the Christmas season. William and I planned to see it together until the war intervened. I found a girl-friend to accompany me so his ticket would not be wasted. At the intermission I was approached by Jules Blackthorn. He identified himself as a solicitor and offered me his card."

"But how could he have known of your impending business deal-ings with Dobson?" Holmes wondered.

"He implied that Dobson had told him."

"Did you mention anything to Dobson about attending that per-formance of *The Nutcracker*?"

"I'm certain I did not."

"And have you conveyed these developments to your husband in a letter?"

She shook her head. "Not yet. His ship would only have arrived in South Africa last week and he has had no time to send me his address. I only pray that he will not be in the front lines of this terrible war."

Presently our train pulled into the station at Rochester and we found Dobson's carriage awaiting us as planned. As in many towns the cathedral was the tallest structure, towering over all else, and we passed it on our way out to the Dobson mansion at Cliffe. Though it was not yet dark when we reached the sprawling cliffside house, a number of carriages were there ahead of ours.

Holmes was the first out and presented his hand to assist the lady down the step to the ground. Already a tall, balding butler had appeared to welcome us and escort us inside. He turned away almost immediately and directed a footman to show us inside. We were led to the rear of the house, to the aptly named Great Hall. Close to a hundred feet long, with a ceiling-scraping Christmas tree and a grand piano at its center, the room had been arranged with three dinner tables on either side. It had windows overlooking the cliffs and flatlands of St. Mary's Marshes. Beyond the marshlands was a majestic view of the mouth of the River Thames, emptying into the North Sea.

Already our fellow guests numbered more than a score, and many of the ladies and gentlemen wore evening clothes. When Edgar Dobson himself appeared he proved to be a short, somewhat scrawny man with puckered eyelids and a flushed face. "My dear child!" he addressed Mrs. Ascott, "I thought you were coming with Mr. Blackthorn. Were you forced to make the journey from London alone?"

"Not at all. May I present my good friend, Mr. Sherlock Holmes, and his companion Dr. Watson."

The little man frowned. "Holmes? Where have I heard that name before?"

"I'm mentioned occasionally in the press," said Holmes with a slight smile.

"Well, I'm pleased you could accompany Mrs. Ascott. It's a lengthy journey to make alone." He turned his attention to her. "Shall we wind up our business before the festivities get under way?"

"I'd like Mr. Holmes to be present as my adviser," she said, taking Dobson by surprise.

"Oh, I'm sure that's not necessary."

"I think it is." Her voice was firm as she spoke the words. "I trust him a great deal more than I do your Mr. Blackthorn."

"Oh, very well. This way, please."

Holmes glanced in my direction but I motioned toward a butler with a tray of beverages. "I believe I'll have a sip of wine."

The three of them disappeared into Dobson's study while I took the wine and walked over to admire the view from the windows. By now it was late afternoon and growing dark. Here and there lights were beginning to come on. "Marvelous, isn't it?" the young man standing next to me said.

"Certainly is," I agreed. "Do you live around here?"

"London." He held out his hand. "Erskine Childers. I'm a committee clerk in the House of Commons." He was a small, neat man, probably not quite out of his twenties. "That's my wife over there in the yellow dress."

"Watson. Medical doctor. I'm down from London too."

"Dr. Watson? You're not the one who chronicles the cases of your friend Sherlock Holmes, are you?"

"I've done that on occasion," I admitted, both gratified and embarrassed that he'd recognized my name.

"Well!" His face brightened. "I've been wanting to try some writing myself. I've joined the City Imperial Volunteers and expect to leave shortly for South Africa. I'm hoping to get a book out of it."

"I wish you luck. The war reports speak of heavy casualties."

"They won't want me in the front lines. I have a slight sciatic limp, acquired from long walks in the Irish countryside."

"You're from Ireland?"

He laughed. "On my mother's side. I spent much of my childhood in Wicklow."

Before we could speak further we were interrupted by a late arrival, a large barrel-chested man with a black beard. "Dr. Watson?" he inquired, his deep voice cutting through our conversation with an accent I couldn't place. I caught a whiff of whiskey on his breath.

"That is correct. What can I do for you?"

"My name is Jules Blackthorn, and I am seeking a woman named Elvira Ascott. The head butler said she arrived with you and Mr. Holmes."

"I believe she is busy at the moment," I replied, trying to prevent any sort of confrontation.

"It is very important that I see her at once!" His voice had risen so that Childers and a few others nearby were looking alarmed.

The balding butler who'd greeted us upon our arrival hurried forward and tried to calm him. Despite the apparent difference in their ages, the butler grabbed him from behind with a strong left arm, catching him in a half nelson. Then he hurried him out of the room with a minimum of commotion.

Erskine Childers grinned and said, "It's nice having wrestlers on your staff."

Edgar Dobson appeared, followed by Elvira Ascott and Sherlock Holmes. "What is it, Samuels?"

The butler went to him for a whispered conversation, turning his face away from Holmes and Mrs. Ascott. Then Dobson said, "Forgive us for the slight altercation," and the party continued.

"Was that about me?" Mrs. Ascott asked. "I heard someone say Blackthorn had been here."

"No, no," our host assured her. "It had nothing to do with you. I'd asked Jules to be our Father Christmas after dinner. Samuels said he'd been drinking too much and had to be removed."

Holmes had an unaccustomed twinkle in his eye. "Perhaps Dr. Watson could offer his services. He was Father Christmas for the Baker Street children just last evening."

I was so startled by his suggestion that I could only murmur, "I'm sure the costume wouldn't fit me."

"We'll try it after dinner," Dobson said. "If it's too big for you, I'm sure Samuels could fill the bill with a bit of padding."

The six tables had been set with six places each, and as the guests took their seats I saw that thirty-five of the chairs were occupied. They'd accommodated me at the last minute, and only Jules Blackthorn was missing. I was at the table with Holmes and Mrs. Ascott, and we'd been joined by Erskine Childers and his wife, an attractive young woman with a pleasant smile. An older woman, a neighbor of Dobson's named Monica Selfridge, rounded out our table.

Elvira glanced over at the next table where their host seemed to be seated without a female companion. "Is Mrs. Dobson here?" she asked the neighbor.

"No, the poor dear died some years back. Edgar has been alone here since then."

Holmes was two seats away from me, with Elvira in between, so it was impossible for me to ask him what had transpired in the meeting with Dobson. Before I knew it the first course was being served and we'd drifted into a discussion of sailing. "Two years ago Erskine and his brother crossed the North Sea on a yacht," his wife told us, "all the way to the Frisian Islands in Germany."

"And what did you find there?" Holmes inquired.

Childers gave a shrug. "Germans."

"As long as they weren't the French," the older woman commented.

"We have nothing to fear from France," Childers insisted. "It is Germany who wants to invade and conquer us."

"Really?" Monica Selfridge drew in her breath. "I'm planning a trip there next summer. Will I be safe?"

"If we're not at war by that time."

"How would they invade us?" asked Holmes.

"By sea, of course. It's the only way. A fleet of small boats hidden among the Frisian Islands could cross the North Sea and land along our coast before we knew what was happening."

A sudden shudder seemed to pass through Elvira Ascott's body. "Please, I don't want to hear any more talk of war. It's bad enough to have a husband volunteer to fight the Boers—"

Childers was immediately interested. "I say, is he down there already? I thought my group would be the first volunteers to go."

"He sailed last week," she said, looking more distressed by the moment. "I wish he were with me now."

I watched Samuels carving roast beef for the main course, holding it with a fork in his right hand while he carved it perfectly with his left. The meat was delicious and after the main course Elvira excused herself. I was able to lean across her chair and ask Holmes quietly, "Was an agreement reached?"

"She put him off, but promised a final decision before she returned to London this evening. I fear she is about to sign away something of value, although the price he offers seems fair enough."

The neighbor, Miss Selfridge, left our table and sat down at the piano. As she played some holiday carols the waiters moved among the tables serving an ice cream dessert in the shape of a Yule log. I was quite impressed, having never seen anything like it before. As I finished the last of it our host came over to my seat and asked if I would try on the Father Christmas costume. "Through that door," he instructed. "Samuels will show you."

The butler pointed me toward an unoccupied sitting room where I found the costume draped across a chair. I removed my shoes but left the rest of my garments in place, quickly determining that the baggy costume would slip on easily over them. A hat with wig and beard attached lay next to the suit, and a pair of black boots stood on the floor. There was even a bed pillow included should I need extra padding around my middle.

I was pulling the Father Christmas pants over my own, silently regretting that I'd allowed myself to be talked into this. Entertaining children was one thing. Parading around in this costume before adults, and strangers at that, was something entirely different. As I bent down to reach for the boots my eye was attracted to a feather on the carpeting. Then I saw another a short distance away. And a third. I checked the pillow but there was no rip in it.

The feathers formed a definite trail across the carpet to a door that I took to be a closet. At the door itself there were two more, and I could not resist the urge to turn the knob and open it.

That was how I came to find the bloodied body of Jules Black-thorn.

I instructed the butler to summon his master and Holmes at once. It was only a moment before he returned with them both. When I revealed my discovery in the closet Dobson was shocked. "How could this be? I thought he'd gone home." He turned to the butler. "Didn't he leave the house, Samuels?"

"I escorted him to the door myself, sir."

Blackthorn had been stabbed twice in the back. The trail of feath-ers was quickly explained when Holmes lifted the body slightly to reveal a slashed pillow beneath the dead man's stomach. It might have been the twin of the one that had been left out for my costume.

"I believe you should notify the local police at once," said Holmes. "They might wish to contact Scotland Yard as well."

"But who could have done this terrible thing?" Edgar Dobson wondered. "Did Blackthorn surprise a thief?"

"This was no thief's act," Holmes pointed out. "If the man really left the house as your butler says, someone must have let him in again. I believe we can reasonably assume that person is the one who killed him."

While we awaited the arrival of the local constable, Dobson made the announcement to his assembled guests. "I'm sorry to report, la-dies and gentlemen, that there has been a serious accident to Mr. Jules Blackthorn, one of this evening's guests. The local constable has been summoned and I suggest that we await his arrival. I'll try to make you as comfortable as possible in the meantime. The waiters will pass among you with after-dinner libations while Miss Selfridge entertains us with some additional carols."

A murmur ran through the three dozen guests, and several insisted they had to be starting home. However the arrival of brandy and cigars soon lured the male guests into the library, while the women stayed to be entertained by the music. As for Holmes and myself, we quickly found ourselves in our host's study along with Elvira Ascott.

"Please understand, Mrs. Ascott," Dobson told her, "that Blackthorn's death makes it more imperative than ever that we complete our transaction."

Holmes merely smile at this. "Would you explain yourself, Mr. Dobson? It seems to me that Blackthorn was nothing more than a cohort of yours, sent to persuade Mrs. Ascott to adhere to your wishes regarding the sale of her land."

"Blackthorn was a principal in the sale. He was putting up a portion of the money for it. I know nothing of his motives. I do know that I am willing to take a worthless parcel of tidal land off your hands for a fair sum of money."

It was night now and all we could see against the windows was our own reflection in the darkened glass. For a full minute no one spoke, and then Elvira Ascott herself broke the silence. "I will sell you the land, Mr. Dobson, just to be rid of it and put an end to this business."

"Not so fast," Holmes cautioned, holding up a hand. "I am acting in your best interests, Mrs. Ascott, when I beg you to delay your decision." He slipped something, a small notebook, from his pocket and held it out to her. "Tell me, have you ever seen this before?"

She took the notebook and opened the cover. On the first page was the notation *Boot*, underlined. It was followed by a column of numbers, each having three digits. Elvira Ascott shook her head. "I know nothing about this. What is it? To whom does it belong?"

"I found it under Blackthorn's body when I lifted it. I believe it slipped out of his pocket."

I studied the notations. "They seem to be a list of boot sizes."

"My dear friend," said Holmes, "have you ever seen boot sizes expressed in just three numbers like that?"

"What else could it mean?"

"I have a suspicion." He turned to our host. "Come now, Mr. Dobson. Isn't it time you told us what you know about all this?"

"I know nothing!" the man insisted.

Just then we were interrupted by a knock at the study door. It opened just a crack, allowing Samuels the butler to announce the arrival of Constable Wallace. As the door was closing again, Holmes called out, "Samuels, could you come in for a moment?"

The tall butler entered the room with some reluctance, his eyes downcast. "Yes, sir?"

"I'd like to ask you about the pillow that went with the Father Christmas costume. I assume it was used if the wearer of the costume needed more girth up front."

"That's correct."

"And the pillow came from one of the upstairs bedrooms?"

"What has this got to do with Blackthorn's murder?" Edgar Dobson wanted to know. "Of course the pillow came from a bedroom, probably one of the guest bedrooms. Why do you ask?"

"Because when the killer stabbed Blackthorn and ripped the pillow, he had to replace it. He had to go up to the second floor of this house and procure another pillow, so the original slashed one could be hidden. That is not something a guest would do, nor one of the servants hired for the party. Certainly your cooks were far too busy in the kitchen at meal time."

"Are you accusing me—?"

"You seemed to be very involved with your guests during the crucial period. There's also the question of your size. If we assume the two men tussled before Blackthorn was fatally stabbed, it seems unlikely you could have overpowered him, Mr. Dobson. Whereas we have seen Samuels here do exactly that this very evening."

The butler's face had gone white at those words. He uttered an oath and turned toward the door, but Holmes was already upon him. "What is this!" he demanded.

"It was you who killed him, you who then replaced the torn pillow. But the police are here now and your conspiracy is at an end!"

I was astounded by this turn of events. "Holmes, are you telling us the butler did it?"

Holmes ripped away the flesh-colored skullcap and fake hair, revealing the head of a much younger man. "Only in a sense, Watson. You see, Samuels the butler is really William Ascott, engaged not in fighting the Boers but in swindling his wife out of her land."

It was not until later, when he was explaining it all to a devastated Elvira Ascott, that I learned the full story from Holmes. Edgar Dobson had been arrested along with Ascott, and we were at the station awaiting the last train back to London when Holmes repeated what he'd told the police.

"My first clue to your husband's involvement was your meeting with Jules Blackthorn at the ballet on the very day that Dobson had made his offer for your land. You insisted you'd not told Dobson of your plans, yet this bogus solicitor was there to accost you. It seemed to me that only your husband, who'd planned to accompany you, knew in advance that you'd be at the ballet. When you said his group of volunteers had only recently departed, and after Erskine Childers indicated he believed he was in the first group, leaving just after

141

New Years, I began to wonder. Was it possible that your husband was still secretly in London, and his New Years departure was the reason Ascott wanted the land deal completed before that date?"

"I-I can't believe that was the case. What did William hope to accomplish?"

"He and Edgar Dobson had entered into a conspiracy with Blackthorn to get that land from you, one way or another. I regret to say this, Mrs. Ascott, but the conspiracy may have existed more than a year ago, even before your marriage."

A sob caught in her throat at his words. "You mean he married me to gain control of that piece of worthless property?"

"It was not worthless to him. Blackthorn was offering a good deal of money for the land. But William learned to his sorrow that even in the case of your death the land would pass to your sister's children in America."

"Do you believe he would have killed me for it?"

"Thankfully, we never had to face that question."

"But how did you know the butler was really my husband?"

"There were a number of things. Chief among them was my observation that he frequently averted his face when in your presence. Even with the false hair and makeup he used in his days as an amateur actor, he feared recognition. Then there was the obvious fact that he was left-handed, demonstrated when he was cutting the meat and when he grabbed Blackthorn with his left hand. In the photograph of your husband that you showed us, he was tall like Samuels and he was firing a pistol with his left hand."

"If Blackthorn was in league with them, why was he killed?" I asked.

"Dobson said it was because they were taking too long to complete the transaction. Blackthorn had been patient for a year, and now his orders were to force you to sign the contract by any means possible. Your husband opposed that. This evening when he forcibly removed Blackthorn from our presence, instead of showing him to the door he took him to that sitting room and stabbed him, using the pillow to protect himself from bloodstains. Then, of course, he had to re-place the pillow for the Father Christmas costume."

"But why was William disguised as a butler in the first place?"

"I believe he'd grown truly fond of you during the year of your marriage. As I indicated, he opposed the use of any force against your person, and insisted on being present while you were at Dobson's house. The butler disguise seemed most practical for his purpose and indeed he did protect you from Blackthorn."

"Why were they so anxious to buy that worthless land from me?" Elvira Ascott wanted to know.

"It wasn't worthless to Dobson. It provided him with a connecting link to the sea. Any boats bringing men to Dobson's estate needed that strip of land to deliver the men without raising a premature alarm."

"Boats?"

"Blackthorn was an agent of the German government. He carried a list of the boat numbers in his notebook. The word *boot* means *boat* in German."

"You mean Germans would have been landing here?" I asked.

Sherlock Holmes nodded. "In large numbers. Our dinner compan-ion tonight, Mr. Childers, suggested that very thing. He was more correct than he knew. But here, I believe our train is approaching at last!"

Ascott and Dobson were convicted of murder and conspiracy, and the German angle to the investigation was never made public. It was not until three years later that our dinner companion Erskine Childers wrote a fictionized version of his suspicions involving a German invasion, titled *The Riddle of the Sands*. It became his most successful novel.

THE MUSIC OF CHRISTMAS

L. B. Greenwood

As I am sure many of my readers know, my wife and I have not been blessed with children. Perhaps this is why we have always chosen to spend Christmas Day alone together, with our own little ritual. We breakfast late, attend church in the afternoon, and then dine out at some more luxurious restaurant than we would ordinarly patronize.

Usually we attend St. John's, convenient as it is to our Bayswater home. For the Christmas of which I write, however, we were going to St. Goddard's because of the pressing invitation of a young patient of mine.

The Carmichaels live half a dozen roads from us, and five years ago I attended the father during his last illness. Mrs. Carmichael was left with a daughter of ten and a son of nine years and very limited finances.

The boy, Hampton, had always been his mother's favourite, and

145

after his father's death he quickly became quite the lord and master of the household. Local schooling was decreed quite insufficient, and Hampton was sent to Garton, to mix with sons of the well-to-do. This necessitated stringent conditions at home for both mother and Emily, willingly made. Hampton had new school uniforms, Emily gowns made from her mother's old garments; both children had excellent voices, but I never heard of Emily's having lessons.

So matters stood in the spring of the year of which I write when Emily contracted typhoid fever. She had inherited her father's weak chest, and for a month I was seriously concerned. Her recovery was slow, her body frail, her spirit weary.

Accordingly, when at Michaelmas she asked my wife and me to attend St. Goddard's for evensong on Christmas, I couldn't refuse. The girl's thin cheeks were glowing with excitement, for Hampton was coming home! Not because of his mother and sister: He would have much preferred to spend his holidays with one of his numerous friends in the Upper Sixth, two forms above his own. He was coming home because the vicar himself had written to ask him to sing a solo in the special music that was being presented, with the collection to go toward a badly needed new organ.

For this, the organist had searched out a nearly unknown cantata from the sixteenth century, "God the Father, Christ the Son." Very moving, I was told by Mrs. Carmichael, yet simple, well within the capabilities of St. Goddard's choir except for the concluding solo by a boy soprano. None of the regular eight boys could sustain this part; for this only Hampton would do.

So, on this Christmas afternoon, Mary and I were attending evensong at St. Goddard's in order to hear Hampton sing.

*　　*　　*

St. Goddard's is a structure of a kind common in London. Of grey stone in a modified Gothic style, not large and without a single outstanding feature, St. Goddard's has been left behind by history and now serves a congregation that ordinarily does little more than half fill it.

Today, however, was quite evidently to be different: Though Mary and I arrived early, we yet had to look for places near the front.

"Good afternoon, Doctor, Mrs. Watson." There was Holmes, sitting near the left of the two pillars, three pews from the altar.

We exchanged seasonal greetings as Mary and I took seats next to him. "I didn't expect to see you here," I remarked.

"I have never heard this cantata performed before," Holmes explained. "In fact, I am sure few have, for it is one of the neglected treasures of the Church. Do you think this young Hampton Carmichael is capable of the demands of the solo? It is considerably more intricate than the choral section."

"His mother and sister assure me that he is," I said, a trifle sourly. "I haven't myself heard him for over a year; certainly the spoilt young coxcomb had a glorious voice then."

While we were speaking, all the seats around us had been claimed, by a well dressed and expectant throng. Obviously Holmes was not the only one attracted by the special music.

The organ began a processional (the instrument was indeed in poor condition), the vicar entered from the door to the left of the altar, and the black-gowned choir from the door to the right. Twelve men and nine boys mounted the three steps to the dais, young Carmichael's sleek, fair head gleaming briefly as he passed under the flaring lamp on the organ.

"Let us pray," the vicar began, and proceded to lead us through the traditional celebration of the holy day. The Gospel According to

147

St. Luke was read, "God Rest Ye Merry" and "It Came Upon a Midnight Clear" were sung, and the collection taken up. I was pleased to see that both plates carefully carried by the verger into the music room were well heaped, with coins peeking out from a large number of notes. The vicar gave a short address, inviting us to unite in the precious beauty of the day, and took his seat. The rest of the service was up to the choir.

The basses began a solemn ode to the love of the Almighty, and the tenors added joyous praise of Christ's sacrifice. The two great themes were then woven together in a harmony that was not elaborate yet was strangely haunting.

Briefly a hush fell, and then from the centre of the front row young Carmichael's voice lifted in glorious praise. It filled the nave and rose to caress the vaulted beams above, sweet, clear and effortless. I could not help thinking that his mother and sister's darling knew little of either love or sacrifice, yet there was no doubt that he could sing.

As the concluding note rang forth, I felt Holmes abruptly stiffen, felt too a tingle of surprise touch here and there among the audience. Even I could tell that that final sound, held perilously long and yet true, dying away under perfect control to the very end, was unexpectedly sombre in resonance. It was at once sad, even tragic, frail as black crystal, and left behind a momentarily stunned audience.

"Let us pray."

The vicar had stepped back into the pulpit and gave the benediction. The organ renewed the processional, and we all stood and ceremoniously turned toward the aisle as the vicar made his way between us toward the main doors. Behind him the choir marched back to the music room. By the clatter, the boys' decorum had begun to break down before they had even left the dais. Well, I thought tolerantly, after all it was Christmas, with supper and the evening's festivities ahead.

"Here, you young varmints, what've you been up to?"

This yell, strident and, after that music, sacriligous in its effect, had come from the music room. "Where've you hid the money? None of you is going anywhere until you cough it up. Now then!"

Some of the congregation had already left the church, the rest were in a throng that had been jovial near the doors. A shocked silence fell on us all, and, as my startled gaze turned back toward the music room, for the first time that afternoon I noticed Emily.

She must have been sitting somewhere at the front, I thought, as of course she would be, as close as she could get to her beloved brother in his moment of triumph. She was now hesitating at the beginning of the main aisle, the dark red plush of her dress and bonnet draining all colour from her thin face. The garments were worn and too small, the skirt hardly covering her ankles or the sleeves her gloved wrists, and the voluminous mantle was a houndstooth drapery that obviously belonged to her mother.

"Vicar!"

That gentleman had already started back down the aisle; this renewed shout from the verger brought him to near running. As he hastened by us, Mary asked in bewilderment, "Whatever can have happened, John? What do you think, Mr. Holmes?"

The last word instantly halted the vicar. "Mr. Holmes! How providential! We have never met, sir, but of course your reputation . . . If you could possibly be so good as to wait a moment? No doubt there is some simple mistake, yet . . ."

"I'll come with you, shall I?" Holmes suggested with a resigned sigh. "And you too, doctor, if Mrs. Watson will permit."

That best of wives agreed at once. I insisted on escorting her to sit with Mrs. Carmichael and Emily, promising to return as soon as I could with news.

Events prevented me from fulfilling this vow.

By the time I caught up with Holmes, the organist had left his instrument to join the choir in the music room, and the vicar had held a hasty conference with the verger. He turned to us with tight face.

"Mr. Holmes, I fear this is indeed serious, very. A matter for the police, in fact, only . . . Surely we can avoid that!

"Simply put, the whole contents of the collection plates have vanished. Vanished somehow during the latter part of the service from the music room. It seems impossible, yet here are the empty plates," (these the verger was holding with shaking hands) "and abundant witnesses that they *were* empty when the choir re-entered the room.

"I'm sure you both saw, as the whole congregation did," the vicar went on, his voice trembling, "the verger carry the full plates into that room—that empty room—at the conclusion of the offertory. He did, as he says (and there is no reason to doubt him, none), as he always does, placed the plates on top of the music cabinet in the corner.

"Ordinarily he would wait until the service was over and the choir dispersed before he would attend to the monies—count and record them and give the whole to me. Today, because of its being Christmas, he naturally wished to leave more promptly, and asked if he could take the plates at once into the vestry and finish his work there."

"The vestry is . . ."

"On the left side of the altar. I leave my coat and hat there. It's a miserable hole," the vicar added, "not much used otherwise."

Holmes stared into space for a thoughtful moment, then took up the lamp from the organ and moved slowly through the choir stalls, the shadows jumping around him in haunting fashion. "I can see nothing of interest," he commented. "If you will be so good, vicar, ask the choir members to take their seats here again so that I can examine the music room."

The organist quickly led in his twelve men and nine boys, all looking serious, most puzzled, the boys apprehensive. Hampton Carmichael was scowling. *No doubt he feels that his merited triumph is being spoiled*, I thought, *and the sprig is right.* Even the glory of his voice seemed to mean little at that moment.

The music room was a mere frame cornering off a prepatory space for the choir, no windows and only the one door. On the floor was very worn drugget; numerous straight chairs were pushed helter-skelter around a battered stand near the walls. In the far corner was the music cabinet, five feet high, with six interior shelves overflowing with piles of sheet music.

To the immediate left of the entry was a large cupboard for the choir gowns. The door facing us opened onto the boys' section, that near the music cabinet onto the men's. Only some old gowns hanging at the back of the rod marked the division between the two.

Holmes made a close survey of the room, spending several minutes in the cupboard. "The carpet is quite dusty in the middle area," he observed as he emerged.

"I don't suppose anyone has gone that far inside for years," the vicar apologized, "and our caretaker is rather rheumatic."

"Like the organ," Holmes observed, wiping his hands on his handkerchief. "Now if the choir would come in one at a time, starting with the organist—"

"Mr. Holmes . . ."

The hesitant voice had come from the doorway: the verger, a small thin man with desperate eyes and haggard face.

"If you'll all excuse me for pushing myself forward like this," he began in a tremulous voice, "there's something I've got to tell Mr. Holmes. It's this, sir: You mustn't pay any attention to what I said at first. What I . . . well, shouted, sir."

"You mean, 'Here, you young varmints, what've you been up to? Where've you hid the money?' "

The verger gulped, though he answered promptly and stoutly. "Yes sir. Because I'd no right to have said any such thing. It was just . . . I was that upset, sir. My head had been so high, you see, because those plates were full. Piled up, you might say.

"This is what you might call a sixpenny congregation ordinarily, sir, but they'd done their church proud today. And there was a lot of visitors of the better-off kind too. Come for the special music, no doubt, and they got their money's worth, for that boy sang a treat."

"How much money was there in total, do you think?"

"I'd say a hundred pounds, easy, sir. Why, there were fivers sticking out all over."

"Well worth stealing, in other words."

I shrank at the suggestion behind Holmes's blunt words, for who else except the verger had been in the music room since the choir left? And there was only the one door, no windows.

The man didn't hesitate. "Well worth stealing, sir. But the boys didn't do it, sir, none of 'em. They were larking about like they always do, only more so, this being Christmas, and so I yelled what I did. But it was only the shock that made me say it, sir, nothing else.

"Well, you saw things for yourself, sir. The boys were all out of the room—and the rest of the choir too—before I even took up the collection, much less put the plates on the music cabinet.

"And, just for the sake of argument, say they were *all* in some

152

plot to make away with the money afterward, they didn't have time to do it. I was right on their heels going back into the room, you see, and they wouldn't have expected me so soon, either."

"Did you notice anything unusual during the whole service?"

"Not that would matter, sir. Just little Wilkins—he's only nine, the youngest of the boys—slipped out of the line on the way back into the room, and ran to his grandmother for a quick hug. She was sitting at the front to the right there, no doubt on purpose. He came running back so fast that he quite barged by me in the doorway."

"On which side was the boy?"

"Why, on my left, sir."

"I see. Thank you."

"Thank *you*, sir. I only hope . . ."

"We'll do our best," Holmes replied. Was that assurance or threat?

After the little man had gone, Holmes turned a questioning look on the vicar. "Your verger: What kind of man is he?"

"An unfortunate one, Mr. Holmes. A sick wife, a son injured in an accident, a daughter who is . . . not living as she should. And I won't deny that the man had the opportunity to have stuffed the collection money into his coat while he was alone in the music room, and to have hidden it goodness knows where since.

"But for all that he is innocent, Mr. Holmes. I would stake more than the contents of the collection plate on that."

"Certainly," Holmes said reflectively, "I have myself evidence of his truthfulness in a small matter. I noticed little Wilkins dash up to an elderly woman in black, exchange a quick hug and rush back. And as he scrambled by the verger, the boy was indeed on his left.

"Well, we must continue. If the organist would be so good as to come in, and ask the choir to follow one at a time."

"Certainly, Mr. Holmes," the vicar replied willingly, "and I will stay in the stalls until you are finished. The boys are probably becoming somewhat restive."

The organist was a tall man of perhaps fifty years, with a gentle manner of which the boys no doubt took full advantage. He told us frankly and immediately that he had no explanation for the disappearance of the money. All he could be positive of was that his choir, men and boys, including Carmichael, had remained in their places from beginning to end of the service.

He added, with reason, that he was sure that the whole congregation would confirm his statement.

As for the solo, the organist agreed that young Carmichael had sung superbly and that that final note, a high E flat, had been quite a surprise.

"The key of the piece," the master explained, "is C, with the concluding chord and final soprano note the same. Turning that note into an E flat meant a venture into a minor chord that was most interesting, almost a . . . a comment on the whole cantata, wasn't it?"

"A most unusual one," Holmes suggested.

"Well, yes, I agree. Of course the boy shouldn't have made such a change on his own, and I shall certainly speak to him about it, but . . . He was showing off a little, and why not?" The organist was smiling. "He had sung like an angel, and it *is* Christmas."

After him came a parade, one by one, of the choir, starting with the adult members. They only confirmed what we already knew.

Several had seen little Wilkins slip out of line during the choir's return processional. The only other boy they had especially noticed was naturally Carmichael, whom they had congratulated in passing as they moved by the crowd of boys to the back of the room. He had kept his eyes down, with a nervous little smile on his face; if he had said anything they hadn't noted it. The rest of the junior choir was "prancing around like Indians," as one of the older tenors resignedly commented, in any case.

The boys followed, starting at Holmes's request with little Wilkins.

The lad was quite on edge, obviously fearful that he was in for what he would doubtless have called a jawing for his leaving his place in line. Assured that we at least considered this a forgiveable sin, he told us that everything had gone "proper, like, sir" and that Carmichael had sung "jolly good."

"At least," the boy added in that judicious way of his age, "he did in the solo."

"Not during the choir's part?"

"He was awfully soft, sir; I hardly heard him at all. P'rhaps he was saving himself for that high note—it *was* ever so splendid, wasn't it, sir?"

"It was indeed. You were the last boy to return to the music room, weren't you? Where was Carmichael when you entered, did you notice?"

"Just sort of standing near the door, sir."

"The cupboard door? Or the door at the room?"

"Both, sir, he was just inside the doorway. There was a terrible scrum going on, sir."

"No doubt. Is that all you have to tell us, Wilkins?"

"Yes, sir."

"Quite sure?"

"Yes, sir." And he would say no more, though he shuffled his feet a great deal under Holmes's continued questioning, and in a few moments was dismissed.

"That lad is holding something back," Holmes remarked, "though quite possibly it is of consequence only to himself. Now for the rest of the boys. We will leave Carmichael to the last, I think."

The young choir members dutifully paraded in, without adding much fresh information. A couple of those at the rear had noticed little Wilkins in his abrupt leaving of the procession; none could remember when he returned. They had been too anxious to get their robes off and be on their way home.

"It's Christmas, sir," they said pleadingly, one after the other. Holmes gave them apologies for their being kept at the church, but made no promises of a quick end to our common ordeal.

Finally only Carmichael was left.

"Have you any theory as yet, Holmes?" I asked before the boy entered.

"Oh yes, doctor, a very fine theory. The problem is that at the moment it appears impossible. After the choir left this room, only the verger came in until they returned at the service's end, with the verger right behind them: true. But suppose there was someone in the room all the time, someone no one saw?"

"Not hidden in the cupboard!" I exclaimed.

Holmes nodded. "In that middle section, behind those old choir gowns."

"Then where did he go? And how? He certainly isn't still in here."

"How do you know?"

"I . . ." I got up, marched to the cupboard door in the men's section, pushed my way past the gowns and emerged from the boys' area. "There is no one in there, Holmes."

He chuckled. "Not now, no. Ah, Carmichael." Holmes' tone became immediately very man-to-man. "I'm afraid the disappearance of the collection money is still a mystery; unfortunately most people are not particularly good observers. Did *you* by any chance notice anything out of the ordinary?"

"I don't think so, sir. Of course I haven't been a regular part of the choir since I've been at Garton."

"Naturally. A good school, is it?"

"Ripping, sir!" There was no doubt about his enthusiasm.

"Strong in music, I suppose?"

"There's a music master," the boy replied quite indifferently, "and he helped me with the solo for today. But music really isn't important, is it, sir?"

"I suppose you find sports of greater interest."

"Not particularly, sir."

"Then what do you most like about Garton?"

"Being among real gentlemen, sir" was the astonishing answer. "The upperclass fellows are super chaps, into everything. A couple of them asked me to go home with them for Christmas, but I had to come home because of the cantata. They couldn't have put it on without me, you see."

I longed to smack the conceited young ass.

"Why did you turn that final chord into a minor key?"

"I just thought I would, sir. A surprise, you know. For Christmas."

Holmes said nothing for a moment, then abruptly asked, "Had your father picked out Garton for you before he died?"

"Oh no, sir, he was only a shopkeeper. I know that's not the thing to say, but it's true. It's terribly good of the Upper Sixth to pay any attention to me at all; they're awfully upper, you know. Is there anything else, sir?"

With which he left.

"Well, Watson?" Holmes leaned back in the rickety old straight chair in which he was seated.

"That boy is on the path to utter ruination," I answered, disgusted, "and his well meaning mother and sister are hastening him on his way."

"No doubt. As for the collection money, who do *you* think took it?"

"I could far more readily give you a list of everyone who couldn't have," I replied ruefully, "starting with the vicar. And going on to the organist, the whole choir, and the complete congregation."

"Always excepting the verger?"

"Yes," I had to admit, with heavy heart. "I'm afraid so."

"Come," Holmes rose, "let us look at the vestry."

"Why?" I protested, though I too had risen. "After the vicar came out, no one else went near the place. We could see that ourselves."

"Strictly speaking, Watson," Holmes said judiciously, leading the way out, "I don't think that is true. At the conclusion of the service, the whole congregation rose; as the vicar started toward the doors at the back of the church, we all turned to face him as he passed. Would you then have noticed small movement of some kind at the front?"

"Perhaps not," I conceded, "though surely the choir would have as they filed out."

"That might depend on what the movements were. Only those nearest him paid any attention to little Wilkins, for instance."

We passed in front of the choir, silently sitting in their stalls; the men looked weary and resigned, the boys weary and subdued. The vicar was stalwartly sitting beside the verger, huddled in a corner of a front pew. Matters did not look good for that poor little man: I was sure that, if he were guilty (and it seemed that he must be), he had been driven to it by need.

The vestry was exactly as the vicar had described, a miserable place. Small, with arched windows at the left and back, admitting more gloom than light at this late hour of a short day. On the floor was more of the worn drugget; furnishings consisted of a much-chipped deal table and two sagging upholstered chairs, on one of which rested the vicar's overcoat and hat. On a wall shelf perched a discoloured brass candlestick with a pair of half burned candles.

These Holmes lit and began to explore the room. "Clean," he observed.

"Why not?" I agreed tiredly. "It's so bare that it wouldn't take even a rheumatic caretaker more than half an hour to do."

"Quite so." Holmes was stooping to look behind the chairs. "What do we have here?" He rose with two straight pins in his fingers.

"Perhaps the young ladies of the congregation hold drawing sessions here," I suggested, "awful though this room is."

"These aren't artist's pins, doctor, merely the ordinary variety that a seamstress holds between her teeth as she works."

"They could have been here for weeks."

"I think not: the carpet has been recently well swept, and these pins were lying right on top of the pile—it is somewhat longer behind the chairs. I cannot see what importance the pins have, yet I shall keep them." Holmes dropped them into one of his ever ready small envelopes and pocketed it. "Now I think we must have another talk with little Wilkins. There is something more he could say, I am sure."

On our way back to the music room Holmes called the boy to follow. Once the door was shut behind us, Holmes said seriously, "I think, Wilkins, you have something else to tell us." The boy looked quite wretched. "Come, tell us."

"I don't want to get anybody into trouble, sir."

"Does your secret have something to do with the missing money?"

"Oh no, sir. I don't know anything about that. I don't, really, sir."

"Then what have you to tell me?" Holmes's tone was kindly, even fatherly.

"Just that . . . while I was coming back here after the service, sir, somebody said . . . 'damn,' sir. I wasn't more than inside the room, sir."

"Shocking. Who was it, do you know?"

The boy shook his head. "I didn't *see* anybody, sir, not separate. We were all pushing and bumping around, trying to get to the cupboard to get our gowns off first. It must have been one of them, sir, because there wasn't anybody else near."

"Not the verger? You bumped together getting into the room, didn't you?"

"Only for a second, like, sir, and then he was off toward the music cabinet. It was after that, right after, that I heard it. And the verger wouldn't swear, sir. Not in church he wouldn't, anyway."

"You mentioned before seeing Carmichael. Could this terrible word have been said by him?"

"Oh no, sir. He was right in front of me, and the . . . the *word* came sort of to my left."

"Was the voice that of a man or boy?"

"I don't know, sir. It was just a whisper. Sort of under your breath."

Holmes thanked the boy, let him out, and returned to the old chair against the wall. He sat teetering there, frowning.

"Holmes," I said finally, "I must ask that Mrs. Carmichael be allowed to take Emily home. The girl is still far from strong, and a long confinement in this chill could seriously worsen her condition."

Holmes was staring at me. "Hampton's sister has been ill?"

"I was seriously concerned for her life last spring. Typhoid fever, and her recovery has been very slow. I fear the household finances are so stringent now that Hampton is going to school that Emily is not receiving as much nourishing food as she needs. Mary takes fruit and other—"

Holmes had let the front legs of the chair drop to the floor with a thud. He sat so for several seconds, silent and still. "Typhoid," he murmured. "Dust in the gown cupboard. Pins on the vestry carpet. Of course. And that concluding E flat . . . I have been much puzzled by that."

He rose, opened the music room door and called. "Carmichael! Would you bring your sister in here for a moment."

Poor Emily looked like a ten-year-old waif, so thin and pale was she, clutching around her the folds of that hideous houndstooth mantle. Hampton escorted her correctly enough and, at Holmes's gesture, took a chair at her side, but his eyes were wary and his mouth sullen.

"I hope we will not have to keep you long, Miss Carmichael," Holmes began, courteously. "Would you tell me if you came to church with your mother this afternoon?"

"No sir," she murmured, "I came early. With Hampton. Because of the choir."

"Was there anyone here then? Ah. When the rest of the choir came, where did you go? To sit with your mother?"

"No sir." She added, looking down, "Mother was sitting with a lot of people, and . . . I haven't been out since I was ill last spring, you see, and I didn't want . . . People stare and *fuss* so, and I hate it."

"Most understandable. Where did you sit?"

"At the front."

"Just where, Miss Carmichael?"

"By that left pillar."

"How strange, for I didn't notice you. Did *you* see Miss Carmichael, doctor? Her red costume would show up well even under the church's poor lighting.''

"I wasn't looking for her,'' I temporised, for I had not noticed the girl until after the verger had called out. Then she had been hovering near the centre aisle, as if uncertain where to go.

Holmes had turned to the boy. "Once you were in your place in the choir stalls, Carmichael, did *you* see your sister sitting by the left pillar?''

"Yes, sir.''

"Well, that settles the matter, doesn't it? Did your mother press your trousers for today, Carmichael?''

This startled him. "Yes, sir.''

"I was sure she would have. Isn't it odd that she didn't also brush them.''

"Of course she did!'' This indigant explosion had come from Emily.

"Then what has your brother done since he left home to cause dust to cling to his trouser bottoms?''

The boy had convulsively jerked his feet under his chair, but not before I had seen that there was indeed dust on the bottoms of his trouser legs.

"The walk was a little dirty,'' he muttered, eyes going everywhere.

"Yet your boots are not soiled,'' Holmes returned sharply, "and your trouser bottoms are covered with grey fluff, *not* dirt. The only area I have found in the front of the church that is dusty is the centre of the cupboard that holds the choir gowns. Between the part for the boys' gowns and that of the men, the carpet is thick with dust. Dust that has been recently crushed, as if someone had been standing there.

"And in the vestry, lying behind the chairs, I found these.''

Holmes brought out the two pins that he had picked up. "Ordinary pins, you will observe, the kind any household has."

Holmes stopped, and the silence gathered.

Emily was parchment white, blazing eyes fixed on her brother.

"If we asked Mrs. Carmichael to come in," Holmes' voice had become very distant, "to ascertain what her daughter is wearing under her dress at the moment, what would we find?"

Only an instant, and Emily was on her feet. She dropped the mantle to the floor, snatched something from her bodice and flung it at her brother. The violence of her actions had pulled up the already short skirt a little: underneath was a pair of boy's trousers, unevenly pinned up, and showing at her throat was the collar of a white shirt. And on the worn drugget between her and her brother now lay a sock full of money.

"Your brother asked you to join him in a prank, didn't he?" Holmes pressed gently. "He told you that you sing as well as he, which is most certainly true, yet I doubt that he had said so before. Last spring when you had typhoid fever your head was shaved; your hair has not grown enough to make you comfortable going out, but it was of perfect length for you to take your brother's place in a poorly lit church, among people who have not seen either of you for several months."

"He said we would look like twins," the poor girl whispered.

"You both came early so that no one would see what you did: leave your dress, bonnet and gloves in the vestry, let down the legs of the trousers you wore underneath, and don your brother's choir gown. He hid himself in the cupboard, the choir gathered, you took his place.

"When did you learn the truth, Miss Carmichael, that you had aided your brother in a theft, not a prank?"

"I heard him," she replied, very low, "just after the verger had left the music room. The sounds weren't very loud, not enough for anyone else to notice, but *I* guessed. I know him too well, you see.

"You're in debt, aren't you, Hamp?" She had swung her accusing young gaze onto her shrinking brother. "What do you think those Upper Sixth fellows want except to get money from a fool cub? Card games and probably horse races too, while mother and I are eating dry bread for tea."

"You didn't expect the verger to go into the room as soon as he did." Holmes added his attack to hers. "You thought that, in the general confusion in this small room, your sister could take off the gown and slip out to the vestry unnoticed, pin up the trouser legs, put on her own clothes again, and join your mother in the company leaving the church.

"As soon as she was out of the room, you would emerge from the cupboard as if you'd just been hanging up your gown, but when you started to step out the verger was right in front of you, heading for the music cabinet where he would find the empty plates. No wonder you said 'damn'—all your plans were shattered.

"All you could think of was to grab your sister before she had escaped, ram the sock—and how keen-witted of you to take an old one with you to hold your loot—into the jacket of yours that she wore, and hustle her out. Your actions would look like part of the scrambling that was going on among all the boys, and you were sure she wouldn't betray you. You were right there.

"Little Wilkins said that Carmichael held his voice back in the choral parts. Did you, Miss Carmichael?"

"I had to," she whispered. "I was crying."

"You mastered yourself for the solo because you were protecting your brother, and, I think, also trying to tell him something: That E

flat turned the whole cantata into a comment on the human condition
that was sad and full of pain. Is that what you meant, Miss Carmichael?"

She nodded. "When I think of poor mother . . . ."

"We can perhaps keep her from knowing." That made both white
young faces turn to Holmes. "Once the money has been returned,
the vicar might agree to let everyone think that the whole sorry episode was only a prank gone wrong, and there is certainly much truth
in that. If *you* wish, Miss Carmichael, I will try to arrange this."

"You aren't going back to that school," the girl told her brother,
her voice cold and firm.

"All right," he whispered. "Only . . . I *do* owe some of the fellows
money, and a gentleman ought to pay his debts."

"A gentleman," Emily retorted, "oughtn't to have debts—that's
just another way of stealing." She took a long breath. "Ever since
term started Mother and I have been putting a little aside for a
Christmas gift for you. You'll use it to pay what you can, and send
the rest later. Bit by bit, out of your pocket money. And my allowance."

"I won't take that," the boy said, and for the first time he looked
manly, more so for the tears in his eyes. "And you're going to have
music lessons—good ones, and a proper piano instead of that tinkle
box in the old nursery. I'll get a post somewhere, errand boy or something, after school."

Holmes rose and picked up the sock full of money. "Then this
will be the best stocking that Father Christmas ever brought.

"Vicar! Come and hear tidings of great joy."

THE ADVENTURE OF THE CHRISTMAS BEAR

Bill Crider

R eaders of these sporadic accounts of the accomplishments
of my friend Sherlock Holmes will no doubt be aware that
the Christmas season seldom brought him joy. His eyes
would come alight at the mention of some nefarious plot or heinous
crime, but they tended to grow dim if anyone brought up a cheerful
holiday topic that he believed related to arrant superstition. It was
not that he was opposed to the experience of joy brought on to others
by the singing of carols or the exchanging of gifts; it was rather that
he achieved his joys, such as they were, from the exercise of his
formidable intellect.

Thus it was that one cold winter's evening some two days before
Christmas I found myself seated at one side of the fireplace listening
to Holmes as he sawed away on his violin at what I am certain was
a tune of his own composition. His intent was to drown out the song
of a group of carolers gathered beneath the windows of 221B Baker

Street. While they sang of Good King Wenceslaus and of snow that was crisp and white and even (quite unlike the snow that presently covered the streets outside), Holmes began a frenzied run up the scale in which I fancied that he missed several of the notes he intended to sound, though I failed to mention that fact to him. At length the carolers moved on, and Holmes immediately put aside his violin.

"My dear Holmes," said I, "I fear that your mood is not in keeping with the festive intent of the season."

He paced distractedly about the room. "The season means little to me, Watson, and it offers no challenges. I am bored. I have not had an adversary worthy of my talents in many weeks." He cast his eyes at the mantelpiece and at the bottle and hypodermic syringe that rested thereon.

I closed the volume of sea stories that I had been reading and said, "I hope that you are not considering some artificial stimulation of your mind, when at any moment someone with a problem needing your attention might come walking through our door."

Holmes paused and turned to give me a speculative look. "I suppose that you are now going to declare some recent acquisition of the powers of clairvoyance and tell me that you can predict to the instant when such a person will appear."

"I make no claims to precognition," I said. "I merely suppose that even at this happy time of year there are those who have their troubles and who might seek the aid of the great Sherlock Holmes."

Even as I spoke, I heard the sound of hoofbeats outside, hoofbeats that came to a stop beneath our window.

"And I presume that is our client now," Holmes said.

"Possibly," I responded. "If so, it is merely a coincidence. Or it could be nothing more than a lost traveler who is seeking directions."

"Of course it would be a coincidence," Holmes said. "It could be nothing more."

He walked over to the frost-rimed bow window, where I joined him in looking out into the dark street. A carriage had stopped in front of 221B, and a rather large gentleman emerged. Without a word to the driver, he entered our building. Shortly there was the sound of a heavy step in the hall, followed almost at once by a knock on our door.

I answered the knock and welcomed our visitor inside. He was even larger than he had appeared from the window, and the room seemed almost to shrink when he entered. He wore a decrepit wide-awake hat on his rather too-long hair and a heavy bottle-green over-coat with a wide fur collar and cuffs. His hands were soft and white, his boots were clean, and his eyes were clear and wide.

He doffed his hat and stood for a moment as he looked around our room. Although Holmes was one of the neatest of men in many ways and certainly had quite tidy habits of mind, neither he nor I made any great pretense to fastidiousness when it came to our lodg-ings. Several unanswered letters from Holmes's correspondents were nailed to the center of the mantel by a jackknife, and there was the strong smell of chemicals and tobacco in the room, which, I confess, could have used a good airing. Books and papers, most of them be-longing to Holmes, who had a positive horror of disposing of any kind of document, were strewn about the hardwood floor, while oth-ers had been tossed into boxes. Two of the cushions from the faded green couch were also on the floor along with the papers, and Holmes's violin lay upon the couch itself. Our bookcase was crammed with maps, charts, and reference books of all kinds, along with Holmes's commonplace books, though the latter, at least, were neatly aligned. Our desks were no less cluttered, and the sideboard was jumbled with cigar boxes, the remains of our cold dinner, and several tumblers, not all of them clean. Our floral wallpaper was marred somewhat on one wall by the pattern of a patriotic V. R. done in bullet-pocks.

It was this last that seemed to draw our visitor's attention. "Ah," said he upon seeing it. "Someone has created an interesting variation in the, um, decor."

"It was I," said Holmes. "But I am sure you did not come here to discuss my house beautiful."

At one time early in my acquaintance with Sherlock Holmes, he had informed me that he wished to possess no knowledge that would not be useful to him. I had deduced from his statement that his knowledge of certain fields was nil, and I had even jotted down a list of those fields for my own amusement. One thing of which I supposed him to know nothing was literature, but afterwards he had more than once surprised me by introducing into our conservation a passing reference to Shakespeare or Pope, to Flaubert or George Sand.

On this occasion, he surprised me once again, and because of his use of a certain phrase, I was fairly certain that he had already discerned the identity of our visitor, as had I, and I decided to put him to the test.

"Holmes," said I, "can you tell me the name of our esteemed guest, or should I reveal it to you?"

"There is no need for you to tell me. I believe that we have the honor of hosting Mr. Oscar Wilde, the lecturer and poet."

"You are correct," Wilde said. He was not surprised at all. It was as if he felt that anyone in London would know him on sight. "Are you familiar with my work?"

"As for me," I responded, "I have seen your picture more than once, and I have attended one of your lectures. It was the one in which you spoke of 'the House Beautiful.' "

He glanced around our room once more, not exactly with approval. "Had I saved a pound for every time I have delivered that lecture, I should be surrounded by luxuries." He smiled. "The necessaries could then take care of themselves."

"And you, Holmes," I said. "How did you know our visitor's identity?" I was quite certain that he had never attended one of Wilde's lectures nor read any of Wilde's works, and I was proved correct by his reply.

"I am not a literary man," said Holmes, "but I have read quite widely in the annals of crime. I believe that Mr. Wilde was involved during his American tour some years ago with a series of quite horrible murders."

I was surprised at Holmes's statement, but Wilde was positively astounded.

"I had not thought that the news of those events had made the return across the Atlantic with me," said he.

Holmes nodded as if in agreement. "It did not. I read the American papers, among many others."

"Ah. I see. Then you are aware of the circumstances. I have indeed come to the right place."

"The right place for what?" Holmes inquired.

"For help," said Wilde. "You see, I believe that someone wants to kill me."

"It would appear," said Holmes, looking far more cheerful than he had at the song of the carolers, "that you have a story to tell. Perhaps we should be seated."

While I retrieved the sofa cushions from the floor, Holmes removed his violin from the couch. I then placed the cushions in their proper places for our visitor, who took a silver cigarette case from a pocket.

When Wilde had lighted a gold-tipped cigarette, Holmes sniffed the air and said, "I believe I detect a hint of clove, do I not?"

"You do," Wilde said, no doubt unaware that Holmes regarded himself as something of an expert on tobacco. "Mixed with Latakia and Virginia. I have them made up—"

"—in Piccadilly," Holmes said. "I'm familiar with the shop."

Smiling at Wilde's surprise, Holmes took some tobacco from the toe of his Persian slipper, packed his pipe, and lit it. Soon he was seated in his chair at the side of the fireplace opposite from my own, puffing contentedly.

"Now, Mr. Wilde," he said, blowing out a stream of white smoke, "let us hear your story. You were saying that someone wants to kill you."

Wilde tried for several seconds to achieve a comfortable position on the couch, without success. He was too tall. Finally he simply leaned forward, puffing airily on his cigarette.

"It all began," he said, "when I saw the bear."

Holmes removed his pipe from his mouth. "A bear? In London?"

Wilde smiled. "Not a real bear. I'm sure of that. But more of a bear than I could bear."

I smiled. Holmes did not. "Either you saw a bear or you did not," said he. "You must be plainer, and restrict yourself to the facts."

"Restricting oneself to the facts," said Wilde, "is not always easy for an artist. Sometimes truth resides in things other than facts."

"Nonsense," said Holmes. "Truth always resides in the facts and nothing more. There *is* nothing more."

Wilde sat a bit straighter and took on the look of the enthusiast. "There is a truth that remains beyond the reach of the facts. It is the truth that is found in art, and sometimes in something beyond even that."

I feared that Holmes might lash out in response to such a statement, but he simply smiled a thin smile and said, "You may have a point. The science of deduction is, in its own way, an art."

"And a consulting detective," said Wilde, "must believe in himself absolutely, as an artist must. Would you not agree?"

"I would," said Holmes. "But we are getting away from your story. Pray proceed."

Wilde appeared readier to discuss art than his troubles, but he said, "Years ago, in America, I had visions of bears. These visions were a prelude to an act of violence against my person and that of another. After that lesson, and others like it, I have come, over the years, to trust my intuition."

"Then you would have us believe that the bear you saw is either art or intuition rather than a fact," said Holmes.

"True," Wilde agreed. "In a way."

"In what way?" I asked, hoping for a straightforward answer.

Wilde returned it. "In the way that what I really saw was a man."

"A man who looked like a bear?"

"Yes. Either that or a vision." He smiled. "Perhaps I should say, a re-vision."

"And do you know the man?" asked Holmes, disregarding all Wilde's statements except the first.

"I believe that I might," said Wilde.

"And does he have a reason for wanting to kill you?"

"He may feel that he does."

"And what would have caused that belief?"

"When I was in America, on that tour of the West that you mentioned," said Wilde, "I encountered two men unlike any I had ever met. They were buffalo hunters."

"You do mean *bison* hunters, I take it," Holmes said.

"Of course, though in America, they call them buffalo. I have no idea why."

"Americans are peculiar that way," said I, and Wilde nodded.

"These particular Americans were very unsavory characters," he said. His nose wrinkled as if he could still smell them. "They . . . did not 'take a liking to me,' as they sometimes say in those parts. In fact, one of them intended to kill me, as well as another person. Instead, the one who wanted to kill me died himself, and his friend fled the scene. I fear that somehow the one who fled has found his way to London, seeking revenge after all these years for the death of his companion."

"Did you kill his companion?" asked Holmes.

"No. That was done by another, someone who came upon the scene and rescued me."

"And the name of this other?"

"It is not one that you would know." Wilde paused to reflect, puffing his cigarette. "Or perhaps you might, but it has no bearing on the present matter."

Holmes nodded. "And has anyone here in London recently made an attempt on your life?"

"I believe so," said Wilde.

Holmes puffed on his pipe, then said, "But is your belief based on fact?"

Wilde smiled. "I cannot be certain," said he. "But as I was walking this morning near my house, a carriage rounded the corner at high speed, careening along as if the Devil himself were at the reins. I am a great admirer of recklessness, especially in others, but I drew back so that I would not be in any danger. At that moment, someone gave me a powerful shove forward, and I stumbled into the street, directly into the path of the careening carriage."

"And yet you sit here before us, calmly telling your story," Holmes observed.

"Not so calmly as it might appear to you," Wilde said. "Although the public might think otherwise, I am generally in control of my emotions. And despite my appearance, I am remarkably nimble, which is why I am sitting here now. I was able to spring aside, and the horses missed me by the narrowest of margins. As I turned back to see who had given me the near-fatal push, I saw the bear turning a corner down the street."

"The man who looked like a bear, you mean," said Holmes.

"Indeed," Wilde responded.

"But he wasn't a bear," said Holmes. "He was a man wearing a winter coat made from the hide of a bison."

Again Wilde was amazed. I, being more accustomed to the work-ings of Holmes's mind, was merely mildly surprised.

"Such would have to be the case," said Holmes. "There was no vision, and there was no bear. But a man wearing a buffalo robe might pass for a bear in London."

"You must be right!" Wilde said. "I'm sure you are. The buffalo hunter is here, as I thought."

"He must be quite conspicuous," said I, though a glance at my visitor's bottle-green coat assured me that one might go about in a London winter in almost any garb and not be thought too outlandish.

"But where can he be spending his time?" asked Wilde. "And how did he come here?"

"It has been several years since your tour of America," Holmes said. "Perhaps he came here out of mere opportunity, without a thought of you in his mind."

"But a man like that," Wilde said. "What opportunity could he have?"

"There is a clue in this very room," said Holmes. "One that you have already remarked upon."

Wilde was puzzled. "I'm afraid I do not understand."

"It is," said Holmes, "simply a matter of reaching a conclusion based on the facts of the matter. Art, I regret to say, does not enter the picture. Why, I suspect that Watson there has already thought the thing through."

It was not often that Holmes expressed any degree of confidence in my abilities, but in this instance he was right to give me the credit, for I had indeed arrived at what I believed to be the correct answer.

"Well, Watson?" said Holmes. I nodded, and he said, "First, the clue."

"It is the patriotic V. R.," I responded.

Holmes applauded silently. "Absolutely correct. Now do you see, Mr. Wilde?"

"I regret to say that I do not. Although the light in your quarters is certainly adequate, I remain entirely in the dark."

Holmes put aside his pipe. "Come now. The queen and an American buffalo. What could the connection possibly be?"

"I have no idea. I . . . wait a moment. Of course! The golden jubilee!"

"Right you are," said Holmes. He reached into a box of papers on the floor beside his chair and withdrew something that he held up for Wilde to see. It was the program that we had brought with us after attending perhaps the most popular attraction of the queen's golden jubilee, *Buffalo Bill's Wild West Show*. The program was quite thick, and Holmes had to thumb through it for several seconds before he found what he was seeking. When he had located it, he read it aloud, emphasizing certain of the words: " 'You will see a *buffalo hunt*, in *all its realistic details*.' Do you remember it, Watson?"

"Indeed I do. It was quite thrilling, actually."

"If not quite realistic," Holmes added. "And do you recall what Colonel Cody told us about his amazing cast of characters?"

That, too, I recalled quite clearly, perhaps because I had considered it such a privilege to meet the great showman himself, bedecked in fringed buckskins and wearing an enormous ten-gallon hat. "He was a true democrat. He said that he hired anyone who would work for him: cowboys, Red Indians, women, children, come one, come all."

"As indeed he would have to do to perform such set pieces as the buffalo hunt. And I am certain that he would not inquire too closely into the background of those he added to his cast. A man such as you have described, Mr. Wilde, might find employment in Colonel Cody's show quite appealing, especially if, since his encounter with you, he had committed other crimes in the United States."

"But why would he still be in England?" asked Wilde. "It has been months since the last performance of the Wild West show."

Holmes nodded agreement. "Let us assume that your enemy was dismissed from the cast for some reason. For indulging in drink, perhaps, or petty theft. Colonel Cody has the reputation of a stern taskmaster and would not tolerate such conduct. Without employment, your friend might not have been able to return to America. He might have been forced to find menial jobs here to support himself. And ask yourself this question: Why has he not attempted your life before now?"

"Do you have the answer?" asked Wilde.

Holmes did not hesitate. "If he is such a person as you describe, the likelihood is that he had not thought of you at all until he tried to kill you. He simply happened to see you on the street, recalled your role in his unhappy life, and took advantage of a sudden opportunity."

Wilde lit another of his cigarettes. "But now he will be thinking of me often. He might very well try again to kill me unless something is done."

"True," Holmes agreed. "And we shall do something tonight."

"But what?"

"We will find this man and put a stop to things immediately. Watson, do you have your revolver?"

I did not, but I told him that I could get it at once.

"Do so. And then we will be on our way."

"But where will we go?" asked Wilde. "We have no idea where to find this person."

"Think about it while we make ourselves ready," answered Holmes. "You may discover that we do indeed have an excellent possibility."

I was as mystified as Wilde, but once we were in the carriage, Holmes directed the driver to the fairgrounds where the Wild West show had been held.

"Where else would a man with little money and few prospects seek refuge?" he asked. "Some structures doubtless remain on the ground, and they would provide a modicum of shelter. He may well be there."

It seemed quite likely that Holmes was correct, as he so often was, and we wound our way through the icy streets, passing carolers singing of animals that would speak in stables at midnight, groups of people giving each other the joy of the season, walls covered with colorful posters advertising dramatic presentations appropriate to the time of year.

One of the latter caught Holmes's attention, and he pointed it out to us. The title of the drama was *The Wolf Shall Lie Down with the Lamb*, which Holmes deemed a ridiculous idea, about as likely as the mountain coming to Mohammed.

"But the drama does not deal with facts," Wilde protested. "The title is an allegorical expression of something that is to be hoped for if not attained."

"And why hope for something unattainable?" Holmes asked.

"Because it is the nature of man to do so," said Wilde. "And it is in the nature of the Christmas season."

Holmes gave him a thin smile. "Explain that to the man who is trying to kill you," he said.

The fairgrounds were dark and apparently deserted. Where once the stagecoach had rumbled and the bison ranged, where the *vaqueros* had roped, where the Indian village had stood, there was now nothing at all. Not even a trace remained. Nor was there a trace of Wilde's supposed enemy or of anyone else. All was loneliness and desolation, covered with a blanket of dirty snow. The icy wind cut through my clothing, and my right hand clutched my revolver.

Sherlock Holmes looked over the scene with chagrin. He rarely makes a mistake, although it has happened before, as even he will admit. It never pleases him, however.

"It appears that I have followed a wrong path in my reasoning," he said. "I was certain that we would find the man here."

Wilde, rather than showing distress, seemed lost in thought. Then he said, "Art. The answer lies in art, and in the science of deduction."

"What do you mean?" I asked.

"That placard we saw," said Wilde. "About the lion and the lamb. Are you familiar with the scriptures?"

I was far from an expert in such matters, and Holmes was equally at a loss. I told Wilde that I failed to see his point.

"The title of the drama is from the book of Isaiah. I do not claim to be a biblical scholar by any means, but I do have some acquaintance with Holy Writ. I cannot recall the passage perfectly, but it says something about the wolf dwelling with the lamb, the leopard lying down with the kid. And they shall be led by a little child."

"I can easily see how the sentiment relates to Christmas," said I. "But not to the current difficulty."

Wilde was happy to elucidate. "The scripture goes on to say that the cow and the *bear* shall feed together, and the lion shall eat straw like the ox."

"Ah," I exclaimed. "Bears again."

"More than bears," said Holmes. "I congratulate you on your deduction, Mr. Wilde. We know that your enemy has an inclination toward the theatrical and that he can appear to be a bear in his buffalo robe. And he needs work if he is not to earn his living by the admittedly dangerous alternative of theft. Clearly, the scripture has broader applications than I had accorded it. But let us waste no more time. It is growing late."

We returned to the carriage and soon located another placard advertising the drama in which we had become so interested. The address of the theater placed it not so very far from Wilde's own residence, as he informed us.

"Then our suppositions are all the more likely to be correct," said Holmes, and he urged the driver to make haste.

* * *

The outside of the rather shabby theater was bedecked with wilting tinsel, and a scrap of paper blew down the nearly deserted street. We had arrived well into the performance, and as there was no one to sell us tickets or to take them from us, we walked straight into the building.

The play had reached its climactic moment. The stage was covered with people representing animals of all kinds: oxen, lambs, panthers, lions, and bears. There were two of the latter, and as I was wondering how we were to determine which of them was the one we wanted, a diminutive actor began declaiming his lines.

" 'For unto us a child is born,' " said he, quoting from Isaiah, as Wilde later informed me. " 'Unto us a son is given: and the government shall be upon his shoulder: and his name shall be called Wonderful, Counselor, the Mighty God, the everlasting Father, the Prince of Peace.' "

I believe that the intention of the playwright at this point was to have the "little child" lead the peaceful animals in what Wilde might have called an "allegorical representation of peacefulness and harmony," but this was prevented by Wilde's pointing at one of the bears and exclaiming "That is the man!"

Wilde had developed quite a sonorous voice for his appearances in the lecture hall. The play came to a standstill, and all eyes turned to the back of the auditorium.

"There!" Wilde said, pointing to the more realistic of the bears, the one nearest the actor playing the child.

At this exclamation the bear leapt up and stared in our direction. The costume, or robe, fell partially away, and I could see that its wearer was a short man with a face shaped like that of a weasel. From the expression in his dark, glittering eyes, it was plain that he recognized the one who had pointed him out.

He threw off his robe and yelled, "You killed my friend, you limey poof!" Then he reached into his boot and pulled out an alarmingly large Bowie knife, quite a popular weapon in the wilds of America, or so I have been told. He waved it over his head and said, "I should have used this on you this morning," in an atrocious accent.

I drew my revolver from my pocket to stop him, but it was already too late. The audience, realizing that what they were seeing had no part in the play, panicked. People stormed toward the exits. To fire the revolver at the man would have been far too risky in the circumstances.

I believe that his thought at that instant was to leap from the stage, charge Wilde, and perhaps disembowel him with the Bowie knife, but he was prevented from doing so for a moment by the stampeding crowd.

Wilde, undeterred by either the knife or the fleeing audience, did not hesitate. Using his great size to advantage, he forced his way through the surging mob, shoving people to the left and right as he cleared a path toward the footlights.

"I never killed your friend," Wilde shouted as he neared the stage. "And I demand that you cease your absurd attempt at revenge."

"Never!" his adversary shouted in reply, and then he leapt.

His bison-hide coat billowed out like the wings of some immense bird, and in one hand he held the knife. I would have attempted a shot, but I was afraid that I might hit Wilde, who was quite close to the stage by that time. All Holmes and I could do was watch as the man landed on Wilde and the two disappeared from our view.

The crowd had mostly disappeared by then, and we worked our way to the spot where the two men lay struggling, concealed by the buffalo robe, which billowed as if a great wind were blowing under it. Then Wilde stood up and threw it away from him. It landed in the first row of seats, and I saw that the man who had worn it was lying on the floor, still clutching his formidable knife by its handle. Unfortunately, the other end of the knife was embedded in his chest.

"I grabbed his arm as he fell," said Wilde, gasping for breath. "I must have twisted it, though I never intended to."

"It was clearly an accident," I said. "And all in self-defense."

Several of the actors gathered at the edge of the stage, still in their costumes.

" 'The cow and the bear shall feed together,' " said Holmes, looking down at the inert form.

"They won't feed together no more," said the cow. "Smelled worse than a bleedin' bear, the fella did. I thought he was a crazy one from the start."

"It was that robe of his that smelled, it was," said the leopard, whose outfit only vaguely resembled the creature it was supposed to represent. "And he never looked like a bear, not really."

"He wasn't a man of cleanly habits," said Wilde. "Of that I am certain. What time it is, Dr. Watson?"

I took out my watch and told him the time.

"Ah, two hours from midnight," said Wilde, looking at Holmes slyly. "And even now the animals are speaking."

"It is not yet Christmas Eve," Holmes pointed out. "They are more than a day early."

"The police will be here at any moment," I reminded them, "summoned no doubt by some of the less panicked members of the audience."

"And we shall have an interesting story to tell them," said Holmes.

Wilde looked at his green overcoat as if checking for specks of blood. "As for me, I am not so sure that I wish to tell my story. It will cause a great deal of talk, I fear."

Holmes smiled. "I should think that for a man such as yourself, the only thing worse than being talked about would be *not* being talked about."

"Very good!" exclaimed Wilde. "In fact, I almost wish I had said that myself." He paused and smiled, then said, "And I will."

Then his smile faded. He looked at the dead man on the floor and said, "I am very sorry that things should have ended this way. Life should be about beauty and peace, and death should not be so ugly."

Holmes looked at him sharply. "I hope that your life is indeed filled with nothing but beauty and peace, but you must know that few lives are."

"Each of us is his own devil," said Wilde. "If we choose to be."

"Then do not choose that way," said Holmes.

"I will not," Wilde responded.

I had the impression that he was going to say more, but at that moment the police arrived, and we had to spend the remainder of the evening explaining about men who looked like bears. And though we heard much of Wilde in latter days, we never encountered him again.

THE ADVENTURE OF THE NATURALIST'S STOCK PIN

Jon L. Breen

*D*uring a recent tour of the Galapagos Islands, one of the Ecua-
dorian guides on our ship took me aside one evening in the
passengers' lounge. After politely chatting about the day's sight-
ings of iguanas, sea lions, frigate birds, and Sally Lightfoot crabs, he asked
me if I would like to read an old manuscript one of his colleagues had
received from a naturalist in England. "Your opinion of its authenticity,"
he said, "would be much valued."

"But I'm not a naturalist," I said. "I can barely tell a blue-footed booby
from a red-footed booby. Maybe my wife . . ."

"Many naturalists have read this manuscript already and given their
opinions. But one of your fellow passengers tells me you are a devotee of
Sherlock Holmes, and no Holmes scholar has yet given us an opinion."

Though calling me a Holmes scholar is a bit of a stretch, I eagerly agreed
to read the document. Never having seen an original Sherlock Holmes manuscript, I didn't recognize Dr. Watson's handwriting. But I could at least

make some comments based on the historical background and the literary style.

Early in my association with Sherlock Holmes, only a few days before Christmas in 1881, I was about to leave the Baker Street rooms for some long-forgotten errand when my friend suggested I might wish to stay.

"I am to be visited by a Mr. Beagle, Watson. He promises to present a case of singular interest. Some diversion might be welcome in this excessively cheery season, don't you agree?"

I agreed only partially. While the Yuletide could be an agent of melancholy in bachelors like ourselves, I was invariably affected with its attendant joy whatever my current circumstances. Still, I had known Holmes long enough to know that cases of interest to him would also be stimulating to me, and I also welcomed an excuse not to venture out in the chill and blustery weather, so I remained.

From our window, we saw Mr. Beagle arrive at Baker Street at the appointed hour. He alighted from a hansom, furtively looking left and right, and moved slowly but purposefully to the door of 221B, with his coat tails flapping in the breeze. He appeared to be an elderly man, and sported an impressive white beard. His hat concealed what facial features the beard did not. When Mrs. Hudson announced Mr. Beagle moments later, Holmes welcomed him in, showed him to a chair before the fire, and offered him a glass of port, which he declined.

"Mr. Holmes, I am grateful you would see me at such short notice," our agitated guest said, after taking a few moments to catch his breath. "I am in a dreadful state. I have become so fearful, so suspicious, I imagined the driver of the cab was an enemy who was carrying me to my doom."

"Why did you suspect him?" Holmes asked.

Our guest waved a hand impatiently. "No good reason. It's just the state of my nerves. City life has that effect upon me. My home is in Kent, where I am . . . ah . . . something in the nature of a country parson. My wife and I get up to London occasionally and are currently here for a short stay with friends. My wife does not know I have come to see you. Much as I dislike deceiving her, I am even more anxious not to give her unnecessary concern."

"Admirable I am sure, Mr. Beagle. What is the nature of your problem?" Our visitor glanced at me with polite suspicion. This was not unusual among Holmes's clients, and he responded in the usual way. "You may speak freely in front of Dr. Watson. He is in my confidence and quite reliable."

"Certainly." Mr. Beagle's nod toward me was apologetic. "I shall state my problem as succinctly as I can. I have received an invitation from a man named Lamburt LeSue, asking me to meet him tomorrow evening at eight o'clock in the private room of The Highwayman's Rest, a pub in Fleet Street. He claims a prior acquaintance, but I do not remember him."

"An unusual name," Holmes mused. "Surely you would remember it if you had heard it before."

"I believe that I would, yes. Normally, of course, I would ignore such an invitation from an unknown person. However, something he said in the invitation makes me want very much to see this man. Still I am wary, and I think with reason."

"Do you have many enemies in London, Mr. Beagle?"

"If you had asked me that question as recently as a week ago, I would have said no. But I have been receiving anonymous messages, signed with names even more unlikely than Lamburt LeSue. Merwin A. Drauss was one of them. Mark Caljane was another."

186

"Do you have these messages with you?"

"I destroyed them immediately."

Holmes passed a pen and the back of a calling card to our visitor. "Please write down those names on this card, Mr. Beagle, with special attention to exact spelling as closely as you can remember."

"Certainly."

"What do you recall of the messages?"

"They were cryptic, nonsensical really, and not precisely threatening. Still, they have made me suspicious even of my friends, mistrustful of anyone outside my family circle. Do I have enemies, you ask? I cannot say with certainty. I dislike to call any fellow human creature an enemy, Mr. Holmes, though many are in profound disagreement with some of my, ah, ideas."

"Your theological ideas, you mean?"

Our visitor looked at Holmes sharply. "Why do you assume that?"

For once I didn't wait for Holmes to elucidate, for surely the reason for the comment was obvious. "You said you were a clergyman, Mr. Beagle," I said.

"Ah, not precisely, though I can see how I might have misled you on that point. My living arrangements and relationship to the community are somewhat like those of a country parson, but I am not a member of the clergy, though at one time in my life it was intended that I should be."

"In any event," I went on, "if you have been invited to a social occasion that for whatever reason is not to your liking, why not simply decline the invitation?"

"I wish it were that simple," our visitor lamented. "As you can see, I am an old man. I have arrived at an age at which the impulse to take on new studies or new projects is tempered by the knowledge that I might not be able to finish them. In so many ways, my life is as wonderful as it could be—I have all the joys brought by family, financial comfort, and intellectual stimulation. Even my health, worrisome my whole life, has enjoyed an unlikely improvement. But still the accumulation of years weighs upon me. Death, if not quite a friend, is a frequently encountered acquaintance, nodded to on a city street, seen from the corner of my eye on public conveyances, glancing over my shoulder even as I take a daily walk on the grounds of my own home. Sometimes I feel that I would welcome death, but I don't relish having life taken from me prematurely by the hand of another. And it may well be that Lamburt LeSue, whoever he is, would like to end my life prematurely, that I am being lured there only to be killed."

"Then why go, Mr. Beagle?" I demanded, becoming impatient. I was so intrigued by our visitor's exasperating reticence that I scarcely noticed Holmes's uncharacteristic silence.

"To get back something that belongs to me. A piece of jewelry, to be precise. A stock pin that was given to me by a ship's captain in commemoration of a journey I once took. It was a completely unique piece. I wore it proudly for many years. Then it vanished, stolen from me, I am grieved to say, in a room full of respectable, distinguished scholars. I had resigned myself to never seeing this stock pin again. But now I want it back. The person who issued this invitation claims to have it."

Holmes spoke at last. "I believe your best course of action, Mr. Beagle, would be to convey your acceptance of the invitation but not to attend."

"If I don't attend, Mr. Holmes, how can I retrieve the property that is mine?"

"Leave that to me. Send word to your host that you will be there, and hie yourself back to Kent with your good wife to enjoy Christmas with your rather large family."

"I made no reference to the size of my family," our guest said with a faint smile.

"You have told us very little but more than enough. Forgive the impertinence, but if you were to accept the invitation and then not attend, it would be consistent with some other major events of your life, would it not?"

Our visitor seemed uncertain whether to be offended or amused. He chose the latter reaction. "I suppose you could say so. But you must understand, Mr. Holmes, often my intentions have been the best, but my body has let me down. It is true I am not at best ease in large gatherings. And the fact that something of value was stolen from me on one of the rare occasions I attended a mass meeting of persons in my field of endeavor might be enough to influence a man to stay away from crowds. But to be more specific to the point I believe you are making, it was the state of my health and not cowardice that caused me to miss that meeting at Oxford in 1860."

"To be sure, to be sure," Holmes agreed. "And Professor Huxley proved a more than adequate stand-in, did he not?"

By this point, I felt myself the object of some sort of game, as Holmes and Beagle airily alluded to matters of which I was ignorant, waiting to see how long it would take me to interpret their conversation. But any person with an awareness of science and public affairs in the England of 1881 would by this time have been afforded enough clues to know the true name of our visitor before Holmes finally deigned to utter it. For once, I was determined to rob Holmes of his dramatic gesture.

"Mr. Beagle," I said, "your theory that music preceded speech in

189

human development is one that Mr. Holmes and I have discussed with interest.''

"Yes, yes," he said, "I'm gratified. But I can no longer take the pleasure in music I once did. Nor art nor poetry. Though I hear my wife's reading of popular romances with pleasure, great literature has closed its pages to me. It is one of the sadnesses of my life.''

"I fear the demands of the clock preclude any more aesthetic discussion,'' Holmes said, somewhat acerbically. "What was the design of this missing stock pin, Professor Darwin?''

Fascinating as it was to listen to an extended conversation between two of the great minds of the nineteenth century, the rest of that conference in Baker Street was only prelude to the real drama of the case. An hour after his arrival, Charles Darwin, author of *The Origin of Species* and one of the most controversial figures in Victorian England, was on his way again. Much information had been exchanged and elaborate plans made, plans which Holmes and I had pledged to carry out. Surely time was of the essence, but when the great scientist had left, Holmes could not resist the opportunity to demonstrate his brilliance yet again.

"Tell me, Watson, exactly when did you guess our distinguished client's identity?''

"It was more than a guess, Holmes, and I must tell you it was well before you called him by name.''

"Why, of course, my dear fellow. I was certain of that.''

"There were several indicators," I said. "The reference to a country home in Kent, to early aspirations to join the clergy, to controversial views, to a large family. And of course, when he mentioned an 1860 meeting at Oxford and you made reference to the arguments of Professor Thomas Henry Huxley, I knew this bearded savant could be only one man, Charles Darwin. And when did *you* know the truth, Holmes?" I added, proud of my deductions but fully expecting to hear that he had been a jump or two ahead of me.

"As soon as he climbed out of his hansom, Watson."

"Then you had prior knowledge."

"My dear fellow, you cut me to the quick! I knew nothing of our client beyond the name he gave. The name alone was enough for a hypothesis, for was not the *Beagle* the ship on which Darwin made his historic five-year voyage? The sight of the white beard and our client's apparent advanced age were enough for hypothesis to become theory. The several pointers you mentioned served only to verify the theory. Now then, Watson, why are we wasting time? There is much to be done and precious few hours in which to do it."

I may have grumbled somewhat testily about my awareness of the urgency, but Holmes did not hear me.

Over our years of friendship, I have seen Sherlock Holmes in many disguises. As readers of my accounts know, some of these impersonations were elaborate enough even to fool me. In the Darwin affair, however, I was in on the impersonation from the beginning. I watched in admiration as Holmes subtly aged himself, donned a white beard, and altered his carriage to suggest advanced years. Before we left Baker Street to fulfill Professor Darwin's social engagement, I expressed my frank amazement.

"It should suffice, Watson," Holmes said, "if, as we have been led to understand, his host does not know Darwin intimately."

Clearly, Darwin was expected to come alone to the scheduled meeting. But shortly before the appointed time, I visited The Highwayman's Rest pub. It was another bitterly cold evening. The pub's sign, depicting the figure of a masked highwayman on horseback under crossed pistols, swayed in the wind. After peering through the round bottle-glass windows at the distorted figures within for a moment, I entered the welcome warmth of the main room, where the glow of the fire glittered off the brass fittings. Holmes had assured me The Highwayman's Rest was an establishment where any service or favour could be had for the right price. He had also provided the name of an employee who would help me if I mentioned the name Sherlock Holmes and showed a palm full of coin. While the establishment had a wealth of small, low-ceilinged rooms that afforded privacy for the various activities of its customers, the phrase "the private room" apparently referred to one in particular. I was shown there and advised where I could conceal myself, firearm at the ready, to listen to the conversation between the ersatz Darwin and the mysterious Lamburt LeSue.

When Holmes, in his Darwinian disguise, arrived at the pub, he was shown into the private room by the same door through which I had entered. I was already waiting behind a rarely-used standing screen. Its apparent purpose was to make the private room even more private when such was requested.

Lamburt LeSue, if indeed it was he who swept dramatically into the room from a rear door a few moments later, cut a remarkable figure. The figure he cut, to be precise, belonged to the traditional Father Christmas, including red suit and white beard, the latter even fuller and much more obviously false than that worn by his prey.

"Happy Christmas!" he roared with manic joviality. "Is this the gift you had hoped for, Professor Darwin?"

The bizarre figure passed to Holmes a small object, presumably the stock pin. Holmes examined it closely to see if it was consistent with the description Darwin had given us. Apparently it indeed contained an insect from Galapagos preserved in amber. He nodded his head.

"It is, sir. I am grateful to you. May I extend my thanks and compliments of the season."

"And does it bring back memories of that historic voyage on which your wonderful brain single-handedly created what has come to be called Darwin's Theory of Evolution?" Father Christmas inquired.

"No, Mr. LeSue, if that is your name, it does not. My work in the field of evolutionary theory took many years after the completion of the voyage of the *Beagle*, and I have never claimed it was mine alone."

"Have you not? My mistake!"

"Might I ask how this pin came into your possession, Mr. LeSue?"

"I did not steal it, if that is what you are wondering. In fact, it was given to me by the man who stole it from you. Professor Isaiah Corcoran. You remember him I am sure?"

"I do indeed," Holmes said. "But as a great scientist, not as a thief."

Father Christmas snorted. "Our experience differs. I know him as a thief. I know him *only* as a thief. I was his student, you see, his assistant for a time, and a discovery I made while working for him, the identification of a rare specimen that would have made my scientific reputation, he published under his own name. The senior researcher's prerogative, I was told. Odd the excuses we make to justify outright thievery. He showed me your stock pin one day, and I knew it could not have come into his hands by legitimate means. He made me a gift of it, an uncharacteristic burst of generosity designed I suppose to make me happier with my lack of credit on a great discovery. I at first determined to give it back to you."

"Which you have done, sir, and I have offered my thanks. Now, if you will excuse me, Mrs. Darwin is waiting, and—"

"No."

"I may not leave?"

"No. As I thought it over, I came to realize how much you, Professor Darwin, symbolized the kind of scientific dishonesty of which I had been the victim. And I realized that my fortuitous possession of the stock pin gave me an opportunity to do a much greater service to mankind than simply to return stolen property. For, you see, some kinds of stolen property cannot be returned. A man's good name, a scientist's reputation, these cannot be returned."

"And what exactly is your name, Father Christmas? Not, I dare to venture, Lamburt LeSue."

"You are correct."

"And it seems doubtful to me you are known as the even more unlikely cognomens Merwin A. Drauss or Mark Caljane."

"There's a tidy puzzle for you in those names, but you aren't going to have time to solve it."

"I've solved it already. They're anagrams. What else could they be?"

"How astute of you. But now I shall at last have my revenge on you, Professor Darwin!"

"What, might I ask, have I done to you?"

"What have you done to me? Better to ask, what have you done to science? And what you do to science, you do to every scientist. If you've solved my anagrams, you should know what I mean."

"I fear I do not."

"Oh, never fear, Professor Darwin, I shall tell you in detail. This pub is noted for its thick walls, discretion, and other services not on the menu. No one will interrupt us. No one will hear us. There is no need to hurry. I can play with you as a cat plays with a mouse."

"If the cat plays too long, the mouse sometimes escapes."

"Rarely, very rarely, and not in this case." Father Christmas laughed nastily. "A friend once asked me, 'Does Darwin keep Christmas, do you think?' And I said after a few moments' thought, 'I should think so. Even if he is an atheist.' "

"I am no atheist," Holmes insisted, a statement consistent with Darwin's public posture.

" 'Whatever his beliefs,' I said to my friend, 'he has a large family and he grew to manhood in a religious tradition, was even intended for the ministry at one time, thinks of his house as a country parsonage. I expect he keeps Christmas, for the children's sake at least.' Then I thought, when I have my revenge on Darwin, when I strike my great blow for truth and reason, why not choose the Yuletide season when I may give a *gift* to the community of science, on behalf of all honest researchers, all who believe in giving and taking credit only where it is due?

"I come before you in the name of Erasmus Darwin, your grandfather and namesake to whose ideas about evolution you added *nothing*. I come to you in the name of Jean Lamarck, another whose researches you plundered and claimed for your own. I come to you in the name of Alfred Russel Wallace, poor deluded man, who did the real original thinking, who had the real new theory, but who through the sleight of hand of you and your cronies Lyell and Hooker was denied it."

"That's not so." Holmes could scarcely have sounded more indignant if his own character had been sullied. "Wallace received full credit. Our papers on species were read together before the Linnean Society."

"Read together, oh, yes, read together, as if a collaboration. But the real original theory was his, not yours. It was Wallace who solved the problem of divergence, Wallace who determined how it is that many different species could have sprung from the same original

195

source, but he could not be allowed to receive his proper credit. You had to be first. So Lyell and Hooker conspired with you to assure that Wallace would be relegated to the backwater of scientific annals."

"We were in constant communication with Wallace. He was consulted at every point."

"Consulted! He was off on his travels, gathering samples, doing the real work of the naturalist and had no one in England to watch out for his interests. So it is in the name of Wallace more than any that I take my revenge today."

"It is true we are alone here," Holmes said. "That does not mean, however, that no one knew I was coming here today. If you kill me, it will be known who arranged for my presence here. And surely the proprietor of this pub, wink though he may at prostitution and other forms of vice, cannot be guaranteed to keep silent where murder is concerned. You will have no hope of escaping arrest, imprisonment, and hanging."

Father Christmas laughed again. "There are ways of escaping beyond the reach of locomotives or clipper ships or courtrooms. And in any event, why should I care? I will have completed my great work. My mission will be finished."

The bearded figure moved menacingly forward, drawing what looked like a dagger from his broad black belt. Now must be the time. I leapt from behind the screen and rode the miscreant to the floor. My inclination would have been to move sooner, but Holmes had made me promise to hear the potential murderer out before I brought him down.

Holmes retrieved the stock pin before we stormed back into the pub's main room and insisted that Scotland Yard be called in to deal with the assailant.

The man in the garb of Father Christmas was eventually identified as Edgar Gamble, a former research scientist with a history of mental disorder. The account of the affair Holmes and I provided the police, making no mention of Charles Darwin, was elaborately conceived but unimportant to this narrative. Holmes was able to return the stock pin, and Darwin, a very wealthy man, expressed his gratitude handsomely.

Back in Baker Street, a few days before the dawn of 1882, I was still troubled by the affair of the stock pin. "Surely, Holmes, Gamble was a madman."

"A clever one, however. Cleverer than the thief he once worked for. Isaiah Corcoran's greatest coup may have been the theft of Darwin's stock pin. He never published anything of real merit, not even the work he stole from his former assistant. Perhaps my claims for Corcoran as a great scientist helped to loosen Gamble's tongue."

"It needed little enough loosening. The same could be said for his wits."

"Gamble had a gift for anagrams, though."

I snorted. "A rather silly game. Merwin A. Drauss. Erasmus Darwin. Mark Caljane. Jean Lamarck. How long do you think it took the fellow to think those up?"

"You forgot the principal one. Lamburt LeSue for Samuel Butler." Butler, the novelist and journalist best known for the novel *Erewhon*, had virtually accused Darwin of plagiarizing his own grandfather and been pointedly ignored by Darwin and his family and friends. Butler had apparently been one of the main inspirations in Gamble's plan of revenge.

"But he was a madman, Holmes. The magnitude of conspiracy he envisioned leaves us no other conclusion. To imply that scientists of the stature of Sir Joseph Dalton Hooker and Sir Charles Lyell should conspire to rob a fellow scientist of his due credit is nothing short of unthinkable.''

"The world of scholarship is a complicated one, Watson, and even the mind that sees conspiracies everywhere might chance on a real one now and then.''

"Holmes, you can't mean—''

"All parties involved may have acted quite honourably in their own minds, Watson. After years of denial, none of them may even believe they were involved in any kind of conspiracy or deception. History will judge matters better than we.''

That was Holmes's last word on the subject. I choose not to believe that Darwin—the family man, the dedicated scientist, the loyal friend—was the sort of person who would claim credit for another's work, but anyone who has run a race of any kind understands the drive to reach the finish line first.

Was the Galapagos manuscript authentic? In many ways, I was the wrong person to decide. I even had to ask my wife what a stock pin was. (A stock, per The Concise Oxford Dictionary, is a "[s]tiff wide band of leather or other material formerly worn round neck, now displaced in general use by collar & tie. . . ." The stock pin, then, even I could figure out was the pin that held it in place—and pictures of Darwin indeed show him wearing such an accessory.)

I told the guide the manuscript read at least somewhat like Watson's work, a first draft perhaps, and I'd like to take a photocopy home with me. When I returned to California, I couldn't let the problem go, plunging into some enthusiastic, if somewhat disorganized, Darwin research of my own.

His biographers record that Darwin cut short his pre-Christmas visit to London in 1881 because of the onset of heart problems. Since his death followed in April 1882, no one has had reason to doubt the truth of this account. Probably it was true, at least in part, but the Galapagos manuscript offers an intriguing alternate possibility.

A frequently repeated anecdote has come to haunt me. While in London the week before Christmas, Darwin called at the house of a friend, George Romanes, who proved to be out. Romanes's butler believed Darwin was not well and asked him to come into the house until a cab could be brought for him. Darwin refused and walked to the cab stand himself, declining the butler's offer to accompany him. Partway there, he was seen to stagger and hold onto a railing for support. The butler saw him turn back toward the house, then change his mind and proceed toward the cab stand.

What does the story mean? Was Darwin genuinely ill or was he faking his discomfort for reasons of his own? Was his indecision about returning to the house based on the admirable qualities friends of Darwin liked to remember: his kindness, consideration for others, and disinclination to give trouble? Or was he somehow suspicious of his friend's butler? Picturing that indecisive Darwin reminds me of one of the unrecorded Holmes cases. Did Darwin fear, if he walked back to his friend's house and crossed the threshold, like Mr. James Phillimore returning to his house for his forgotten umbrella, he would never be seen again in this world? Too fanciful? No doubt.

THE ADVENTURE OF THE
SECOND VIOLET

Daniel Stashower

In glancing through my notes for the year 1899, I find record of three remarkable cases which arose to challenge the singular gifts by which my friend Mr. Sherlock Holmes was distinguished. The first was the extraordinary affair of the weeping coachman, which so perplexed the Sussex constabulary and the citizens of Godalming. The second concerned the curious business of the ox, the aster and the ivory eyepiece, which threatened to bring a scandal on one of Europe's reigning families. But of all the cases which crossed our threshold in Baker Street that year, perhaps none presented my friend with such a baffling problem—or threw his talents into such brilliant relief—as that of the unhappy Mrs. Violet Oldershot, née Hunter.

I had arisen late upon a Tuesday morning in the second week of December to find Holmes lost in contemplation of the morning newspapers. The columns were filled with accounts of the mounting tensions in South Africa, and of the intractable views of Mr. Kruger, the leader of the Dutch Boer settlers.

"A bad business, Watson," said Holmes, throwing down the *Times*.

"Surely the matter will be over in a matter of weeks?" I answered. "These Boers are simple farmers."

"These farmers will show themselves to be the most formidable antagonists who ever crossed the path of Imperial Britain," Holmes declared. "Napoleon and all his veterans never treated us so roughly as will these hard-bitten farmers with their ancient theology and their inconveniently modern rifles."

"But Holmes—" I began.

"In any case," he said, "there are matters closer to home which commend themselves to our attention. What do you make of this?" He passed across a sheet of notepaper which had evidently just arrived in the morning post. Taking it from his outstretched hand, I read:

Dear Mr. Holmes:

I trust that you will recall the episode at the Copper Beeches when you rendered such invaluable service to my wife, the former Miss Violet Hunter. I fear that she is once again in need of your assistance, though she shows no inclination to seek you out on her own behalf. I assure you that the present matter is no less grave—perhaps even more so. May I call at 9:00?

Yours faithfully,
—Mr. Henry Oldershot

"Violet Hunter!" I exclaimed.

"Indeed," said Holmes. "An intriguing prospect, is it not?"

It was seldom that Holmes had occasion to offer his services twice to the same client. Almost by definition, the problems which were brought to him were singular and exceptional, and therefore of a type unlikely to occur twice in the lifetime of any given client. It was notable indeed, then, that we should have found ourselves once again entertaining the difficulties of the woman we had first known as Miss Violet Hunter.

Some of my readers will recall the remarkable episode which first brought Miss Hunter to Baker Street, an episode which I have chronicled as *The Adventure of the Copper Beeches*. Miss Hunter had been engaged as a governess by a Mr. Jephro Rucastle, who had insisted as a condition of her employment that she sacrifice her luxuriant chestnut hair. It subsequently emerged that Mr. Rucastle secretly intended that Miss Hunter would impersonate his own daughter, whom he had imprisoned in an isolated chamber of the house, so as to discourage the attentions of a persistent suitor. Only the timely intervention of Sherlock Holmes brought this disagreeable business to a satisfactory conclusion.

We had heard that Miss Hunter had gone on to become headmistress at a private school for girls at Walsall, where she enjoyed a very notable success until her marriage some little time later. Indeed, Holmes had been so impressed by the spirit and intelligence of Miss Hunter that I recall expressing some disappointment at the time that he himself evinced no further interest in her, as I had not yet fully apprehended the degree of his bachelorhood.

Now, studying the note from Mr. Henry Oldershot, I naturally wondered what fresh difficulty had brought Miss Hunter back within our horizons. "What sort of problem do you suppose has so agitated this gentleman?" I asked.

"I can think of any number of possibilities," Holmes answered, "but in the absence of corroboration I would imagine—ah! There is our client's ring. We shall have our answer shortly."

Holmes rose and opened the door to admit a tall, broad-shouldered young man with pale-reddish close-cropped hair, a strong chin and clear green eyes. He stood in the doorway for a moment nervously fingering the brim of a worn bowler. "I am Henry Oldershot," he said, extending his hand. "You must be Sherlock Holmes."

"I am," said my companion, "and this is my colleague Dr. Watson."

"Of course," he said, stepping into the room. "Violet has spoken of you both so often that I feel we are already acquainted."

"Pray sit down, Mr. Oldershot," said Holmes, as I took the young man's hat and coat. "We are most interested to hear the nature of the difficulty which has brought you to Baker Street. Apart from the fact that you are a school teacher, that you have recently sold your pocket watch, and that you have lately suffered a financial reversal which you are anxious to conceal, I know nothing."

Mr. Oldershot dropped into an armchair by the fire with an expression of frank wonder upon his features. "I see that Violet has not exaggerated your abilities, Mr. Holmes. I consider myself a reasonably intelligent man, but I'm afraid I can't conceive of how you were able to arrive at those conclusions."

Holmes raised his eyebrows at me. "Watson?"

I studied our visitor and attempted to apply my friend's methods. "The ink stain?" I asked.

"Excellent, Watson!" cried he. "You are coming along nicely." He turned to Mr. Oldershot to explain. "Your marriage to Miss Hunter naturally suggested some connection to the school at Walsall. The stain of Pressman's Blue ink on your left shirtcuff—a variety commonly found in school inkwells—indicates that you are employed in the classroom, rather than the headmaster's office. The dusting of chalk along the inner sleeve of your coat confirms the notion."

"But the watch?" asked our visitor. "And the financial difficulties?"

Holmes glanced at me. I shook my head to indicate that I had not followed his reasoning that far. "Simplicity itself," said Holmes, turning back toward our client. "You are a schoolmaster, a profession which requires a certain degree of punctuality, and yet you arrived here at our lodgings seventeen minutes past the appointed hour, a fact you confirmed by glancing at our mantel clock rather than at your own pocket watch. The inevitable conclusion is that you have either sold your watch or sent it out for repair. The fact that you still wear a leather watch strap on your waistcoat suggests the former alternative—that your watch has been sold, and that you do not wish to call attention to this fact. It naturally follows, therefore, that you have endured a financial blow which you are eager to conceal."

Our visitor's stunned expression confirmed the accuracy of all that Holmes had said. "I must confess," Mr. Oldershot said at length, "that your words have amazed me. All that you say is quite true, though it brings me no pleasure to admit it. In fact, my recent—my recent embarrassments lie at the root of the problem which brings me here today."

"I imagined as much," said Holmes. "Pray let us have the details." He settled back in his armchair and closed his eyes.

"Very well," said Mr. Oldershot. "I am not a wealthy man, as you have surmised, Mr. Holmes. My schoolmaster's salary has been enough to provide a comfortable existence for the two of us, and my wife is not of a disposition to complain. In the two years since our marriage I have had everything to make a man's happiness complete—an interesting and challenging profession, a devoted partner and my good health. You will recall that my wife is a most remarkable woman, and no man has ever been graced with a more gentle or amiable companion. Indeed, many are the nights when I find myself sitting beside her at the fire and thinking myself the most favored man in the whole of Britain, or perhaps even the entire—"

"I'm sure that is most gratifying," said Holmes, without opening his eyes. "Please state the nature of your difficulty."

"Of course," said Mr. Oldershot with a start. "I will not waste any more of your time than necessary. I should explain, however, that at the time of our marriage I enjoyed the income of a small bequest from my late uncle. I chose to invest these funds in a small publishing concern, as I have some modest ambitions in that arena. Unfortunately, my efforts to launch a literary journal have not met with any great success. We have now been thrown back on my salary alone, which should have been sufficient but for the outstanding business debts which I am now forced to honour. I had sought to ensure our future, but instead I have placed a severe strain on what little remains of our resources."

"I see," said Holmes. "And your wife knows nothing of this?"

"On the contrary, she has been steadfast in her support of my literary aspirations. I might have wished to spare her the anxiety of my misfortunes, but in the circumstances I could scarcely conceal them from her. She has faced the challenge very bravely, and we are attempting to reduce our expenses wherever possible. She had even suggested that she might return to her previous post at the Walsall Academy for Girls, but of course this was impossible."

Holmes opened his eyes and sat forward in his chair. "You object to the prospect of employment for your wife?"

"I should not have enjoyed seeing my wife return to work, if that's what you mean, Mr. Holmes, but I would not have stood in her path if she desired it. No, the Academy would have forbidden her return so long as I remained at the boys' school."

"I see," said Holmes, reaching across toward his pipe rack.

"We soon resolved to manage as best we could until our circumstances improved. If we no longer ate quite as well or as often, or enjoyed entertainments in the evening, we still had enough to be content. Or so I thought until last Sunday evening."

Holmes snatched up his oily black clay and began filling it with tobacco. "And what happened on Sunday evening?"

"I had just finished correcting some exam papers when Violet suggested that we take a walk along the High Street. The shop windows had all been dressed for the holidays and we were admiring the displays when a strange man hurried toward us from the opposite direction. He was a small man, and rather fat, with a strange trick of hopping from foot to foot as he walked. Although I had never seen him before, he appeared to recognize my wife. Lifting his hat, he said, 'Good evening, Miss. Have you had a chance to reconsider my offer?' "

"Did your wife acknowledge this greeting?" Holmes asked.

"She did not. She simply gripped my arm and urged me forward, without giving a response of any kind. But as we walked on, I heard his voice calling after us. 'That's all right, my dear,' he said, 'I shall hold the offer open until tomorrow.' " Mr. Oldershot winced at the memory.

"How did your wife explain this encounter?"

"She insisted that the fellow must have mistaken her for someone else. But when I looked back as we crossed the next street, he stood looking after us with the most unpleasant expression one could imagine, like a fox gloating over a plump hen."

Holmes stood up and walked to the mantelpiece. "Can you tell us anything else of this gentleman's appearance?"

"That's just it, Mr. Holmes. He looked for all the world like Mr. Jephro Rucastle, the villain who employed my wife at the Copper Beeches!"

"Surely not!" I ejaculated.

"Of course I cannot be certain, having never laid eyes on the fellow. But he strongly resembled your own description of him, Dr. Watson, from the account you published at the time. 'A prodigiously stout man with a very smiling face.' Was that not how Violet described him to you? Those words would have fit this man perfectly."

Holmes picked up a glowing ember with the fireplace tongs and used it to light his pipe. "Forgive me, Mr. Oldershot, but I could easily walk to our front window and point out some half dozen other men who match that vague description."

"I am aware of that, Mr. Holmes, although you would not be so quick to dismiss my fears had you seen the look of absolute revulsion on Violet's face. I assure you, however, that I would not have travelled all the way down to London to consult you simply because my wife brushed up against a stranger in the street."

"Ah," said Holmes, drawing at his pipe, "there was a second encounter?"

"There was. Yesterday afternoon an unexpected thunderstorm cancelled the scheduled cricket match at the school. I took advantage of my sudden liberty to do a bit of holiday shopping in the town. I had just completed my purchases when I happened to glance across the road. To my utter astonishment, there stood my wife in earnest conversation with this very same man—the man she had so vehemently denied knowing."

Holmes folded his hands. "Did you confront her?"

"I was too astonished to do so. Instead I turned and walked through the village for some little while, wondering how best to deal with the situation. I had all but convinced myself that I had entirely exaggerated the matter, but when I returned to our flat my darkest fears were confirmed. It is now clear to me, Mr. Holmes, that the man in the street was indeed Mr. Jephro Rucastle, and that my wife has once again fallen under his malign influence." Our young client looked earnestly into Holmes's face, gathering his resolve before he continued. "Mr. Holmes, when I returned home that evening, I found that my wife had cut off all of her hair."

"Again!" I cried.

"Just so. As you know, my wife's hair is of a particularly captivating chestnut shade. It is her greatest vanity and, if I may say so, her strongest feature. You are familiar with the extraordinary circumstances which led her to sacrifice it the first time—when Mr. Rucastle intended that she should serve as an unwitting substitute for his own daughter. Those events, you will grant, were most exceptional. In her ignorance of Mr. Rucastle's true intentions, one can understand how my wife might have been influenced to wear her hair in a certain way. But would she do so a second time? I have cudgelled my brains, and I cannot imagine how or why she would agree to such a thing. Is it possible that Mr. Rucastle—if, indeed, it is he—has persuaded her to resume the impersonation of his daughter for some purpose?"

I looked over at Holmes. His eyes were shining as he pressed the tips of his fingers together. "Did she offer no explanation?" he asked eagerly.

"To the contrary, she would not even entertain my questions on the subject. Instead, she attempted to turn the conversation."

"How do you mean?"

"Her attention seemed fixed on our reduced circumstances. She would speak of nothing else."

"Was there anything specific in what she said?"

"I hesitate to tell you, Mr. Holmes, for you will think that my wife has lost her reason. She made repeated reference to mutton chops."

"Indeed?"

"Mutton chops, my pocket watch and Madame de Maintenon."

"Pardon?" I said. "Madame de Maintenon?"

"The second wife of Louis XIV," he explained, "though why this had any bearing on the matter is entirely beyond my reach."

"How extraordinary!" I exclaimed.

Holmes appeared to be gazing intently at the fire coals. "She refused to give any explanation for having cut her hair?"

"None. I pressed her repeatedly on the point, but she would answer only in terms of mutton. At last I lost my temper and stormed out of the flat. When I returned several hours later, Violet had gone. I have not seen her since." Mr. Oldershot stared down at his hands, his eyes rimmed with tears. "Mr. Holmes, I am at the end of my wits."

Holmes had been leaning against the mantelpiece as our client finished this remarkable narrative. Now he began pacing a short line before the hearth, his hands clasped behind his back. His expression had changed little, but I, who knew his moods and habits so well, could see that his interest had been keenly aroused.

"Mutton chops, you say?"

"Yes, Mr. Holmes."

He sent a cloud of pipe smoke toward the ceiling and looked after it for several moments. "Your case is not without features of interest," he said at last.

"Will you help, Mr. Holmes? As to your fee, I'm afraid—"

Holmes gave a peremptory wave of his hand. "We shall discuss my fee upon a satisfactory resolution of the problem. At present I can do nothing. However, if you will return at 7:00 this evening, I believe I may be able to shed some light on the matter."

"But I don't—"

"Good day to you, sir. Dr. Watson will show you out." Holmes turned abruptly and stretched out both hands to lean against the mantelpiece, his eyes fixed on a point at the center of the fire. I rose to conduct our visitor to the door.

"One last thing, Mr. Oldershot," Holmes called over his shoulder.

"Yes?" The young man halted in the doorway.

"Are you especially fond of mutton?"

"Why, yes. I am, sir. But—"

"Very well, then. I shall have an answer for you this evening." Holmes returned his attention to the fire.

I closed the door behind our visitor and turned to question Holmes further about the case. He refused to be drawn out, but launched instead into a lengthy discourse on the merits of body armour for front-line soldiers in South Africa.

"Of course, one objects to the added weight under trying conditions," he informed me, "but this difficulty is easily surmounted. It is largely a question of—"

"Holmes," I cried, with some asperity, "will you tell me nothing of Mr. Oldershot's dilemma?"

He disappeared behind the Chinese screens which shaded his chemical deal table from the rest of the room. "Only the vital body centers need be covered," he called cheerily, "so there would be no loss of mobility. You may set your mind at rest upon that point."

"Holmes—"

"I will be occupied for most of the day, Watson," he said, emerging from behind the screen. "Might I impose upon you to join me when Mr. Oldershot returns this evening?"

"Holmes, if you are going to the Copper Beeches to look for Mrs. Oldershot, I would not think of allowing you to go alone. Jephro Rucastle is still a dangerous man. If you'll give me a moment, I'll fetch my service revolver and—"

"Jephro Rucastle is dead, Watson."

"What?"

"He died seven months ago, of influenza. I thought you knew."

"But why did you not say?"

"If my surmises are correct, Mrs. Oldershot would have preferred that I remain silent. No, Watson, I shall not need you today."

"But then where—?"

"After all," he said, "there have been innumerable cases where a Bible, a cigarette case, or some other chance article has saved a man's life by stopping a bullet. Why has this not set us scheming so as to do systematically what has so often been the result of a happy chance?" With this, he turned and disappeared down the stairs, leaving me gazing after him in confusion.

I was kept busy with my rounds for much of the day, and did not return to Baker Street until shortly before the hour of our appointment with Mr. Oldershot. I entered our rooms to find that Holmes had preceded me. "Ah, Watson!" cried he, emerging from behind the Chinese screens. "You are just in time!"

"Have you had any success?" I asked. "Have you located Mrs. Oldershot?"

"All in good time, dear fellow. I believe I hear our client's tread upon the stair."

He opened the door to admit our young client, who appeared even more downcast than he had been that morning. "Good evening, Mr. Oldershot!" cried Holmes with hearty good cheer. "Take a seat by the fire, there is a chill in the air this evening. Will you join me in a cigar?"

"That's very kind of you, Mr. Holmes, but I won't impose any further upon your hospitality. If you would please tell me—"

"A glass of sherry, perhaps?"

"Thank you, no. I apologize if I seem curt, Mr. Holmes, but I am on fire to know the results of your enquiries. Have you any news of my wife?"

"I have spoken with her at some length."

"You have! Where is she?"

"I shall be pleased to tell you, of course," Holmes said, cutting the end of a black lunkah. "But first I must ask you a question."

"Anything!"

He lit a taper in the fire and used it to warm the end of his cigar. "I'm afraid the question is a rather intimate one."

"If it will assist you in clearing this matter, I will answer as fully as I am able."

"Very well. Tell me, Mr. Oldershot, do you love your wife?"

Our visitor sprang from his chair, his pale cheeks flashing an angry red. "Mr. Holmes! That is outrageous and insulting!"

Unperturbed, Holmes lit his cigar and let out a long stream of smoke. "Your wife believes that she has alienated your affections. She has concluded that you ceased to love her the moment you found that she had cut her hair."

"Ridiculous!"

"Then why did you react with such violence at the sight of her shorn hair?"

"I've told you—I feared for her safety! I took it as an indication that she had entered into a renewed arrangement with her former employer!"

"Why did you not explain this to her last night?"

"I tried to do so. She would not hear me."

"Are you certain that you made yourself understood? 'Violet, what have you done—it is ruined, ruined!' Were those not the words you used?"

"Ruined? I—I did not mean—I was not referring to her appearance! She cannot have thought—" Mr. Oldershot sank back into his chair. "Mr. Holmes, I believe I will take a glass of sherry, if you don't mind. Thank you, Dr. Watson." He took a sip from the glass I passed him as he struggled to collect his thoughts. "Mr. Holmes, if I did say such a thing, I am deeply ashamed. It was only the shock of the thing, you see. I did not mean that Violet had ruined her hair, I meant only that she had ruined the surprise I had planned for her. You see, when I happened across my wife talking to Mr. Rucastle—or the man I thought was Mr. Rucastle—I had just been shopping for her Christmas gift. She has long admired a particular set of tortoise shell combs in the window of a shop in the square, as they were just of a shade to flatter her particular coloring. Of course she never dreamed of owning them, but I could not resist, though it meant pawning my watch in the bargain. That watch had been a legacy from my grandfather, and was my most prized possession. So it was rather a blow, you see, to return home having traded the watch for the combs only to find that Violet no longer had any use for the combs. But if I spoke sharply—"

He broke off at the sound of a woman's gasp. I turned to see the young lady I had known as Violet Hunter step from behind the Chinese screens. She had the same bright, quick face that I remembered so well, freckled like a plover's egg, and her newly-cropped hair was arranged in stylish ringlets. Mr. Oldershot was at her side in an instant. "Violet!" he cried. "Please forgive me. I—"

She placed a fingertip to his lips to silence him. "Don't you understand, Henry? I sold my hair to buy a chain for your watch."

"You—you what?"

"You've always seemed so ashamed of that old leather strap. I saw a magnificent gold chain at the shop in town, you see, just the thing for your grandfather's watch, and I—"

"But—but how did you—?"

"I sold my hair to the Hair Goods shop. My type of hair is much in demand for a particular style of wig known as the Madame de Maintenon, so it fetched a very good price. It took me several days to make up my mind, and that's why Mr. Harker—the gentleman from the shop—stopped us the other day, although of course I could not tell you so at the time. He dealt with me very fairly, I must say. There was even enough money left to purchase some nice mutton chops for our Christmas dinner. I tried to tell you all of this last night, but you were in too much of a state to hear."

Mr. Oldershot stood for several moments clutching his wife's hands. A slow tide of comprehension spread across his features, which gradually resolved itself into a broad, almost beatific smile. "You sold your hair to buy me a watch chain," he said with quiet wonder, "and I sold my watch to buy combs for your hair. That beats everything, Violet. Truly it does."

Holmes, who had watched this scene unfold with great merriment, stepped forward to ring the bell for Mrs. Hudson. "I believe we have brought your problem to a satisfactory conclusion, Mr. Oldershot. Now we would be most obliged if you would join us for a spot of dinner. You will find that Mrs. Hudson's mutton is excellent. Afterward, you may wish to examine that parcel on the mantelpiece. It contains something I picked up at the pawn shop in Walsall."

"Mr. Holmes," said Mrs. Oldershot, favoring my companion with a radiant smile, "we cannot possibly repay your kindness."

"Or compensate you for your services," added her husband.

"You shall do both soon enough," Holmes replied. "Earlier today you mentioned your literary aspirations, Mr. Oldershot. May I suggest that the events of the past two days might provide something in the way of inspiration? Of course, you may not wish to publicize these events over your own name, as this might cause some little embarrassment for your wife, but a simple pen name would serve your purpose nicely. Perhaps an inversion of your own name?" He paused to consider the matter.

"Yes," he said, "I think the name 'O. Henry' should do nicely."

THE HUMAN MYSTERY

Tanith Lee

This story is respectfully dedicated to the memory of the late, unique Jeremy Brett, a fine actor, and a definitive Sherlock Holmes.

1

Although I have written so often of the genius of Mr. Sherlock Holmes, a reader may have noticed, it was not always to Holmes's satisfaction. With that in mind, I suspect the reader may also have wondered if, on occasion, certain exploits were never committed to paper. This I confess to be true.

The causes are various. In some instances the investigation had been of so delicate a nature that, sworn to secrecy myself, as was Holmes, I could not break my vow. Elsewhere Holmes had perhaps acted alone, and never fully enlightened me, due mostly, I believe, to a certain boredom he often exhibited, when a case was just then complete. Other adventures proved ultimately dull, and dullness I have never readily associated with Sherlock Holmes.

Otherwise a small body of events remain, rogues of their kind.

They would not please the more devoted reader, as indeed at the time they had not pleased Holmes, or myself. I do not mean to imply here any failure, anything dishonourable or paltry on the part of Holmes. Although he has his faults, that glowing brain of his, when once electrically charged, transcends them. In this, or in any age, I daresay, he would be a great man. Nevertheless, certain rare happenings have bruised his spirit, and in such a way that I, his chronicler, have let them lie.

A year has gone by, however. An insignificant item in the newspaper brings me to my pen. No other may ever read what it writes. It seems to me, even so, that what was a distasteful, sad curiosity, has become a tragedy.

Holmes, although he will, almost undoubtedly, have seen the item, has not alluded to it. I well remember his sometime comment that more recent work pushes from his memory the ventures of the past. It is therefore possible he has forgotten the case of the Caston Gall.

One winter afternoon, a few days before Christmas, Holmes and I returned to our rooms from some business near Trafalgar Square. The water in the fountain had been frozen, and I had great sympathy with it. The Baker Street fire was blazing, and the lamps soon lit, for the afternoon was already spent and very dark, with a light snow now falling.

Holmes regarded the snow from the window a moment, then turning, held out to me a letter. "I wonder if the weather will deter our visitor?"

"Which visitor is that?"

"This arrived earlier. I saved it to show you on our return."

Dear Mr. Holmes,

I should like to call upon you this afternoon at three o'clock.

Hopefully, this will be of no inconvenience to you. Should it prove otherwise, I will return at some more favourable hour.

I looked up. "How unusual, Holmes. A client who fails to assume you are always in residence, awaiting them!"

"Indeed. I also was struck by that."

The letter continued:

I am divided in my mind whether or not to ask your opinion. The matter at hand seems strange and foreboding to me, but I am acutely conscious your time is often filled, and perhaps I am fanciful. Finally I have decided to set the facts before you, that you may be the judge. Please believe me, Mr. Holmes, if you can assure me I have no cause for fear, I shall depart at once with a light heart.

"Good heavens!" I exclaimed.

Holmes stood by the window. "She sets great store by my opinion, it seems. She will allow me to decide her fate merely on hearsay."

"She? Ah yes, a lady." The signature read "Eleanor Caston." It was a strong, educated hand, and the paper of good quality.

"What do you make of it, Watson?" Holmes asked, as was his wont.

I told him my views on the paper, and added, "I think she is quite young, although not a girl."

"Ah, do you say so. And why?"

"The writing is formed, but there is none of the stiffness in it which tends to come with age. Nor does she seem querulous. She has all the courteous thought of someone used to getting her own way. Conversely, she knows of and trusts you. Wisdom, but with a bold spirit. A young woman."

"Watson, I stand in awe."

"I suppose," I added, not quite liking his tone, "an elderly lady will now enter the room."

"Probably not. Mrs. Hudson caught sight of her earlier. But do go on."

"I can think of nothing else. Except I have used this writing paper myself. It is good but hardly extravagant."

"Two other things are apparent," said Holmes, leaning to the letter. "She wears a ring slightly too large for her, on her right hand. It has slipped and caught in the ink, here and here, do you see? And she does not, as most of her sex do, favour scent."

I sniffed the paper. "No, it seems not."

"For that reason, I think, Watson, you at first deduced the letter had been penned by a man. A faint floweriness is often present in these cases. Besides, her writing is well-formed but a trifle masculine."

Below, I heard the bell ring. "And here she is."

Presently Eleanor Caston was admitted to the room.

She was slim, and quite tall, her movements extremely graceful. She wore a tawny costume, trimmed with marten fur, and a hat of the same material. Her complexion was white and clear, and she had fine eyes of a dark grey. Her hair was decidedly the crowning glory, luxuriant, elegantly dressed, and of a colour not unlike polished mahogany. I was surprised to note, when she had taken off her gloves, that contrary to Holmes's statement, she wore no rings.

Although her appearance was quite captivating, she was not, I thought, a woman one would especially notice. But I had not been in her company more than five minutes, before I realized hers was a face that seemed constantly changeable. She would, in a few moments, pass from a certain prettiness to an ordinariness to vivid flashes of beauty. It was quite bewitching.

"Thank you, Mr. Holmes, Doctor Watson, for allowing me this interview today. Your time is a precious commodity."

Holmes had sat down facing her. "Time is precious to all of us, Miss Caston. You seem to have some fear for yours."

Until that moment she had not looked directly at him. Now she did so, and she paled. Lowering her eyes, she said, rather haltingly, "You must forgive me. This is, as you suspect, perhaps a matter of life or death to me."

Without taking his eyes from her, Holmes signalled to me. I rose at once and poured for her a glass of water. She thanked me, sipped it, and set it aside.

She said, "I have followed many of your cases, Mr. Holmes, in the literature of Doctor Watson."

"Literature—ah, yes," Holmes remarked.

"The curiosity of it is, therefore, that I seem almost to be acquainted with you. Which enables me to speak freely."

"Then by all means, Miss Caston, speak."

"Until this summer, I have lived an uneventful life. My work has been in the libraries of others, interesting enough, if not highly remunerative. Then I was suddenly informed I had come into a house and an amount of money which, to me, represents a fortune. The idea I need no longer labour for others, but might indulge in study, books and music on my own account, was a boon beyond price. You see, a very distant relative, a sort of aunt I had never known I had, died last Christmas, and left all her property to me, as her only relation. You will note, I am not in mourning. As I say, I did not know her, and I dislike hyprocrisy. I soon removed to the large house near

Chislehurst, with its grounds and view of fields and woodland. Perhaps you can envisage my happiness."

She paused. Holmes said, "And then?"

"Autumn came, and with it a change. The servants, who until then had been efficient and cheerful, altered. My maid, Lucy, left my service. She was in tears and said she had liked her position very well, but then gave some pretext of a sick mother."

"And how could you be sure it was a pretext, Miss Caston?"

"I could not, Mr. Holmes, and so I had to let her go. But it had been my understanding that she, as I, was without family or any close friends."

At this instant she raised her head fiercely, and her eyes burned, and I saw she was indeed a very beautiful woman, and conceivably a courageous one. Despite her self-possession, it was obvious to me that Holmes made her shy and uneasy. She turned more often to me in speech. This phenomenon was not quite uncommon, I must admit. She had admitted after all to reading my histories, and so might have some awareness of Holmes's opinion of women.

"Presently," she went on, "I had recourse to my aunt's papers. I should have explained, a box of them had been left for me, with instructions from my aunt to read them. That is, the instruction was not directed solely at me, but at any woman bearing the Caston name, and living alone in the house. Until then I had put the task off. I thought I should be bored."

"But you were not," said Holmes.

"At first I found only legal documents. But then I came to these. I have them here." She produced and held out to him two sheets of paper. He read the first. Then, having got up and handed both papers to me, Holmes walked about the room. Reaching the window, he stayed to look out into the soft flurry of the falling snow and the darkness of impending night. "And she had died at Christmas?"

"Yes, Mr. Holmes, she had. So had they all."

The first paper was a letter from Miss Caston's aunt. It bore out my earlier amateur theory, for the writing was crochety and crabbed. The aunt was a woman in her late sixties, it seemed, her hand tired by much writing.

To any female of the Caston family, living in this house a single life, unwed, or lacking the presence of a father or a brother: Be aware now that there is a curse put on the solitary spinsters of our line.

You may live well in this house at any time of year save the five days which forerun and culminate in Christmas Eve. If you would know more, you must read the following page, which I have copied from Derwent's *Legends of Ancient Houses*. You will find the very book in the library here. Take heed of it, and all will be well. It is a dogged curse, and easy to outwit, if inconvenient. Should you disregard my warning, at Christmas, you will die here.

I turned to the second paper. Holmes all this while stood silent, his back to us both. The young woman kept silent too, her eyes fixed on him now as if she had pinned them there, with her hopes.

"Watson," said Holmes, "kindly read Derwent's commentary aloud to me."

I did so.

In the year 1407, the knight Hugh de Castone is said to have left his bane on the old manor-farm at Crowby, near Chislehurst.

A notorious woman-hater, Sir Hugh decreed that if any Castone woman lived on the property without husband, father or brother to command her obedience, she would die there a sudden death at Yuletide. It must be noted that this was the season at which de Castone's own wife and sister had conspired to poison him, failed, and been mercilessly hanged by his own hands. However, the curse is heard of no more until the late seventeenth century, when Mistress Hannah Castone, her husband three months dead, held a modest festival in the house. She accordingly died from choking on the bone of a fowl, on Christmas Eve. One curiosity which was noted at the time, and which caused perplexity, was that a white fox had been spotted in the neighbourhood, which after Mistress Castone's burial, vanished. A white fox it seems, had been the blazon of Sir Hugh de Castone, as depicted on his coat of arms.

I stopped here and glanced at Miss Caston. She had turned from us both and was gazing in the fire. She appeared calm as marble, but it occurred to me that might be a brave woman's mask for agitation.

"Watson, why have you stopped?" came from the window.

I went on.

Again the curse fell dormant. It may be that only married ladies thereafter dwelled at the farm, sisters with brothers or daughters with their fathers. However, in 1794, during the great and awful Revolution in France, a French descendant of the Castons took refuge in the house, a woman whose husband had been lost to the guillotine. Three nights before the eve of Christmas, charmed, as she said, by glimpsing a white fox running along the terrace, the lady stepped out, missed her footing on the icy stair, and falling, broke her neck. There has in this century been only one violent death of a Caston woman at the house in Crowby. Maria Caston, following the death of her father the previous year, set up her home there. But on the evening preceeding Christmas Eve, she was shot and killed, supposedly by an unwanted lover, although the man was never apprehended. It is generally said that this curse, which is popularly called the Caston Gall, is abridged by midnight on Christmas Eve, since the holiness of Christmas Day itself defeats it.

I put down the paper, and Holmes sprang round from the window. "Tell me, Miss Caston," he said, "are you very superstitious?"

"No, Mr. Holmes. Not at all. I have never credited anything which could not be proved. Left to myself, I would say all this was nonsense."

"However?"

"The lady I call my aunt died on Christmas Eve, about eleven o'clock at night. She had had to break her own custom. Normally she would leave the house ten days before Christmas, staying with friends in London, and returning three days after St. Stevens. But this year she fell ill on the very day she was to leave. She was too unwell to travel, and remained so. I heard all this, you understand, from the servants, when once I had read the papers in the box, and questioned my staff firmly."

"How did she die?"

"She was asleep in her bed, and rallying, the doctor believed. The maid slipped out for a moment, and coming back found my aunt had risen as if much frightened, and was now lying by the fireplace. Her face was congested and full of horror. She was rigid, they told me, as a stone."

"The cause?"

"It was determined as a seizure of the heart."

"Could it not have been?"

"Of course her heart may have been the culprit."

Holmes glanced at me. His face was haughty and remote but his eyes had in them that dry mercurial glitter I connect with his interest.

"Mr. Holmes," said Eleanor Caston, standing up as if to confront him, "when I had questioned my servants, I put the story away with the papers. I engaged a new maid to replace Lucy. I went on with my improved life. But the months passed, and late in November, Lucy wrote to me. It was she who found my aunt lying dead, and now the girl told me she herself had also that day seen a white fox in the fields. It would be, of course, an albino, and our local hunt, I know, would think it unsporting to destroy such a creature. No, no. You must not think for a moment any of this daunted me."

"What has?"

"Three days ago, another letter came."

"From your maid?"

"Possibly. I can hardly say."

On the table near the fire she now let fall a thin, pinkish paper. Holmes bent over it. He read aloud, slowly, " 'Go you out and live, or stay to die.' " He added, "Watson, come and look at this."

The paper was cheap, of a type that might be found in a thousand stationers who catered to the poor. Upon it every word had been pasted. These words were not cut from a book or newspaper, however. Each seemed to have been taken from a specimen of hand-writing, and no two were alike. I remarked on this.

"Yes, Watson. Even the paper on which each word is written is of a different sort. The inks are different. Even the implement used to cut them out, unless I am much mistaken, is different." He raised the letter, and held it close to his face, and next against the light of a lamp. "A scissors here, for example, and there a small knife. And see, this edge—a larger, blunter blade. And there, the trace of a water-mark. And this one is very old. Observe the grain, and how the ink has faded, a wonder it withstood the paste—Hallo, this word is oddly spelled."

I peered more closely and saw that what had been read as 'out' was in fact 'our.' "Some error," said Holmes, "or else they could not find the proper word and substituted this. Miss Caston, I trust you have kept the envelope."

"Here it is."

"What a pity! The postmark is smudged and unreadable—from light snow or rain, perhaps."

"There had been sleet."

"But a cheap envelope, to coincide with the note-paper. The writing on the envelope is unfamiliar to you, or you would have drawn some conclusion from it. No doubt it is disguised. It looks malformed." He tossed the envelope down and rounded on her like an uncoiling snake.

"Mr. Holmes—I assure you, I was no more than mildly upset by this. People can be meddlesome and malicious."

"Do you think that you have enemies, Miss Caston?"

"None I could name. But then, I have been struck by fortune. It is sometimes possible to form a strong passion concerning another, only by reading of them say, in a newspaper. I gained my good luck suddenly, and without any merit on my part. Someone may be envious of me, without ever having met me."

"I see your studies include the human mystery, Miss Caston."

Her colour rose. One was not always certain with Holmes, if he complimented or scorned. She said, rather low, "Other things have occurred since this letter."

"Please list them."

She had gained all his attention, and now she did not falter.

"After the sleet, there was snow in our part of the country, for some days. In this snow, letters were written, under the terrace yesterday. An E, an N and an R and a V. No footsteps showed near them. This morning, I found, on coming into my study, the number five written large, and in red, on the wall. I sleep in an adjoining room and had heard nothing. Conversely, the servants say the house is full of rustlings and scratchings."

"And the white fox? Shall I assume it has been seen?"

"Oh, not by me, Mr. Holmes. But by my cook, yes, and my footman, a sensible lad. He has seen it twice, I gather, in the last week. I do not say any of this must be uncanny. But it comes very near to me."

"Indeed it seems to."

"I might leave, but why should I? I have gone long years with little or nothing, without a decent home, and now I have things I value. It would appal me to live as did my aunt, in flight each Christmas, and at length dying in such distress. Meanwhile, the day after tomorrow will be Christmas Eve."

2

After Miss Caston had departed, Holmes sat a while in meditation. It seemed our visitor wished to collect some rare books, as now and then she did, from Lightlaws in Great Orme Street. We were to meet her at Charing Cross station and board the Kentish train together at six o'clock.

"Well, Watson," said Holmes at length, "let me have your thoughts."

"It appears but too simple. Someone has taken against her luck, as she guesses. They have discovered the Caston legend and are attempting to frighten her away."

"Someone. But who is that someone?"

"As she speculated, it might be anyone."

"Come, Watson. It might, but probably things are not so vague. This would seem a most definite grudge."

"Some person then who reckons the inheritance should be theirs?"

"Perhaps."

"It has an eerie cast, nonetheless. The letters in the snow: ENRV. That has a mediaeval sound which fits Sir Hugh. The number five on the study wall. The fox."

"Pray do not omit the rustlings and scratchings."

I left him to cogitate.

Below, Mrs. Hudson was in some disarray. "Is Mr. Holmes not to be here for the festive meal?"

"I fear he may not be. Nor I. We are bound for Kent."

"And I had bought a goose!"

Outside the night was raw, and smoky with the London air. The snow had settled only somewhat, but more was promised by the look of the sky.

On the platform, Miss Caston awaited us, her parcel of books in her arm.

Holmes did not converse with us during the journey. He brooded, and might have been alone in the carriage. I was glad enough to talk to Miss Caston, who now seemed, despite the circumstances, serene and not unhappy. She spoke intelligently and amusingly, and I thought her occasional informed references to the classics might have interested Holmes, had he listened. Not once did she try to break in upon his thoughts, and yet I sensed she derived much of her resolution from his presence. I found her altogether quite charming.

Her carriage was in readiness at Chislehurst station. The drive to Crowby was a slow one, for here the snow had long settled and begun to freeze, making the lanes treacherous. How unlike the nights of London, the country night through which we moved. The atmosphere was sharp and glassy clear, and the stars blazed cold and white.

Presently we passed through an open gateway, decorated with an ancient crest. Beyond, a short drive ran between bare lime trees, to the house. It was evident the manor-farm had lost, over the years, the greater part of its grounds, although ample gardens remained, and a small area of grazing. Old, powerful oaks, their bareness outlined in white, skirted the building. This too had lost much of its original character to a later restoration, and festoons of ivy. Lights burned in tall windows at the front.

Miss Caston's small staff had done well. Fires and lamps were lit. Upstairs, Holmes and I were conducted to adjacent rooms, supplied with every comfort. The modern wallpaper and gas lighting in the corridors did not dispell the feeling of antiquity, for hilly floors and low ceilings inclined one to remember the fifteenth century.

We descended to the dining room. Here seemed to be the heart of the house. It was a broad, high chamber with beams of carved oak, russet walls, and curtains of heavy plush. Here and there hung something from another age, a Saxon double-axe, swords, and several dim paintings in gilded frames. A fire roared on the great hearth.

"Watson, leave your worship of the fire, and come out on to the terrace."

Somewhat reluctantly I followed Holmes, who now flung open the terrace doors and stalked forth into the winter night.

We were at the back of the house. Defined by snow, the gardens spread away to fields and pasture, darkly blotted by woods.

"Not there, Watson. Look down. Do you see?"

Under the steps leading from the terrace—those very steps on which the French Madame Caston had met her death—the snow lay thick and scarcely disturbed. The light of the room fell full there, upon four deeply incised letters: ENRV.

As I gazed, Holmes was off down the stair, kneeling by the letters and examining them closely.

"The snow has frozen hard and locked them in," I said. But other marks caught my eye. "Look, there are footsteps!"

"A woman's shoe. They will be Miss Caston's," said Holmes. "She too, it seems, did as I do now."

"Of course. But that was brave of her."

"She is a forthright woman, Watson. And highly acute, I believe."

Other than the scatter of woman's steps, the letters themselves, nothing was to be seen.

"They might have dropped from the sky."

Holmes stood up. "Despite her valour, it was a pity she walked about here. Some clue may have been defaced." He looked out over the gardens, with their shrubs and small trees, towards the wider landscape. "Watson, your silent shivering disturbs me. Go back indoors."

Affronted, I returned to the dining room, and found Miss Caston there, in a wine-red gown.

"They will serve dinner directly," she said. "Does Mr. Holmes join us, or shall something be kept hot for him?"

"You must excuse Holmes, Miss Caston. The problem always comes first. He is a creature of the mind."

"I know it, Doctor. Your excellent stories have described him exactly. He is the High Priest of logic and all pure, rational things. But also," she added, smiling, "dangerous, partly unhuman, a leopard, with the brain almost of a god."

I was taken aback. Yet, in the extreme colourfulness of what she had said, I did seem to make out Sherlock Holmes, both as I had portrayed him, and as I had seen him to be. A being unique.

However, at that moment Holmes returned into the room and Miss Caston moved away, casting at him only one sidelong glance.

The dinner was excellent, ably served by one of Miss Caston's two maids, and less well by the footman, Vine, a surly boy of eighteen or so. Miss Caston had told us she had dispensed with all the servants but these, a gardener and the cook.

I noticed Holmes observed the maid and the boy carefully. When they had left the room, he expressed the wish to interview each of the servants in turn. Miss Caston assured him all, save the gardener, who it seemed had gone elsewhere for Christmas, should make themselves available. The lady then left us, graciously, to our cigars.

"She is a fine and a most attractive woman," I said.

"Ah, Watson," said Holmes. He shook his head, half smiling.

"At least grant her this, she has, from what she has said, known a life less than perfect, yet she has a breeding far beyond her former station. Her talk betrays intellect and many accomplishments. But she is also womanly. She deserves her good fortune. It suits her."

"Perhaps. But our mysterious grudge-bearer does not agree with you." Then he held up his hand for silence.

From a nearby room, the crystal notes of a piano had begun to issue. It seemed very much in keeping with the lady that she should play so modestly apart, yet so beautifully, and with such delicate expression. The piece seemed transcribed from the works of Purcell, or Handel, perhaps, at his most melancholy.

"Yes," I said, "indeed, she plays delightfully."

"Watson," Holmes hissed at me. "Not the piano. Listen!"

Then I heard another sound, a dry sharp scratching, like claws. It came, I thought, from the far side of the large room, but then, startling me, it seemed to rise up into the air itself. After that there was a sort of soft quick rushing, like a fall of snow, but inside the house. We waited. All was quiet. Even the piano had fallen still.

"What can it have been, Holmes?"

He got up, and crossed to the fireplace. He began to walk about there, now and then tapping absently on the marble mantle, and the wall.

"The chimney?" I asked. "A bird, perhaps."

"Well, it has stopped."

I too went to the fireplace. On the hearth's marble lintel, upheld by two pillars, was the escutcheon I had glimpsed at the gate.

"There it is, Holmes, on the shield. De Castone's fox!"

3

To my mind, Holmes had seemed almost leisurely so far in his examination. He had not, for example, gone upstairs at once to view the study wall. Now however, he took his seat by the fire of the side parlour, and one by one, the remaining servants entered.

First came the cook, a Mrs. Castle. She was a large woman, neat and tidy, with a sad face which, I hazarded, had once been merry.

"Now, Mrs. Castle. We must thank you for your splendid dinner."

"Oh, Mr. Holmes," she said, "I am so glad that it was enjoyed. I seldom have a chance to cook for more than Miss Caston, who has only a little appetite."

"Perhaps the former Miss Caston ate more heartily."

"Indeed, sir, she did. She was a stout lady who took an interest in her food."

"But I think you have other reasons to be uneasy."

"I have seen it!"

"You refer—?"

"The white fox. Last week, before the snow fell, I saw it, shining like a ghost under the moon. I know the story of wicked old Sir Hugh. It was often told in these parts. I grew up in Chislehurst Village. The fox was said to be a legend, but my brother saw just such a white fox, when he was a boy."

"Did he indeed."

"Then there are those letters cut in the snow. And the number upstairs, and all of us asleep—a five, done in red, high upon the wall. The five days before Christmas, when the lady is in peril. A horrible thing, Mr. Holmes, if a woman may not live at her own property alone, but she must go in fear of her life."

"After the death of your former employer, you take these signs seriously."

"The first Miss Caston had never had a day's indisposition until last Christmas. She always went away just before that time. But last year her carriage stood ready on the drive every day, and every day the poor old lady would want to go down, but she was much too ill. Her poor hands and feet were swollen, and she was so dizzy she could scarce stand. Then, she was struck down, just as she had always dreaded."

"And the fox?" Holmes asked her.

The cook blinked. She said, "Yes, that was strange."

"So you did not yourself see it, on that former tragic occasion?"

"No, sir. No one did."

"But surely, Mrs. Castle, the present Miss Caston's former maid, Lucy, saw the white fox in the fields at the time of the elder lady's death?"

"Perhaps she did, sir. For it would have been about," Mrs. Castle replied ominously.

"Well, I must not keep you any longer, Mrs. Castle."

"No, sir. I need to see to my kitchen. Some cold cuts of meat have been stolen from the larder, just as happened before."

"Cold meat, you say?"

"I think someone has been in. Someone other than should have been, sir. Twice I found the door to the yard unlocked."

When she had left us, Holmes did not pause. He called in the footman, Vine. The boy appeared nervous and awkward as he had during dinner. From his mumblings, we learned that he had seen the white fox, yesterday, but no other alien thing.

"However, food has been stolen from the kitchen, has it not?"

"So cook says," the boy answered sullenly.

"A gypsy, perhaps, or a vagrant."

"I saw no one. And in the snow, they would leave their footprints."

"Well done. Yes, one would think so."

"I saw the letters dug out there," blurted the boy, "and Miss Caston standing over them, with her hand to her mouth. Look here, she says to me, who has written this?"

"And who had?"

The boy stared hard at Holmes. "You are a famous gentleman, sir. And I am nothing. Do you suspect me?"

"Should I?"

Vine cried out, "I never did anything I should not have! Not I. I wish I never had stayed here. I should have left when Lucy did. Miss Caston was a hard mistress."

I frowned, but Holmes said, amiably, "Lucy. She was obliged to care for her ailing mother, I believe."

Vine looked flustered, but he said, "The mistress never mourned her aunt, the old woman. Mistress likes only her books and piano, and her thoughts. I asked her leave to go home for the Christmas afternoon. We live only a mile or so distant, at Crowby. I should have been back by nightfall. And she says to me, Oh no, Vine. I will have you here."

"It was your place to be here," I said, "at such a time. You were then the only man in the house."

Holmes dismissed the boy.

I would have said more, but Holmes forestalled me. Instead we saw the maid, Reynolds, who had waited at dinner. She had nothing to tell us except that she had heard recent noises in the house, but took them for mice. She had been here in old Miss Caston's time, and believed the old woman died of a bad heart, aggravated by superstitious fear. Reynolds undertook to inform Holmes of this without hesitation. She also presented me with a full, if untrained, medical diagnosis, adding, "As a doctor, you will follow me, I am sure, sir."

Lastly Nettie Prince came in, the successor to Lucy, and now Miss Caston's personal maid. She had been at the house only a few months.

Nettie was decorous and at ease, treating Holmes, I thought, to his surprise, as some kind of elevated policeman.

"Is your mistress fair to you?" Holmes asked her at once.

"Yes, sir. Perfectly fair."

"You have no cause for complaint."

"None, sir. In my last employment the mistress had a temper. But Miss Caston stays cool."

"You are not fond of her, then?"

Nettie Prince raised her eyes. "I do not ask to love her, sir. Only to please her as best I can. She is appreciative of what I do, in her own way."

"Do you believe the tales of a curse on the Caston women?"

"I have heard stranger things."

"Have you."

"Miss Caston is not afraid of it, sir. I think besides she would be the match for any man, thief or murderer—even a ghost. Old Sir Hugh de Castone himself would have had to be wary of her."

"Why do you say that?"

"She talks very little of her past, but she made her way in the world with only her wits. She will not suffer a fool. And she knows a great deal."

"Yet she has sent for me."

"Yes, sir." Nettie Prince looked down. "She spoke of you, sir, and I understand you are a very important and clever gentleman."

"And yet."

Nettie said, "I am amazed, sir, at her, wanting you in. From all I know of Miss Caston, I would say she would sit up with a pistol or a dagger in her lap, and face anything out—alone!"

"Well, Watson," said Holmes, when we were once more by ourselves in the parlour.

"That last girl, Nettie Prince, seems to have the right of it. An admirable woman, Miss Caston, brave as a lioness."

"But also cold and selfish. Unsympathetic to and intolerant of her inferiors. Does anything else strike you?"

"An oddity in names, Holmes."

Holmes glanced my way. "Pray enlighten me."

"The letters in the snow, ENRV. And here we have a Nettie, a Reynolds and a Vine."

"The E?"

"Perhaps for Eleanor Caston herself."

"I see. And perhaps it strikes you too, Watson, the similarity between the names Castle and Caston? Or between Caston and Watson, each of which is almost an anagram of the other, with only the C and the W being different. Just as, for example, both your name and that of our own paragon, Mrs. Hudson, end in S.O.N."

"Holmes!"

"No, Watson, my dear fellow, you are being too complex. Think."

I thought, and shook my head.

"ENR," said Holmes, "I believe to be an abbreviation of the one name, Eleanor, where the E begins, the N centres, and the R finishes."

"But the V, Holmes."

"Not a V, Watson, a Roman five. A warning of the five dangerous days, or that Miss Caston will be the fifth victim of the Gall. Just as the number five is written in her study, where I should now like to inspect it."

Miss Caston had not gone to bed. This was not to be wondered at, yet she asked us nothing when she appeared in the upper corridor, where now the gas burned low.

"The room is here," she said, and opened a door. "A moment, while I light a lamp."

When she moved forward and struck the match, her elegant figure was outlined on the light. As she raised the lamp, a bright blue flash on the forefinger of her right hand showed a ring. It was a square cut gem, which I took at first for a pale sapphire.

"There, Mr. Holmes, Doctor. Do you see?"

The number was written in red, and quite large, above the height of a man, on the old plaster of the wall which, in most other areas, was hidden by shelves of books.

"Quite so." Holmes went forward, looked about, and took hold of a librarian's steps, kept no doubt so that Miss Caston could reach the higher book shelves. Standing up on the steps, Holmes craned close, and inspected the number. "Would you bring the lamp nearer. Thank you. Why, Miss Caston, what an exquisite ring."

"Yes, it is. It was my aunt's and too big for me, but in London today it was made to fit. A blue topaz. I am often fascinated, Mr. Holmes, by those things which are reckoned to be one thing, but are, in reality, another."

"Where are you, Watson?" asked Holmes. I duly approached. "Look at this number." I obeyed. The five was very carefully drawn, I thought, despite its size, yet in some places the edges had run, giving it a thorny, bloody look. Holmes said no more, however, and descended from the steps.

"Is it paint, Holmes?"

"Ink, I believe."

Miss Caston assented. She pointed to a bottle standing on her desk, among the books and papers there. "My own ink. And the instrument too—this paper knife."

"Yes. The stain is still on it. And here is another stain, on the blotting paper, where it was laid down."

Holmes crossed the room, and pulled aside one of the velvet curtains. Outside the night had again given way to snow. Opening the window, he leaned forth into the fluttering darkness. "The ivy is torn somewhat on the wall." He leaned out yet further. Snow fell past him, and dappled the floor. "But, curiously, not further down." He now craned upwards and the lamplight caught his face, hard as ivory, the eyes gleaming. "It is possible the intruder came down from the roof rather than up from the garden below. The bough of a tree almost touches the leads just there. But it is very thin."

"The man must be an acrobat," I exclaimed.

Holmes drew back into the room. He said, "Or admirably bold."

Miss Caston seemed pale. She stared at the window until the curtain was closed again. The room was very silent, so that the ticking of a clock on the mantle seemed loud.

Holmes spoke abruptly. "And now to bed. Tomorrow, Miss Caston, there will be much to do."

Her face to me seemed suddenly desolate. As Holmes walked from the room, I said to her, "Rest as well as you can, Miss Caston. You are in the best of hands."

"I know it, Doctor. Tomorrow, then."

4

The next morning, directly after breakfast, Holmes dispatched me to investigate the hamlet of Crowby. I had not seen Miss Caston; it seemed she was a late riser. Holmes, abroad unusually early, meanwhile wished to look at the bedchamber of the deceased elder Miss Caston. He later reported this was ornate but ordinary, equipped with swagged curtains and a bell-rope by the fire.

As I set out, not, I admit, in the best of humours, I noted that the sinister letters and the Roman number five had been obliterated from the ground below the terrace by a night's snow.

Elsewhere the heavy fall had settled, but not frozen, and in fact I had a pleasing and bracing walk. Among the beech coppices I spied pheasant, and on the holly, red berries gleamed.

Crowby was a sleepy spot, comprising two or three scattered clusters of houses, some quite fine, a lane or two, and an old ruin of a tower, where birds were nesting. There was neither a church nor an inn, the only public facility being a stone trough for the convenience of horses.

Vine's people lived in a small place nearby, but since Holmes had not suggested I look for it, or accost them, I went round the lanes and returned.

My spirits were quite high from the refreshing air, by the time I came back among the fields. Keeping to the footpath, I looked all about. It was a peaceful winter scene, with nothing abnormal or alarming in it.

When I came in sight of the house, I had the same impression. The building looked gracious, set in the white of the snow, the chimneys smoking splendidly.

Indoors, I found Vine, Reynolds and Nettie engaged in decorating the dining room with fresh-cut holly, while a tree stood ready to be dressed.

Holmes and Miss Caston were in the side parlour and I hesitated a moment before entering. A fire blazed on the parlour hearth, and a coffee pot steamed on the table. Holmes was speaking of a former case, affably and at some length. The lady sat wrapt, now and then asking a sensible question.

Seeing me, however, Holmes got up and led me in.

"I have been regaling Miss Caston with an old history of ours, Watson. It turns out she has never read your account of it, though nothing else seems to have escaped her."

We passed an enjoyable couple of hours before luncheon. I thought I had seldom seen Holmes so unlike himself in company, so relaxed and amenable. Miss Caston cast a powerful spell, if even he was subject to it. But presently, when he and I were alone, he changed his face at once, like a mask.

"Watson, I believe this interesting house is no less than a rat-trap, and we are all the rats in it."

"For God's sake, Holmes, what do you mean?"

"A plot is afoot," he said, "we must on no account show full knowledge of."

"Then she is in great danger?" I asked.

He glanced at me and said, coldly, "Oh, yes, my dear Watson. I do believe she is. We are dealing with high villainy here. Be on guard. Be ready. For now, I can tell you nothing else. Except that I have looked at the elder Miss Caston's papers myself, and made an obvious discovery."

"Which is?"

"The warning or threatening letter which was sent my client had all its words cut from various correspondence kept here. I have traced every word, save one. No doubt I would find that if I persisted. They were part of bills and letters, one of which was written in the early seventeenth century. Our enemy effaced them without a care. One other incidental. The footman, Vine, resents the dismissal of his sweetheart, Lucy, who was Miss Caston's former maid."

"His sweetheart?"

"Yes, Watson. You will remember how Vine spoke of his employer, saying that she was a hard mistress."

"But surely that was because she would not let him go off for Christmas."

"That too, no doubt. But when he mentioned her hardness, it was in the past tense, and in the same breath as Lucy's dismissal. He declared he 'should have left when Lucy did.' "

"She was not dismissed, Holmes. She went of her own accord."

"No. During our morning's friendly conversation, I put it to Miss Caston that she had perhaps sent Lucy away due to some misconduct with Vine. Our client did not attempt to deceive me on this. She said at once there had been trouble of that sort."

"That then furnishes Vine and Lucy with a strong reason for malice."

"Perhaps it does."

"Did she say why she had not told you this before?"

"Miss Caston said she herself did not think either Lucy or Vine had the wit for a game of this sort. Besides, she had not wanted to blacken the girl's character. Indeed, I understand she gave Lucy an excellent reference. Miss Caston expressed to me the opinion that Lucy had only been foolish and too ardent in love. She would be perfectly useful in another household."

"This is all very like her. She is a generous and intelligent woman."

Reynolds alone attended to us at lunch. The hall was by now nicely decked with boughs of holly. Miss Caston announced she would dress the tree herself in the afternoon. This she did, assisted by myself. Holmes moodily went off about his investigations.

My conversation with her was light. I felt I should do my part and try to cheer her, and she seemed glad to put dark thoughts aside. By the time tea was served, the tree had been hung with small gold and silver baubles, and the candles were in place. Miss Caston lit them just before dinner. It was a pretty sight.

That night too, Mrs. Castle had excelled. We dined royally on pheasant, with two or three ancient and dusty bottles to add zest.

Later, when Miss Caston made to leave us, Holmes asked her to remain.

"Then, I will, Mr. Holmes, but please do smoke. I have no objection to cigars. I like their smell. I think many women are of my mind, and sorry to be excluded."

The servants had withdrawn, Vine too, having noisily seen to the fire. The candles on the tree glittered. Nothing seemed further from this old, comfortable, festive room than our task.

"Miss Caston," said Holmes, regarding her keenly through the blue smoke, "the time has come when we must talk most gravely."

She took up her glass, and sipped the wine, through which the firelight shone in a crimson dart. "You find me attentive, Mr. Holmes."

"Then I will say at once what I think you know. The author of these quaint events is probably in this house."

She looked at him. "You say that I know this?"

"Were you not suspicious of it?"

"You are not intending to say that after all I believe Sir Hugh de Castone haunts me?"

"Hardly, Miss Caston."

"Then whom must I suspect? My poor servants? The affair with Lucy was nothing. She was too passionate and not clever enough. Vine was a dunce. They were better parted."

"Aside from your servants, some other may be at work here."

Just at that moment the most astonishing and unearthly screech burst through the chamber. It was loud and close and seemed to rock the very table. Holmes started violently and I sprang to my feet. Miss Caston gave a cry and the glass almost dropped from her hand. The shriek then came again, yet louder and more terribly. The hair rose on my head. I looked wildly about, and even as I did so, a scratching and scrabbling, incorporeal yet insistent, rushed as it seemed through thin air itself, ascending until high above our heads in the beamed ceiling, where it ended.

I stood transfixed, until I heard Holmes's rare dry laughter.

"Well, Watson, and have you never heard such a noise?"

Miss Caston in her turn also suddenly began laughing, although she seemed quite shaken.

"A fox, Watson. It was a fox."

"But in God's name, Holmes—it seemed to go up through the air—"

"Through the wall, no doubt, and up into the roof."

I sat and poured myself another glass of brandy. Holmes, as almost always, was quite right. A fox has an uncanny, ghastly cry, well known to country dwellers. "But then the creature exists?"

"Why not?" said Holmes. "White foxes sometimes occur hereabouts, so we have learnt from Mrs. Castle, and from Derwent's book. Besides, in this case, someone has made sure a white fox is present. Before we left London, I made an inquiry of Messrs Samps and Brown, the eccentric furriers in Kempton Street, who deal in such rarities. They advized me that a live albino fox had been purchased through them, a few months ago."

"By whom?" I asked.

"By a man who was clearly the agent of another, a curious gentleman, very much muffled up and, alas, so far untraceable." Holmes looked directly at Miss Caston. "I think you can never have read all the papers which your aunt left you. Or you would be aware of three secret passages which run through this house. None is very wide or high, but they were intended to conceal men at times of religious or political unrest, and are not impassable."

"Mr. Holmes, I have said, I never bothered much with the papers. Do you mean that someone is hiding—in my very walls?"

"Certainly the white fox has made its earth there. No doubt encouraged to do so by a trail of meat stolen from the larder."

"What is this persecutor's aim?" she demanded fiercely. "To frighten me away?"

"Rather more than that, I think," said Holmes, laconically.

"And there is a man involved?"

"It would seem so, Miss Caston, would you not say?"

She rose and moved slowly to the hearth. There she stood in graceful profile, gazing at the shield above the fireplace.

"Am I," she said at last, "surrounded by enemies?"

"No, Miss Caston," I replied. "We are here."

"What should I do?"

Holmes said, "Perhaps you should think very clearly, Miss Caston, delve into the library of your mind, and see what can be found there."

"Then I will." She faced him. She was not beseeching, more proud. "But you mean to save me, Mr. Holmes?"

He showed no expression. His eyes had turned black as two jets in the lamplight. "I will save whomever I can, Miss Caston, that deserves it. But never rate me too highly. I am not infallible."

She averted her head suddenly, as if at a light blow. "But you are one of the greatest men living."

So saying, and without bidding us good night, she gathered her skirts and left the room. Holmes got up, and walked to the fire, into which he cast the butt of his cigar.

"Watson, did you bring your revolver?"

"Of course I did."

"That is just as well."

"Tomorrow is Christmas Eve," I said, "according to the story, the last day of the Gall."

"Hmm." He knocked lightly on the wall, producing a hollow note. "One of the passages runs behind this wall, Watson, and up into the attics, I am sure. The other two I have not yet been able to locate, since the plans are old and hardly to be deciphered. Just like the postmark on the letter sent to Miss Caston. Did you notice, by the by, Watson, that although the envelope had been wetted and so conveniently smudged, no moisture penetrated to the letter itself?"

I too tossed my cigar butt into the flames.

"Fires have the look of Hell, do you think, Watson? Is Hell cheerful after all, for the malign ones cast down there?"

"You seem depressed. And you spoke to her as if the case might be beyond you."

"Did I, old man? Well, there must be one or two matches I lose. I am not, as I said, infallible."

Leaving me amazed, he vacated the room, and soon after I followed him. In my well-appointed bedchamber, I fell into a restless sleep, and woke with first light, uneasy and perplexed.

5

I now acknowledged that Holmes was keeping back from me several elements of the puzzle he was grappling with. This was not the first occasion when he had done so, nor would it be the last. Though I felt the exclusion sharply, I knew he would have reasons for it, which seemed wise to him, at least.

However, I checked my revolver before breakfast. Going downstairs, I found I would eat my toast and drink my coffee alone. Miss

Caston, as yesterday, was above, and Holmes had gone off, Vine grudgingly told me, on his own errands.

I amused myself as I could, examining the old swords, and finding a distinct lack of newspapers, tried the books in the library. They proved too heavy for my present scope of concentration.

About noon, Holmes returned, shaking the snow off his coat and hat. A blizzard was blowing up, the white flakes whirling, hiding the lawns, trees and fields beyond the windows. We went into the dining room.

"Read this," said Holmes, thrusting a telegram into my hands. I read it. It came from the firm of Samps and Brown, Furriers to the Discerning. A white fox had been purchased through their auspices on 15th October, and delivered to the care of a Mr. Smith.

"But Holmes, this was the very information you relayed last night."

"Just so. It was the information I expected to get today. But the telegram was kept for me at Chislehurst Village."

"Then why—"

"I gambled for once on its being a fact. I dearly wanted to see how Miss Caston would take it."

"It frightened her, Holmes, I have no doubt. What else?"

"Oh, did it frighten her? She kept a cool head."

"She is brave and self-possessed."

"She is a schemer."

He shocked me. I took a moment to find words. "Why on earth do you say so?"

"Watson, I despair of you. A lady's charms can disarm you utterly. And she well knows that, I think."

"She speaks more highly of you," I angrily asserted.

"I am sure that she does, which is also a way of disarming you, my dear fellow. Sit down, and listen to me. No, not there, this chair, I suggest, away from the fire."

I obeyed him. "You believe someone listens in the secret passage behind the wall there?"

"I think it possible. But this is a peculiar business and certainly its heroine has got me into a mode of distrust."

We sat down, and Holmes began to talk: "Miss Caston came to us, Watson, well-versed in all your tales of my work, inaccurate and embellished as they are. She brought with her the legend of the Caston Gall, which legend seems to be real enough, in as much as it exists in Derwent and elsewhere. Four Caston women, widows or spinsters, have apparently died here on one of the five days before Christmas. But the causes of Miss Caston's recent alarm—the writing in the snow, the number on the wall, the warning letter, the white fox—all these things have been achieved, I now suppose, by the lady herself."

"You will tell me how."

"I will. She had easy access to the letters and documents of her aunt, and herself cut out the words, using different implements, and pasting them on a sheet of cheap paper which may be come on almost anywhere. She was impatient, it is true, and used the word 'our' where 'out' eluded her. In her impatience, too, she hired some low person of no imagination to procure the fox and bring it here—Mr. Smith, indeed. Then she herself took cold meat from the larder to lure the animal to a tenancy inside the passageway, where it has since been heard scratching and running about. The door of the kitchen was found—not forced, nor tampered with, I have checked—but unlocked, twice. And if unlocked from the outside, why not from the inside? Again, her impatience perhaps, led her to this casualness. She would have done better to have left some sign of more criminal work, but then again, she may have hoped it would be put down to the carelessness of her staff. The letters in the snow she scratched there herself, then stood over them exclaiming. Hence her footsteps mark the snow, but no others. The abbreviation of her name and the use of the Roman five are not uningenious, I will admit—she has been somewhat heavy-handed elsewhere. In the study, she herself wrote the number five upon the wall. Standing on the librarian's steps, I had to lean down some way, the exact distance needed for a woman of her height, on those same steps, to form the number. You noticed the five, though drawn carefully, was also three times abruptly smeared, particularly on the lower curve. This was where her blue topaz ring, which at that time did not properly fit her, slipped down and pulled the ink, just as it had on her note to me. The ivy she herself disarranged from the window, with an almost insolent lack of conviction."

"Holmes, it seems to me that this once you assume a great deal too much—"

"At Baker Street I watched her in the window as she looked at me. My back was turned to her, and in her obvious unease, she forgot I might see her lamplit reflection on the night outside. Her face, Watson, was as predatory as that of any hawk. I fancied then she was not to be trusted. And there is too much that fits my notion."

"When the fox screamed, I thought she would faint."

"It is a frightful cry, and she had not anticipated it. That one moment was quite genuine."

"Vine," I said, "and Lucy."

"I have not decided on their rôle in this, save that the boy is obviously disgruntled and the girl maybe was not sensible. As for the letter Lucy is said to have written to Miss Caston, that first warning which so unfortunately was thrown away, being thought at the time of no importance—it never existed. Why should Lucy, dismissed from her employment and her lover, desire to warn the inventor of her loss?"

"Perhaps Lucy meant to frighten her."

"An interesting deduction, Watson, on which I congratulate you. However, you must look at the other side of the coin. If the inventor of Lucy's loss received a sinister warning from her, would she too not conclude it was an attempt to frighten?"

"Very well. But the deaths, Holmes. I too have read Derwent. The elder Miss Caston undeniably died here. The other three women certainly seem to have done."

"There is such a thing as coincidence, Watson. Mistress Hannah Castone choked on a chicken bone. The French lady slipped on the icy stair. Maria Caston was shot by a spurned and vengeful suitor. The aunt was apoplectic and terrified out of her wits by having to remain in the house at Christmas. You as a doctor will easily see the possibility of death in such a situation."

"She had left her bed and lay by the fireplace."

"In her agony, and finding herself alone, she struggled to reach the bell-rope and so summon help."

"And the bell-rope is by the fire."

"Phenomenal, Watson."

"By God, Holmes, for once I wish you might be in error."

"I seldom am in error. Think of our subject, Watson. She has come from a miserable life, which has toughened her almost into steel, to a great fortune. Now she thinks she may have anything she wants, and do as she wishes. She flies in the face of convention, as exemplified in her refusal to wear mourning for the old lady. She prefers, now she can afford better, an inferior writing-paper she likes—a little thing, but how stubborn, how wilful. And she has got us here by dint of her wiles and her lies."

"Then in God's name why?"

"Of that I have no definite idea. But she is in the grip of someone, we may be sure of it. Some powerful man who bears me a grudge. He has a honed and evil cast of mind, and works her strings like a master of marionettes. Certain women, and often the more strong among their sex, are made slaves by the man who can subdue them. And now, old chap, I shall be delighted to see you later."

I was so downcast and irascible after our talk, I went up to my room, where I wrote out the facts of the case up to that point. These notes have assisted me now, in putting the story together at last.

When I went down to lunch, I found Holmes once more absent, and Miss Caston also. She sent me her compliments by Nettie, who said her mistress was suffering from a cruel headache to which she was prone. Naturally I asked if I could be of any help. I was rather relieved, things standing as now they did, when Nettie thanked me and declined.

Vine waited on me at lunch, in a slapdash manner. Afterwards I played Patience in the side parlour, and was soundly beaten, as it were, nothing coming out. Beyond the long windows which ran to the floor, as they did in the dining room, the snow swirled on with a leaden feverishness.

Finally I went upstairs again to dress for dinner. I had on me, I remember, that sensation I experienced in my army days when an action was delayed. Some great battle was imminent, but the facts of it obscured. I could only curb my fretfulness and wait, trusting to my commander, Sherlock Holmes.

Outside, night had thickened, and the snow still fell. Dressed, I kept my revolver by me. Tonight was the fifth night of the Caston curse, and despite Holmes's words, perhaps because of them, I still feared not only for my friend, but for Eleanor Caston.

As I went down the corridor, for some reason I paused to look out again, through a window there. Before me on the pale ground I saw something run glimmering, like a phantom. Despite what we had learned, I drew back, startled. It was the Caston fox, pure white, its eyes flashing green in the light of the windows.

"Yes, sir. The beast exists."

I turned, and there stood the footman, Vine. He was clad, not in his uniform, but in a decent farmer's best, and looked in it both older and more sober.

"The fox is not a myth," I said.

"No, sir."

"Why are you dressed in that way?"

"I am going home. I have given her my notice. I have no mind to stay longer. I will take up my life on the land, as I was meant to. There is a living to be made there, without bowing and scraping. And when I have enough put by, I shall bring Lucy home, and marry her."

From a bad-tempered boy he had become a man, I saw. My instinct was to respect him, but I said, "And what of your mistress, Miss Caston?"

"She may do as she pleases. There was love, but nothing improper between Lucy and me. That was her excuse. Miss Caston threw Lucy out on account of her reading—and I will say it now, on account of you, sir, and Mr Holmes."

Dumbfounded, I asked what he meant.

"Why, sir, when Miss Caston came here, she would rather have read the coal-scuttle than anything of yours."

"Indeed."

"Any popular story was beneath her. She likes the Greek philosophers and all such. But when she had her headaches, Lucy read to her, and one day it was a tale of yours, sir, concerning Mr. Holmes. And after that, Lucy read others, since Miss Caston asked for them."

My vanity was touched, I confess. But there was more to this than my vanity.

"She made a regular study of Mr. Holmes, through your tales, Doctor. And then, this last September, she said Lucy must go, as her conduct with me was unseemly, which it never was. Even so, she gave my girl a fine reference, and Lucy has work now in a house better than this one."

I was searching in my mind for what to say, when the lad gave me a nod, and walked away. There was a travelling bag in his hand.

"But the weather, the snow," I said.

"This is a cold house," said he. "Snow is nothing to that." And he was gone.

Downstairs, I found Holmes, as I had hoped to. He stood by the dining room hearth, drinking a whisky and soda.

"Well, Watson, some insight has come your way."

"How do you know?"

"Merely look in a mirror. Something has fired you up."

We drew back from the hearth, mindful of a listener in the secret place behind it, and I told him what Vine had said.

"Ah, yes," said Holmes. "She has studied me. This confirms what I suspected. I think you see it too, do you not?"

"It is very strange."

"But the man who is her master, despite all my efforts, with which I will not tax you, he eludes me. What is his purpose? His name? It is a long way round to come at me."

Just then, Eleanor Caston entered the room. She wore a gown the dark colour of the green holly, which displayed her milk-white shoulders. Her burnished hair was worn partly loose. Seldom have I seen so fetching a woman.

Our dinner was an oddity. Only Reynolds waited on us, but efficiently. No one spoke of the affair at hand, as if it did not exist and we were simply there to celebrate the season.

Then Miss Caston said, "At midnight, all this will be over. I shall be safe, then, surely. I do believe your presence, Mr. Holmes, has driven the danger off. I will be for ever in your debt."

Holmes had talked during the meal with wit and energy. When he set himself to charm, which was not often, there was none better. Now he lit a cigarette, and said, "The danger is not at all far off, Miss Caston. Notice the clock. It lacks only half an hour to midnight. Now we approach the summit, and the peril is more close than it has ever been."

She stared at him, very pale, her bright eyes wide.

"What then?" she asked.

"Watson," said Holmes, "be so kind, old man, as to excuse us. Miss Caston and I will retire into the parlour there. It is necessary I speak to her alone. Will you remain here, in the outer room, and stay alert?"

I was at once full of apprehension. Nevertheless I rose without argument, as they left the table. Eleanor Caston seemed to me in those moments almost like a woman gliding in a trance. She and Holmes moved into the parlour, and the door was shut. I took my stance by the fireplace of the dining room.

How slowly those minutes ticked by. Never before, or since, I think, have I observed both hands of a clock moving. Through a gap in the curtains, snow and black night blew violently about together. A log settled, and I started. There was no other sound. Yet then I heard Miss Caston laugh. She had a pretty laugh, musical as her piano. There after, the silence came again.

I began to pace about. Holmes had given me no indication whether I should listen at the door, or what I should do. Now and then I touched the revolver in my pocket.

At last, the hands of the clock closed upon midnight. At this hour, the curse of the Gall, real or imagined, was said to end.

Taking up my glass, I drained it. The next second I heard Miss Caston give a wild shrill cry, followed by a bang, and a crash like that of a breaking vase.

I ran to the parlour door and flung it open. I met a scene that checked me.

The long doors stood wide on the terrace and the night and in at them blew the wild snow, flurrying down upon the carpet. Only Eleanor Caston was in the room. She lay across the sofa, her hair streaming, her face as white as porcelain, still as a waxwork.

I crossed to her, my feet crunching on glass that had scattered from a broken pane of the windows. I thought to find her dead, but as I reached her, she stirred and opened her eyes.

"Miss Caston—what has happened? Are you hurt?"

"Yes," she said, "wounded mortally."

There was no mark on her, however, and now she gave me an awful smile. "He is out there."

"Who is? Where is Holmes?"

She sank back again and shut her eyes. "On the terrace. Or in the garden. Gone."

I went at once to the windows, taking out the revolver as I did so. Even through the movement of the snow, I saw Holmes at once, at the far end of the terrace, lit up by the lighted windows of the house. He was quite alone. I called to him, and at my voice he turned, glancing at me, shaking his head, and holding up one hand to bar me from the night. He too appeared unharmed and his order to remain where I was seemed very clear.

Going back into the dining room I fetched a glass of brandy. Miss Caston had sat up, and took it from me on my return.

"How chivalrous you always are, Doctor."

Her pulse was strong, although not steady. I hesitated to increase her distress but the circumstances brooked no delay. "Miss Caston, what has gone on here?"

"Oh, I have gambled and lost. Shall I tell you? Pray sit down. Close the window if you wish. He will not return this way."

Unwillingly I did as she said, and noted Holmes had now vanished, presumably into the icy garden below.

"Well then, Miss Caston."

She smiled again that sorry smile, and began to speak.

"All my life I have had nothing, but then my luck changed. It was as if Fate took me by the hand, and anything I had ever wanted might at last be mine. I have always been alone. I had no parents, no friends. I do not care for people much, they are generally so stupid. And then, Lucy, my maid read me your stories, Doctor, of the wonderful Mr. Holmes. Oh, I was not struck by your great literary ability. My intimates have been Dante and Sophocles, Milton, Aristotle and Erasmus. I am sure you do not aspire to compete with them. But Holmes, of course—ah, there. His genius shines through your pages like a great white light from an obscure lantern. At first I thought you had invented this marvellous being, this man of so many parts: chemist, athlete, actor, detective, deceiver—the most effulgent mind this century has known. So ignorant I was. But little Lucy told me that Sherlock Holmes was quite real. She even knew of his address, 221B Baker Street, London."

Miss Caston gazed into her thoughts and I watched her, prepared at any moment for a relapse, for she was so blanched, and she trembled visibly.

"From your stories, I have learned that Holmes is attracted by anything which engages his full interest. That he honours a mind which can duel with his own. And here you have it all, Doctor. I had before me in the legend of this house, the precise means to offer him just such a plot as many of your tales describe—the Caston Gall, which of course is a farrago of anecdote, coincidence and superstition. I had had nothing, but now I had been given so much, why should I not try for everything?"

"You are saying you thought that Holmes—"

"I am saying I wanted the esteem and friendship of Mr. Sherlock Holmes, that especial friendship and esteem which any woman hopes for, from the man she has come to reverence above all others."

"In God's name, Miss Caston! Holmes!"

"Oh, you have written often enough of his coldness, his arrogance, and his dislike of my sex. But then, what are women as a rule but silly witless creatures, geese done up in ribbons. I have a mind. I sought to show him. I knew he would solve my riddle in the end, and so he did. I thought he would laugh and shake my hand."

"He believed you in the toils of some villain, a man ruthless and powerful."

"As if no woman could ever connive for herself. He told me what he thought. I convinced him of the truth, and that I worked only for myself, but never to harm him. I wanted simply to render him some sport."

"Miss Caston," I said, aghast, "you will have angered him beyond reason."

Her form drooped. She shut her eyes once more. "Yes, you are

quite right. I have enraged him. Never have I seen such pitiless fury
in a face. It was as if he struck me with a lash of steel. I was mistaken,
and have lost everything."

Agitated as I was, I tried to make her sip the brandy but she only
held it listlessly in one hand, and stood up, leaning by the fireplace.

"I sent Lucy away because she began, I thought, to suspect my
passion. There has been nothing but ill-will round me since then.
You see, I am becoming as superstitious as the rest. I should like to
beg you to intercede for me—but I know it to be useless."

"I will attempt to explain to him, when he is calmer, that you
meant no annoyance. That you mistakenly thought to amuse him."

As I faltered, she rounded on me, her eyes flaming. "You think
you are worthy of him, Watson? The only friend he will tolerate.
What I would have offered him! My knowledge, such as it is, my
ability to work, which is marvellous. All my funds. My love, which I
have never given any other. In return I would have asked little. Not
marriage, not one touch of his hand. I would have lain down and let
him walk upon me if it would have given him ease."

She raised her glass suddenly and threw it on the hearth. It broke
in sparkling pieces.

"There is my heart," said she. "Good night, Doctor." And with
no more than that, she went from the room.

I never saw her again. In the morning when we left that benighted
house, she sent down no word. Her carriage took us to Chislehurst,
from where we made a difficult Christmas journey back to London.

Holmes's mood was beyond me, and I kept silent as we travelled.
He was like one frozen, but to my relief his health seemed sound.
On our return, I left him alone as much as I could. Nor did I quiz
him on what he did, or what means he used to allay his bitterness

and inevitable rage. It was plain to me the episode had been infinitely horrible to him. He was so finely attuned. Another would not have felt it so. She had outraged his very spirit. Worse, she had trespassed.

Not until the coming of a new year did he refer to the matter, and then only once. "The Caston woman, Watson. I am grateful to you for your tact."

"It was unfortunate."

"You suppose her deranged and vulgar, and that I am affronted at having been duped."

"No, Holmes. I should never put it in that way. And she was but too plausible."

"There are serpents among the apples, Watson," was all he said. And turning from me, he struck out two or three discordant notes on his violin, then put it from him and strode into the other room.

We have not discussed it since, the case of the Caston Gall.

A year later, this morning, which is once more the day of Christmas Eve, I noted a small item in the paper. A Miss Eleanor Rose Caston died yesterday, at her house near Chislehurst. It is so far understood she had accidentally taken too much of an opiate prescribed to her for debilitating headaches. She passed in her sleep, and left no family nor any heirs. She was twenty-six years of age.

Whether Holmes, who takes an interest in all notices of death, has seen this sad little obituary, I do not know. He has said nothing. For myself, I feel a deep regret for her. If we were all to be punished for our foolishness, as I believe Hamlet says, who should 'scape whipping? Although crime is often solvable, there can be no greater mystery than that of the human heart.

About the Authors

As the creator of historical mysteries with her Charlotte and Thomas Pitt novels, *Anne Perry* is indisputably one of the world's most popular mystery writers. She lives in a small fishing village on the remote North Sea coast of Scotland.

Peter Lovesey is well known to mystery readers the world over as the creator of Victorian-age police officers Sergeant Cribb and Constable Thackeray. Other creations include using King Edward VII as a sleuth in another take on the Victorian age. In between these series he has also written dozens of short stories, as well as several television plays. A winner of both the Silver and Gold Dagger awards from the Crime Writers Association, he recently added another laurel to his list of honors by winning the Mystery Writers of America story contest with his short story "The Pushover."

Barbara Paul has a PhD in Theatre History and Criticism and taught at the University of Pittsburgh until the late seventies when she became a full-time writer. She has written five science fiction novels and sixteen mysteries, six of which are in the Marian Larch series. Her most recent book is *Jack Be Quick and Other Crime Stories*.

Loren D. Estleman is the author of forty-seven books, including the Amos Walker detective series, several Westerns, and the Detroit historical mystery series, including *Whiskey River*, *Motown*, *King of the Corner*, and *Thunder City*. His first Sherlock Holmes pastiche, *Sherlock Holmes vs. Dracula*, has been in print for twenty years.

Like many lawyers these days, *Carolyn Wheat* has put her legal skills, honed by the Brooklyn chapter of the Legal Aid Society, to good use in her novels, which feature Cass Jameson. She has taught mystery writing at the New School in New York City, and legal writing at Brooklyn Law School. Recent novels include *Mean Streak* and *Troubled Waters*. An Adventuress of Sherlock Holmes, Carolyn's investiture is The Penang Lawyer.

Edward D. Hoch makes his living as a writer in a way that very few other people can attest to—he works almost entirely in short fiction. With hundreds of stories primarily in the mystery and suspense genres, he has created such notable characters as Simon Ark, the 2,000-year-old detective, Nick Velvet, the professional thief who only steals worthless objects, to the calculating Captain Leopold, whose appearance in the short story "The Oblong Room" won his creator the Edgar award for best short story.

L. B. Greenwood's fiction has appeared in *Malice Domestic, Malice Domestic III*, and *Malice Domestic IV*. She is also one of the few women to take up the mantle of Sherlock Holmes in novel form. Her pastiches include *Sherlock Holmes and the Case of the Raleigh Legacy* and *Sherlock Holmes and the Thistle of Scotland*. She lives in British Columbia, Canada.

Bill Crider is the author of more than twenty mystery, Western, and horror novels as well as numerous short stories. *Too Late to Die* won the Anthony Award for favorite first mystery novel in 1987, and *Dead on the Island* was nominated for a Shamus Award as best first private eye novel.

Jon L. Breen has written six mystery novels, most recently *Hot Air* (1991), and over seventy short stories; contributes review columns to *Ellery Queen's Mystery Magazine* and *The Armchair Detective*; was short-listed for the Dagger Awards for his novel *Touch of the Past* (1988); and has won two Edgars, two Anthonys, a Macavity, and an American Mystery Award for his critical writings.

Daniel Stashower is the author of *Teller of Tales: The Life of Arthur Conan Doyle*, as well as a Sherlockian pastiche, *The Adventure of the Ecto-plasmic Man*. He is a winner of The Raymond Chandler Fulbright Fellowship in Detective and Crime Fiction Writing. He lives in Washington, D. C.

Tanith Lee has made her reputation by successfully mixing science fiction, heroic fantasy, and fairy tales into a unique mix all her own. Often turning fantasy conventions upside down, her examination of the ambiguities of moral behavior can be found in her novels *Death's Master*, *Dark Dance*, and *Darkness, I*. A World Fantasy Award winner, Lee lives in East Sussex, England.